stasis

kim fielding

DSP PUBLICATIONS

Published by

DSP Publications

5032 Capital Circle SW, Suite 2, PMB# 279, Tallahassee, FL 32305-7886 USA
www.dreamspinnerpress.com

Stasis
© 2016 Kim Fielding.

Cover Art
© 2016 Reese Dante.
http://www.reesedante.com
Cover content is for illustrative purposes only and any person depicted on the cover is a model.

ISBN: 978-1-63476-829-0
Digital ISBN: 978-1-63476-830-6
Library of Congress Control Number: 2015953082
Published May 2016
v. 2.0
First Edition published by CreateSpace, 2009.

Printed in the United States of America

This paper meets the requirements of
ANSI/NISO Z39.48-1992 (Permanence of Paper).

For Dennis, who cheered me on.

Acknowledgments

MANY THANKS to Mabel Marsters for reading my draft and giving me helpful comments and to Karen Witzke for her eternally patient assistance. My family and friends may have thought I was crazy to try to write a novel during the single month of November, but they were also very supportive and tolerant of my (temporary) insanity. I'm grateful to the NaNoWriMo organizers for giving me the motivation to write this. And special thanks to all of you who have read my writing and encouraged my muse with your kind and encouraging comments!

stasis

kim fielding

prologue

THIS FAR down, he didn't so much hear the waves as feel them patiently pounding against the stone foundations, rumbling and crashing without rest. It was disconcerting. Ennek felt as if the building could give way any moment, tumbling him and everything he knew into the unforgiving brine. At the same time, though, the battering of the sea comforted him, because it was as if the ocean was alive. Certainly it seemed more alive than the body now stretched before him, pale as marble, suspended in a webbing of ropes.

Ennek stood next to the wizard, Thelius, who ran his fingertips over the arm of the inert man. It reminded Ennek of the way his father, the Chief, would stroke absently at his big oak desk, worrying at many decades' worth of gouges and scratches and dents. Thelius's motion made Ennek's stomach churn uncomfortably, and the Chief noticed and scowled at him. But Thelius only inclined his head a little and kept on speaking.

"So you see," the wizard said, "they remain like this until their sentence is completed."

Ennek's brother lifted his hand as if he meant to touch the prisoner, then let it drop.

"Oh, it's quite all right, Larkin. Feel if you like." When the Chief's older son didn't react, Thelius gently grasped Larkin's large hand in his bony one and set it on the prisoner's unmoving chest.

"It's cold," Larkin said in a near whisper.

"Yes. They remain at room temperature, as their hearts no longer pump blood through their bodies."

Ennek had taken a half step back, as if he might be forced to touch the man as well. "Do... do they dream?" he asked.

The Chief made a rumbling sound of disapproval deep in his throat, but Thelius only shook his head. "No, young man, they do not. They're not asleep. They don't breathe, they don't eat or drink, they don't age, they don't sense anything around them, and they don't think. It's as if they are frozen in a single moment, you see?"

Ennek nodded, but his stomach felt no better, especially when Thelius's fingers made another proprietary little motion across the white skin.

Larkin's hand was still on the man's chest. "How long has he been like this?" His voice was calm, almost disinterested, but Ennek knew his brother well and could tell by the slight flush in his cheeks and the way his breathing had become a little too rapid that Larkin found the concept of Stasis interesting, exciting even.

"This one has been here for slightly over seventeen years. He has thirteen more years remaining." Thelius's dry voice crackled like old sticks.

"And when he... wakes up?"

"Then the world will have moved on, beyond whatever foolish ideas he was trying to spread. He's been forgotten already, I'm sure. And I'm certain the Chief will find an appropriate position for him, some way for him to repay his debt to society."

The Chief nodded gravely at this.

"How many are there?" Larkin asked.

"Not many, not anymore," the wizard said. "Only a score. In times past, when things were rather more... chaotic... traitors were much more common. But most of them served their sentences and were released many years ago. As you know, under wiser leadership, treachery is rare." He inclined his head a little at the Chief, and the Chief blinked back. "I'm quite certain that when it is your own turn to take the office, you will be a strong Chief as well."

"Thank you," Larkin said, clearly pleased by the compliment and, perhaps, even more pleased when the Chief did not contradict his wizard's praise.

The four of them stood for several moments, looking down at the prisoner's bare body. Ennek wondered whether he'd been that skinny before or if he'd become that way under Stasis. He'd never seen a grown man naked before and now gazed with frank curiosity at the man's genitals. He wondered if they all looked like this, shrunken and vulnerable.

"What's the longest any of them have been here?" It took him a second to realize the voice asking the question was his own. He hadn't intended to speak.

Thelius gave him a long look, but Ennek couldn't make out what the man was thinking. Finally Thelius said, "One man has been here for nearly three hundred years."

Larkin gasped. Maybe Ennek did as well. "Why?" he said.

Thelius shrugged. It was an odd gesture on him, like watching a ladder unfold. "I suppose he did something particularly egregious. I don't know. His sentence is one thousand years."

Ennek tried to imagine what it would be like to awaken after such an unimaginably large amount of time. For him, just the stretch from one New Year to the next seemed like an eternity. He shuddered, catching another angry glance from the Chief.

"Can we see him?" Larkin asked eagerly. "The one who's been here so long?"

Thelius and the Chief exchanged looks. It was the Chief who spoke. "No. This is enough. You both have studies to return to, especially Ennek, who shouldn't have been here at all."

Ennek bowed his head, wondering if he'd face some punishment for begging to come along. But he'd known that if he didn't accompany Larkin now, he might never be allowed down here. After all, he wasn't the heir. He had no need to know what was going on Under.

Almost regretfully, Larkin took his hand off the man. Thelius did not, however. He gripped the bony shoulder tightly enough to make Ennek wonder if the prisoners in Stasis could bruise.

The Chief began walking toward the door of the cell. "Come on," he ordered. "I have work to do."

They followed him down the stone corridor, first Larkin and then Ennek, with Thelius bringing up the rear. Their boots clomped and echoed, and the gaslights sputtered fitfully in their sconces. Ennek counted the narrow doors as they went, forty-eight by the time they came to the entrance. Forty-eight cells, each capable of holding a person trapped like an insect in a web. The Chief used one of his heavy keys to unlock the big wooden door, they filed through, and Thelius locked it behind them. They marched up the long stairway single file and through another locked door, where a pair of guards saluted the Chief smartly.

They were back above now, and again Ennek could hear the ocean, could smell salt and fish instead of just damp rocks. He would have thought he'd be relieved, and he was, a little; but as he walked away to find his tutor, numbers tumbled through his head. Forty-eight cells. Twenty prisoners. Three hundred years.

BAVELLA WAS angry with him, but that was nothing new. Her emotions toward him generally ranged from annoyed through irritated, stopping just short of enraged. Usually it was because he hadn't done his lessons or because his mind had wandered as she droned on and she'd had to repeat herself for the third or fourth time. "Twelve years old and still cannot properly name the principal cities along the Great Road or do his sums," she'd hiss at him. "It's a disgrace! Your brother could do these things before he was ten."

"My brother has to know these things because he'll be Chief. I don't."

"Even a younger son should not be ignorant."

He'd cross his arms on his chest and set his jaw. He knew what kind of future awaited him, a life very like his uncle Sopher's. Sopher had an official title, of course—he was the Censor—but he left the work to his underlings and spent his time sailing the bay in his bright little boat, or hunting in the headlands to the north, or playing in the Gentlemen's Room at the gaming house.

Today, though, it wasn't Ennek's inattention that had brought the wrath of his tutor but rather the questions he had asked her. About traitors and punishments, mostly.

The frown line between her light brows deepened. "That is none of your concern."

"But this morning I was Under, and—"

"You shouldn't—" She bit back the rest of the sentence, apparently unwilling to criticize the Chief's decision. She took a deep breath, then went on. "You were permitted to accompany your brother only because you pestered so thoroughly, and only because the Chief was in a generous mood. You should be thankful you were allowed so much."

Ennek wasn't thankful. In fact, he regretted the tour. He kept seeing that unmoving white flesh before him, the man's face not looking asleep or dead but something else altogether. Kept hearing the din of the waves, feeling the little trickle of dampness as it ran down uneven stone and dripped onto the floor. And kept seeing the long corridor lined with doors, and imagining the uncomfortable possibilities behind them. Were they imprisoned in the dark, he wondered. They must be—what need did those in Stasis have for light?

He shivered, and Bavella narrowed her eyes. "We were discussing history. The line of accession for Praesidium that leads directly to the Chief. This is your own family, boy!"

"A bunch of angry-looking old men," he muttered, ignoring her scandalized gasp. "I don't want to know about them. I want to hear about the others, the ones who questioned them."

"Nobody remembers *them*," she answered coldly. "That is, after all, the point of Stasis. They're locked away Under until even their names have been lost, and then they live out the rest of their days as bond-slaves, just more wretches cleaning the filth from the streets or digging in the quarries. And it's a fate too good for them, I think. Daring to question their betters!"

"But—"

"Enough! Recite, or I shall have to report your lack of progress." She pounded her finger against the open book.

Ennek glowered, but he began to read. He didn't much feel like being punished today.

"IF THIS automated wagon of theirs is perfected, then Horreum will be able to convey shipments quickly without even needing the bay, and then what will become of us?" The chief of Nodosus sounded worried, but then, he always did.

Ennek's father snorted dismissively and swallowed a mouthful of beef. "If, *if* this folly of theirs actually works—and I have grave doubts about that—and if it actually proves capable of hauling cargo, then they're going to rely on the polises over the mountains to supply the coal to run the thing, and the polises between to allow their contraptions passage. Horreum has no treaties with those states, or very weak ones at best. Even if they can negotiate something, much of Horreum's power and profits will be whittled away."

"But—"

"And!" The Chief silenced the other man with a gesture of his fork. "And in any case, other polises would still rely on the bay for overseas trade. Where else would the great ships dock? Among the rocks to our south? Or perhaps the even bigger rocks to our north?"

"Yes, yes. But if Horreum has the most efficient way of transporting overland, they could gain a monopoly on it, and then their power might eventually rival yours."

It was Larkin who responded to the visiting leader. "Sir, I doubt very much there's any danger of that, especially when we have such good allies as yourself."

The chief of Nodosus beamed at the compliment, and a quick look of satisfaction flashed over the Chief's face. Even Ennek could tell that Larkin made a good diplomat, but still he rolled his eyes theatrically at his friend Gory, who sat across the table from him, stuffing bread into his face. Gory grinned back and then gestured with his head toward the door.

"Excuse me, sir," Ennek said to the Chief. "May I be excused?"

The Chief nodded absently and then started pontificating about the perils of steam engines. Ennek took a last gulp of watered wine, wiped his mouth, and rose from the table. He jogged to his own chambers, thankful that, while he was old enough to have to attend these dinners now, at least he didn't have to stay for the endless, boring discussions that always followed. In his room, he considered changing into slightly less formal clothes—his new suit was itchy and not very comfortable—but decided instead to just throw on his warmest coat. He clattered back through the hallways, sometimes nodding to guards and various functionaries as he passed, until he ascended a steep, winding stairway.

Gory was already waiting for him on the roof. His corn-silk hair was whipping around, and his handsome face was tilted in its usual smirk. Ennek could see his tan even in the moonlight; Nodosus was a day's ride inland, where the sun shone almost all the time.

"That brother of yours has been practicing sucking up," Gory said by way of a greeting.

"Yeah. He's getting pretty good at it."

"Well, dear old Dad sure ate it up."

They walked to one edge of the roof and bent over the railing to look at the water. The foam was phosphorescent, as otherworldly as the moon. They had to raise their voices a little to be heard. "You ever swim in it?" Gory asked.

Ennek shook his head. "No. Too cold."

Gory sneered. He was eighteen months older than Ennek and six inches taller. Someday he would be a chief too. He pointed at Rennis

Island, the lights of which were just visible through the gathering fog. "I bet I could swim out there. It's not that far."

"It's cold," Ennek repeated. "And there are sharks."

Gory flapped his hand, whether at sharks or at people who were afraid of them, Ennek wasn't sure. "I could do it. I swim in the river all the time, even in the spring when it's all melted snow, and *that's* cold, boy. And there are things that live in the river, too, deadlier things than sharks."

Ennek didn't know if this was true. He'd never been beyond the walls of Praesidium, unless you counted an afternoon or two sailing in the bay or the one time Sopher had taken him to hunt deer.

He trailed Gory as the older boy stomped across the roof to the other side. Gory had a pocketful of pebbles, and he began dropping them over the edge onto the helmets of the guards below, pulling back out of sight when the guards looked up. "Here," he said, laughing and holding out a few small stones. "You try."

Ennek imagined the Chief's face if he found out. "No, thanks," he mumbled.

"Aw, c'mon."

Ennek found himself taking some of the smooth little things in his hand, then creeping to the railing. When the next guard walked by on his rounds, Ennek let go, and two pebbles plunked loudly off the man's head. Ennek crouched down, giggling.

"How about this?" Gory said. Now he was holding a larger chunk of stone, almost as big as his fist. It looked as if it had crumbled off the battlements.

"I'm not gonna drop that on someone's head!"

"Why not? They're wearing helmets. It's not like you're gonna kill anyone."

But Ennek shook his head, and Gory let the stone fall to his feet with a sizable *clomp*. A loud silence followed, Gory's full lips pulled up on one side, his lean hips cocked just so, one perfect eyebrow arched high.

"I went Under last month!" Ennek suddenly blurted.

Gory's eyes widened and then immediately narrowed. "You did not."

"I did! The Chief took Larkin to see and I was invited along." It wasn't quite far enough from the truth to be a lie.

Gory came very close to him, looked him up and down, and then leaned against the stone railing. He was trying for nonchalant but not quite managing, to Ennek's great delight. "What was it like?" Gory finally asked. Nodosus had no Under. Its worst criminals were simply hung, which was rather efficient but, the Chief had said, barbaric. Not to mention dangerous—a dead traitor could too easily become a martyr. But Nodosus's wizard was much less powerful than Praesidium's, as was fitting because Nodosus itself was much less powerful than the great polis to the west. Nodosus's wizard undoubtedly lacked the skill for Stasis.

Ennek looked at the way Gory's hair hung in his face, almost covering his eyes. He wondered what his own hair would look like if he allowed it to grow so long. Not the same, of course. Ennek's hair was thick and curly and nearly black. He imagined Gory's must feel very soft. "It was no big deal," he said.

"Oh?"

"Thelius showed us one of the prisoners. He was…. He looked kind of like a statue or… or a doll." That wasn't quite right, but it was as close as he could get. "And he was naked," he added in a near whisper.

"Really?" Gory's eyes shone in the cold moonlight.

"Really. He was in this sort of hammock thing. Thelius said their skin wears through if they're just left on the ground. Not that they'd feel it, but they would when they woke up."

"So you could do, like, anything to them, and they wouldn't know?"

"Yeah, I guess."

Gory chewed at his lip for a moment. "I want to see one!" he announced.

"Um, I guess your chief could ask mine."

"No. You know they'd never let me."

"Well, maybe someday when you're chief, you could—"

"That's a million years away, Ennek! I want to see now. Tonight."

Ennek swallowed. "No way."

Gory stood in front of him, stooping slightly so they were eye to eye. "Come on. Just a peek. We can go after everyone's asleep and nobody will ever know."

"But what if they found out?"

"They won't," Gory huffed. "Don't be a baby. I've snuck into tougher places than this plenty of times."

Ennek was skeptical about that. Besides, even if it was true, Gory had done his sneaking back home, where he was heir and the Chief had no authority. Ennek was going to say no again, was going to just turn away and go back inside, actually, when Gory stuck out his arm and clutched Ennek's shoulder with his tanned, man-sized hand. "Come on," Gory purred.

And to his own dismay, Ennek heard himself agreeing to meet his friend outside the dining hall in three hours.

"THAT'S YOUR spy outfit?" Gory scoffed.

Ennek looked down at himself. He was wearing a pajama top tucked into a pair of old trousers that were now a little short on him. He'd pulled on a sweater too, a lumpy gray one his mother had knitted for Larkin years ago, and a pair of old boots. "What difference does it make if nobody's going to see us anyway?" he countered.

"Well, *I* have to see you." Gory had on a pair of sharply creased wool pants, a dark red shirt of silky cotton, and shiny black shoes. He was going to be cold if they actually made it Under, but Ennek didn't tell him so.

Ennek shrugged, his eyes downcast.

"Did you at least get the keys?"

Ennek looked up and grinned, then pulled a heavy iron ring from his pocket. It was Larkin's, the set of keys he'd been given on his eighteenth birthday. Ennek had made enough secret forays into his brother's room to know where they'd be hidden, and also to know that Larkin would be sound asleep after a heavy meal and several glasses of wine. Ennek wasn't absolutely positive that one of the bits of metal would work on the door to Under, but he certainly wasn't going to try to steal the Chief's keys, or the wizard's for that matter.

He led Gory through the empty halls of the keep. It was kind of a creepy place this late at night, when nobody scurried by with arms full of papers. There were a few guards posted here and there, of course, and a bond-slave or two down on his knees, scrubbing at the floors, but they were easy enough to avoid.

The door that led Under was well out of the way, tucked at the end of a long corridor that held mostly storerooms full of mops and towels and old furniture. It would have been completely unremarkable if it weren't for the single guard leaning against the wall, nodding sleepily.

"How are we going to get by him?" Ennek whispered after he peeked around the corner.

"Simple." Gory held out his hand. There were two candies there, red and sticky-looking. "Sleeping potion. My dad takes one every night. I just nicked a couple."

"But how are you going to get the guard to take them? And when he wakes up, won't he know he's been drugged?"

"You'll see, and yeah, he will, but he's not gonna tell anyone, because then he'd get in trouble for not doing his job. Right?"

Ennek nodded doubtfully, then caught his breath as Gory marched confidently around the corner and down the hall. The guard jerked awake and stared at the approaching youth. "Hi," said Gory.

The guard said nothing, just watched until Gory was standing a few feet away.

"Do you know who I am?"

The guard shook his head. He wasn't much older than Gory, really, maybe Larkin's age. His helmet looked uncomfortable where the strap dug into his skin, and he had dark circles under his eyes.

"Name's Gory. I'm the heir of Nodosus."

The guard straightened his shoulders until he was almost standing at attention. "Yes, sir," he said, so quietly Ennek could barely hear.

"Have you ever been to Nodosus?"

"No, sir. I've never left Praesidium, sir."

"That's too bad. Maybe someday you can manage a visit. We have real summers, you know, with the sun blazing hot and the grass all golden, and tomatoes sweet as candy when you eat them right off of the vine."

"Yes, sir."

"We have traditions too. Like giving small gifts to those who work for us. Here." He held out his palm.

The guard looked down at it. "Thank you, sir, but I really couldn't. We're not allowed, and—"

"Aw, it's just a little candy. No big deal. You wouldn't want to hurt my feelings, would you?"

Ennek was beginning to feel sorry for the man. He was about to step around the corner and end the whole thing when the guard said, "No, sir, of course not."

"C'mon, then. They're good."

As Ennek peeked around the wall, he saw the guard hesitate, then gingerly pick the candies up and pop them into his mouth. "Thank you, sir," he said with his mouth full.

"Sure thing. You have a good night now." Gory walked back toward Ennek, who ducked out of sight.

They stood there awhile, fidgeting restlessly, until they heard a loud rustle. When Ennek chanced another look, the guard was sitting, his legs straight out in front of him and his back up against the wall. As Ennek watched, the guard slowly, slowly slumped to the side.

"Got him." Gory grinned triumphantly and marched down the hall with Ennek at his heels. In front of the door, Gory stopped to prod the guard with his shoe. The man's mouth hung open and a thin line of drool was running down his cheek. He snored lightly.

Ennek produced the keys again. After a few minutes of fumbling, he found one that fit the lock, which turned a little stiffly. It seemed very loud, as did the door when he swung it open. There was a light switch just inside, and when Ennek pushed the button, a row of small gas lamps hissed to life, illuminating the stairway. He locked the door behind them, noting with a thrill of satisfaction Gory's unnaturally pale face, and led the way down.

When they were finally in the long, dank corridor, Gory let out a low whistle. "Is there somebody behind every door?"

"No. At least, not anymore. Thelius said there are only about twenty left."

"Well, let's see one!"

Ennek wasn't sure which cell he'd been in before, but he didn't suppose it mattered. He stepped—much more confidently than he felt—to the nearest door and unlocked it. Wincing slightly, he swung the door open.

There was nobody in the cell. Both boys let out sighs, maybe of mixed relief and disappointment. One of the hammock things was there, but it was empty, and there was nothing else in the room except one tiny light affixed to the bumpy walls.

Gory walked inside and, with slight hesitation, touched the ropes. "Is this what they lie in?" he asked. His voice was quiet and a little hoarse, as if he needed to clear his throat.

"Yeah."

"It's soft. The ropes, I mean, they're soft, like silk."

"I suppose that protects their skin."

"Yeah, I guess so." He gave the webbing an experimental tug. "Strong. Okay, let's try another."

The next room was even emptier, without any ropes inside, and Gory clucked. "I'm beginning to think there's nobody here at all."

But the next room was occupied.

It might have been the same cell he'd been in before. Certainly the prisoner looked similar, but then, maybe they all looked like that after a while—skeletal, colorless, ageless. He hung suspended, with his eyes closed in such a way that the lids seemed almost sealed. His head was completely hairless, as was the rest of him. Ennek hadn't noted that the last time. He wondered if the prisoners were shaved for some reason, or if it was some side effect of Stasis. It made him look less human, sexless almost, despite the penis and scrotum clearly visible between his legs.

Ennek and Gory stood on either side of the prisoner, looking down at him, for a long time. Then Gory raised his arm and, very hesitantly, touched just one fingertip to the man's bicep before quickly snatching his hand away. The man didn't respond, of course. So Gory moved forward a bit, and this time he laid his palm flat against the unmoving chest.

Not to be outdone, Ennek rested his own hand on the man's shoulder.

"He feels like a corpse," Gory said.

"No, he doesn't."

Gory looked up sharply, but Ennek didn't elaborate. Two years ago he'd been on his way to the stables when he heard his mother scream. He'd dashed back to the keep and had discovered a dozen people—guards and passersby—gathered around her body, broken on the hard cobblestones beneath her window. Nobody else seemed certain what to do, so he was the first to touch her, to gather her into his arms and brush the blood-soaked hair from her face. Even in his horror and grief, he'd known she was dead, the form he was cradling nothing but an empty shell. The prisoner didn't feel like a shell. His shoulder was sharp bones and cold slick skin, but somehow Ennek could sense the spark of life still inside.

After several minutes, Gory seemed to work up more courage and allowed himself to explore the prisoner's body. Ennek watched uncomfortably as his friend rubbed the man's bald head and parted his bloodless lips with his fingers. Then Gory slapped the man's chest quite hard and looked with interest as no redness resulted. Ennek turned his head away. "Don't!" he said urgently.

"Why not? He doesn't care."

"It's... disrespectful."

"Disrespectful? This guy probably plotted to kill your father, or maybe your grandfather. He doesn't deserve respect."

Ennek took his hand off the man's shoulder, shoved it into his pocket, and shifted from foot to foot. "It's... it's wrong."

"I'm just curious, that's all."

Ennek turned his back and stood facing the open door, staring at the identical door across the way, pretending his belly wasn't lurching uncomfortably.

After several minutes, Gory huffed out a heavy breath and stomped over to where Ennek still had his back to the cell.

"You ready, then?" Ennek said gruffly. The thought of his own bed, warm and safe and familiar, had never been so welcome.

"Do you think there are any... female prisoners? We could just take a peek."

Ennek gritted his teeth and growled, "I don't know."

"Let's find out." Gory pushed past Ennek. Gory didn't have the keys, though, and wouldn't be able to open any more cells. Ennek could just leave right now, *should* leave right now, and Gory would have to comply or face being locked down here by himself, in the dark. Ennek was pretty certain Gory wasn't prepared to face that.

Gory waited impatiently at the next door down the corridor. "C'mon, Ennek. We don't have all night."

Ennek looked back and forth between the other boy and the door leading to the stairs. Gory was shivering with cold—just as Ennek had predicted—but his face was flushed with excitement and his blue eyes were sparkling brilliantly in the gaslight. "Just one more," Ennek sighed, and Gory let out a small whoop of triumph.

Something made Ennek pause before he unlocked the door, but Gory pounded his back. "Hurry!" he said, his breath hot against Ennek's neck.

Ennek unlocked the door to find another man. Gory made a disappointed sound and grabbed Ennek's arm, as if he was going to drag him away, probably to try another cell. But Ennek was drawn forward. There was something different about this prisoner, despite the fact that he looked like the others suspended in white ropes, pale, hairless, and skinny.

Ennek reached for him, intending, perhaps, to touch his shoulder. But just before their skin made contact, the man's eyelids opened.

Behind him, Gory screamed and scrambled away, but Ennek was too petrified to move. The man's eyes were the color of the sea, all greens and grays, and although the pupils seemed unnaturally large, Ennek thought the man's gaze was focused on him. His eyes were pools of anguish. The prisoner twitched then, just a tiny movement of his upper body, and made a small sound somewhere between a moan and whimper.

"Are you awake?" Ennek rasped.

The man twitched again and gasped. And then his eyelids fell closed and he was as still as death.

"Are you awake?" Ennek repeated, but there was no response. He steeled himself and, with all the courage he could muster, touched the man's cold cheek. Nothing happened.

"Ennek! Let's get the hell out of here!" Gory sounded like he might be about to cry, and he tugged again on Ennek's arm, more frantically this time.

Ennek brushed the man's cheek again, softly. Then he turned and let Gory haul him away.

chapter one

THE MAN named Wick was cheating. He wasn't all that good at it, but Ennek supposed Wick was too drunk to concentrate. Ennek was not drunk. Not yet anyway. He preferred to wait until he was in his own chambers for that, ever since the time he'd had almost a full bottle of whiskey and had serenaded the innkeeper's son. Someone had called the guard, the guard had recognized him and notified the Chief, and the Chief had had him dragged back to the keep and kept under lock and key for a month. He could still picture the startling color of the Chief's face the next day, almost purple. "You will *not* dishonor me or this family or the office I hold. Do not think that blood ties will protect you from punishment."

Ennek had had a flash of memory then. A cold stone room. A web. The sea. He didn't know what it meant, but it made him shudder.

Taking a deep breath as if to calm himself, the Chief had come so close that he was looming over the chair in which Ennek sat. "You haven't traveled beyond those sleepy little inland cow towns. You don't know what the other great port cities of the world are like. They are pits of vice and degradation, filthy cesspools of corruption and depravity. What makes this polis the greatest in the world isn't our propitious location but the rules with which we live, the laws that ensure order and morality."

Ennek had nodded to show he was listening. He fought the urge to look down at his lap like a chastened child and instead stared directly ahead at the Chief's orderly desk. It loomed as vast as a playing field.

"I am the hand of the law. The last place I will tolerate disgrace is in my own keep, in my own home. Is this understood?"

"Yes, sir."

"This will be the last time we have this discussion."

So now Ennek spent his evenings at the inns or the gaming house and drank only sparingly until the night was waning and the proprietors were eyeing him impatiently. Then he'd stalk home through fog-shrouded streets and climb the hill, nod to the guards at the entrance of the keep, and find his way to his chambers. He'd shuck his coat and kick off his boots and, if the fire in his room burned hot enough, discard the rest of his clothing as well, and he'd sit on his leather chair and drink good red wine until his mind was as murky as the streets. Then he'd crawl into bed and pass out. The Chief undoubtedly knew about this but didn't seem to care, as long as Ennek remained sober and controlled in public.

Wick glanced slyly at him from under lowered lashes and slid a card out of his sleeve, using it to replace another that he quickly palmed and hid away. Ennek pretended not to see, instead bobbing his head absently at the music that trickled in from the common room.

The two other men at the table knew what was going on. They'd played with Ennek many times before and, unlike Wick, were well aware of who he was. But this was Wick's first time in the Gentlemen's Room. He owned a small ship, he said, and had recently sold a cargo of exotic cloth for a tidy profit, enough to allow him to move up in the world. These two men didn't bother to tip the newcomer off. Instead they played conservatively, folding early, waiting and watching to see what the Chief's younger son would do.

Wick splayed his cards face up on the table and smiled. "Three kings," he said.

Ennek put his own cards down. He had nothing but a pair of sevens. He smiled back as Wick scooped up the pile of chips in the center. "You're having quite a run of luck," he said easily.

"Well, beginner's luck maybe, seeing as how I'm new here."

"Maybe," Ennek agreed.

One of the other men dealt the next hand, and this time Ennek won with a full house. Wick had folded early, though, and lost only a little.

The next time around, Wick again replaced a card with one from his sleeve. He was fairly good at it, actually, might even have pulled it off if he hadn't overindulged from the bar. When he put his cards down this time, he grinned triumphantly over a straight, queen high. Ennek had three aces. He waited until Wick had again scooped up his winnings and then chuckled. "You're cleaning me out, friend. I'm going to have to call it a night."

"Maybe you'll win next time," Wick said. His teeth were crooked and yellow, like a rat's. His blue suit, though, was very fine. It wouldn't fit Ennek—Wick was only a little taller, but much scrawnier, apart from the bulge of his belly—but it was worth a small fortune, probably. The buttons were gleaming silver, the cloth rich and well dyed.

"I'll tell you what," Ennek said. "One more hand. But instead of money, let's wager something else."

Wick's expression sharpened with interest. "What did you have in mind?"

"Your suit. I'll wager your suit against this." He slid a heavy gold ring off his finger and set it on the table. It had been his eighteenth birthday gift—a fancy bauble in place of the keys of office—and it was inset with a large red stone imported from overseas. It was worth far more than the clothing.

Wick's eyes grew very wide, and he stared at the ring as if mesmerized. The other two men sat back comfortably in their seats. Their faces were neutral, but they knew the denouement of the evening's little drama was close at hand.

"All right," Wick said. His voice shook a little.

The man to Ennek's right began to shuffle the cards. Ennek hummed quietly. Just as the man cut the deck, a split second before he began to deal, Ennek said, "Did you hear what the Chief did last night?"

"No, what?" said the dealer, not quite suppressing a smile.

"He found four men guilty of cheating—three at cards, one at dice. He sentenced them all to ten years as bond-slaves."

Wick swallowed audibly.

The man to Ennek's left said, "Well, the Chief has little patience for swindlers. I've heard he's told the guard to keep an eye out for them. Is that true, Ennek?"

Ennek watched as the dealer handed a card to Wick, who took it distractedly. He'd grown pale.

Ennek smiled and shrugged. "I don't know. I don't keep very close tabs on what my father's doing."

All three men looked worried as Wick had a sudden choking fit. "Can I get you some water?" Ennek asked politely.

"No… um… I'm fine. Just fine."

"Well, then, let's play this hand, shall we? It's getting late."

Ennek whistled as he walked home. It was earlier than usual for him, and a few people still strolled the streets. At the bottom of Keep Hill, he passed a freedman who was pushing a small wagon, probably laden with whatever junk he'd managed to scavenge for sale. Ennek handed the bundle of blue clothing over to the astonished man. "Here you go." He smiled. "Doesn't fit me well, I'm afraid. But it looks about your size."

As the man gaped, Ennek continued on his way, his whistling interrupted by guffaws as he pictured Wick scuttling home wearing only his underclothes beneath his coat.

"YOU NEED a job," Larkin said.

Ennek put his feet on the low table of carved cherrywood with inlaid mother-of-pearl. Ugly as hell, he thought, but very expensive. Larkin scowled at him.

"I have a job."

Larkin leaned back and crossed his arms. "Oh? And what exactly is that, dear brother?"

"I read over treaties now and then. And when I'm not, I am the official Degenerate and Dissipated Younger Son."

"You read over treaties maybe twice a year. And the rest—that's going to get you in trouble."

"I do it quietly, now. Mostly."

Larkin sighed. "Why can't you just find some pretty girl and get married and—"

"That's my new job? Breeding? Carrying on the family line? I thought that was your purview, Lark." The heir's wife had just delivered their third child.

"That's not what I meant. You're not a kid anymore, En. You need to settle down. You don't have to adore the girl, just—"

Ennek looked his brother in the eyes. "I can't. Wouldn't be fair to her, whoever she might be, would it?"

Larkin opened his mouth, then closed it. This was as near as they'd ever come to saying the truth, the real reason Ennek hadn't settled down and never would. They'd go no further, certainly not here in the keep, certainly not when Larkin himself would sometime soon be charged with enforcing the Morality Code.

Larkin shook his head sadly. "Fine. But I do have a job for you, a real one. Something that could keep you busy if you let it."

"What?"

"Portmaster."

Ennek thought he'd misheard. "Say again?"

"Portmaster," Larkin repeated patiently.

"Busy, huh? Keeping track of every ship in and out, inventorying and taxing the cargos, overseeing the stevedores and longshoremen, maintaining the docks… sounds like a little more than busy to me."

Larkin waved his hand. "You can have assistants do most of that on a day-to-day basis. You just check in on them as often as you want to. Watch out for corruption, make sure everything's running smoothly."

Ennek shifted his feet a little and gazed at the faded tapestry hanging above Larkin's head. It was seven hundred years old, he'd been told once. Priceless. It depicted a harbor in which ships stuffed with every imaginable food and luxury sailed peacefully in and out under cloudless skies. "Is this a request or a command?"

"A command" was the quiet answer. "From the Chief himself, not me."

Ennek jumped to his feet. "Then I guess I'll have to comply. Wouldn't want to defy orders and end up a bond-slave or something."

It must have been the sourness of his tone that made Larkin lose his usually serene temper. "Keep up the disrespect and it'll more likely be Stasis for you," he spat.

Ennek glared and left without saying another word.

WHEN ENNEK had turned eighteen, he moved out of the small chamber in which he'd spent most of his life and into a larger suite. It was still in the private part of the keep, but farther from the Chief and Larkin and his family. It had one very large room with windows that looked out to the bay, a bathroom with reasonably modern plumbing, and another room whose windows had a view of the open sea. The larger room served as his bedroom and lounge and private library, while he'd set up the smaller to exercise in. He had weights to lift and an ingenious machine that permitted him to run in place. He would have preferred to run outside, but the Chief had forbidden it. Too distracting, he said. The guard might mistake him for a thief or worse. Ennek knew that was nonsense—the guard would soon get used to him running, as they'd long since grown accustomed to the way he rode his horse at a gallop or, on a whim, commandeered one of the keep's small boats so he could cross the bay and hike in the wild headlands. But the Chief's word was the law, and so Ennek ran indoors, looking out at the endlessly shifting waves.

One of the gifts Ennek had received from his forebears was a strong, solid build. He was a little shorter than average, but his shoulders were broad and his bones heavy, and he had thick slabs of muscle across his chest, arms and legs, and back. He also worked hard to keep his belly trim, not for the looks he'd collect—admiration from women and envy from men—but rather because his body was one thing over which he had control. Exercise kept him occupied and prevented him from thinking too hard, and afterward he was pleasantly exhausted and able to sleep more soundly, sometimes without needing alcohol's soothing effects.

But tonight, even though he'd run and stretched and lifted weights until his breaths came in gasps and his body dripped with sweat, he couldn't find peace. Larkin's words kept echoing in his head. Not the part about the job—Ennek didn't really mind about that. It would keep him busy in a good sort of way, and the docks were always interesting, full of action and exotic sights and sounds. He liked the sailors, their rough accents, and the tales of their travels. They were one of the reasons he so often visited the inns, even the ones the Chief said were below his station.

No, what was gnawing at Ennek tonight, as he tossed and turned in his fine sheets, was his brother's angry threat. Stasis. Ennek hadn't thought of it for years, not since he was a boy. He'd pleaded to tag along on a tour Under then, and something unpleasant had happened. He didn't quite remember what—he'd been burying those events as deeply as possible for a very long time. But he thought it was probably related to the dream, the nightmare that came to him sometimes and left him screaming in his bed.

The dream was always the same. There were endless stairs, down and down and down, perhaps into the bowels of hell itself, only cold. There was the wizard, Thelius, ageless and gaunt as death, with unnaturally long fingers that wandered and grasped like pale spiders. Spiders that spun enormous sticky webs that trapped men inside. There was a boy, smiling, holding red candy in his palm. And there was the ocean, pounding and crashing—not mindlessly, not even malevolently, but desperately, fearfully, as if it were trying to escape. What could the sea need to escape?

This was the dream that led him to drink so heavily, because sometimes if he drank himself into a stupor, the dream wouldn't come.

Tonight, though, he was pretty sure it would.

chapter two

"The *Eclipse* is ready to sail at dawn, sir. Pending your approval, of course."

Ennek looked up from the pile of manifests and met his assistant portmaster's grin with one of his own. He'd heard rumors that Mila's father had been a pirate, and looking at her now, he could well believe it. She was getting on in years—closer to sixty than fifty—but still trim and fit, with iron-gray hair that frizzed around her head no matter how she tried to tame it, a jaunty uniform that was always impeccably clean and pressed, and a sparkle of mischievous glee in her green eyes.

"They've fixed their little problems?"

"So the captain says. But I thought perhaps you'd like to do the final inspection yourself."

"The *new* captain, yes?"

"Yes, sir." Her smile ratcheted up a notch or two.

"I'll be right with you."

Mila waited patiently, gazing at the paintings of ships that hung on the office walls, while he read another few pages and then signed them with a flourish. He grabbed his coat and put it on. It was a little gaudy for his tastes, with shiny brass buttons and miles of golden braid, but it was required when he acted in his official capacity. And besides, it was nice and warm.

Ennek and Mila left the office, walked past his secretary, who nodded at them briskly, and stepped out the door and onto the wooden planks that led to the piers. Ennek paused for a moment to take a deep breath of salty air—he'd been inside most of the day, inhaling woodsmoke and dust. Then they walked down to where the *Eclipse* was berthed.

She was a sleek three-masted clipper that had arrived two weeks earlier with a cargo of tea and spices. Her holds were now filled with almonds and cotton and wool fabrics, and she'd been meant to sail two days earlier. But for no particular reason, Ennek had decided to inspect this ship himself. As he'd totaled up the export duties owed, he'd seen an odd gleam in the captain's eyes, and it made him suspicious. Ever since prospectors had discovered gold in the mountains three days' ride to the east, there had been a marked increase in attempts to smuggle valuable cargo through the port without paying appropriate taxes.

Ennek had wandered the deck with the captain in tow until they drew very close to a knot of the *Eclipse*'s sailors who were repairing some rigging. "Now, Captain," he said, rather more loudly than necessary, "I'm sure you're aware of the penalties for gold smuggling."

The captain paled a little. "Yes. A fine of triple the tax."

"No, that's the penalty for ordinary smuggling. The Chief has increased the punishments for gold specifically. It's been a real problem, you see. So many people eager to profit without paying their dues."

"What's the fine for gold?" The captain tried for nonchalance and failed.

"Oh, it's not a fine. It's twenty years as a bond-slave for officers and ten for every other man aboard." Out of the corner of his eye, he saw the sailors exchange nervous looks.

"That's quite harsh, sir," said Mila, who knew exactly what was going on.

"No more than the scurvy dogs deserve," he countered. He was glad he'd been able to maintain a straight face. He disembarked shortly afterward, taking care to inform Mila—within earshot of the sailors—that he'd be in his office for the next hour.

Fifteen minutes later his secretary informed him that three sailors from the *Eclipse* were asking to see the portmaster about a matter of great importance. Ennek smiled and told the secretary to let them in.

He recognized them immediately as members of the group who heard the onboard conversation. They stood in his office for a moment, filling it with the reek of cheap whiskey and nudging one another nervously. Then one of them stepped forward, a bald man with a deeply lined face and a scar across one cheek.

"Sir, um, begging your pardon."

"Yes?" Ennek tapped his pen impatiently on his desktop.

"About the punishment for smuggling gold, sir."

"Ten years. Yes?"

"Would it still apply, if, er, the ship hadn't left port yet? Sir?"

"Yes, it would, as long as it was evident that an attempt had been made to hide its presence."

"But what if… what if someone was to let you know about it, like? Would that man be punished?"

Ennek allowed a slight frown to settle on his face. "If the gold were disclosed before sailing, only the captain would be penalized."

Less than twenty minutes later, Ennek and Mila and members of the guard were looking at several pounds of gold ingots that had been hidden behind a false wall. The captain was taken into custody, the ship's owner notified and a hefty fine collected from him, and the first officer was promoted. Ennek made sure nobody else was punished. Most of them probably hadn't known about the gold anyway.

As Ennek boarded the ship now, the new captain was there to greet him with a smile and a handshake. "You'll find all cargo properly listed on the manifest, sir," he said.

"I'm pleased to hear that. I value honesty a great deal, Captain."

The man nodded and looked him in the eyes. "Yes, sir. I can ensure that's what you will receive from me."

Ennek made a quick tour of the ship. It was possible that there was more gold hidden elsewhere, but he doubted it, and in any case, the former captain's predicament would surely discourage at least some future misdeeds.

After walking the hold from end to end, Ennek climbed back to the deck and, with a broad smile, signed the certificate that permitted the *Eclipse* to set sail at her pleasure. He shook the captain's hand once again. "Have a safe journey, Captain."

"Thank you, sir. I shall look forward to meeting again on our next visit."

Ennek walked down the gangplank and spent several minutes standing next to Mila, watching longshoremen carry boxes and bales and crates and bins onto and off ships. Men rowed a launch to a windjammer anchored in the middle of the bay, waiting for a suitably sized berth to become available. Off in the distance, a small fleet of smacks sailed inland, no doubt taking some of today's catch to the evening markets in Beneventum and Mareota. At the narrow mouth of the bay, a thick layer of clouds was building, ready to roll inward and blanket the polis. As always, the sight of the gray-green water both soothed and unsettled him.

Mila turned to him. "That was good of you, sir. Not to punish the crew, I mean."

He shrugged. "This worked better. The word will get out, I'm sure. Besides, we could use more sailors than slaves."

"That captain will be bound, though, sir. For twenty years."

"True enough. He shouldn't have broken the law."

"He'll be an old man when he's free, if he survives that long."

He crooked his head at her, but she was looking at the bay, not at him. "It's the law, Mila. It's the basis of our civilization. It makes us strong."

"Yes, sir."

There was a long pause, and then he sighed. "I think I'll take the rest of the day off. Mila, it's all yours."

"Thank you, sir. Enjoy your afternoon."

He stopped in his office to exchange the flashy coat for a more staid navy wool. He'd walked rather than ridden to the port that morning—it was only about twenty minutes away, if he moved briskly—but now, suddenly in a hurry, he had a guard hail a hackney carriage. The coachman must have recognized him, because he was especially fawning until Ennek ordered him to just get a move on.

At the keep, Ennek told the coachman to wait. He dashed upstairs to his chambers and rooted in a wardrobe until he unearthed a canvas bag, into which he shoved a change of clothing. He toed off his shiny portmaster's shoes and replaced them with a pair of sturdy dun-colored boots. Then he ran back downstairs and out of the keep.

"Back to the port," he commanded. "Quickly!"

The ride took less than five minutes, despite the afternoon crowds in the streets. Ennek threw the coachman some coins and trotted to the headquarters of the port guards, a squat stone building a hundred yards from his office. The lieutenant was inside, discussing something with an underling, and he jumped a little when Ennek slammed through the door.

"I need a boat," Ennek announced.

"Yes, sir. Fifteen minutes. Would you like a drink while you wait?"

"No."

In fact, Ennek refused the lieutenant's invitation to sit by his fire, instead choosing to lean against the outside of the building and watch the guards scurry to prepare the catboat with the red-striped sail. They knew what he expected of them by now, and within twelve minutes, he was clambering onto the boat while a dour-faced guard held the tiller and the lieutenant himself untied the mooring line from the bollard.

Ennek didn't speak to the guard as they sailed across the bay. He just stared at the waves that peaked and bobbed beside the boat, and then up at the gulls that wheeled optimistically overhead.

They soon found their way to a small pier tucked into a tiny cove under the hulking rocks of the headlands, and the guard tied up the boat. After a brief order to set up camp, Ennek marched away.

He'd come this way many times, so he immediately found the rough little trail and scrambled upward through thickly scented scrub, past stunted trees and furry-leaved flowers. At one point the path turned inland a bit and traveled through a small sheltered canyon where redwoods towered and small creatures rustled about. Soon enough, though, he'd reached the top of the hill. Here there were mostly grasses, newly green under the autumn rains. Far overhead, hawks hovered and banked.

Ennek plopped onto the ground. He could see the keep from here, dark and looming at the entrance to the bay, and beneath it, the streets that strove vainly for order among the polis's steep hills. There was the *Eclipse*, waiting to sail in the morning, and several score of large ships, as well as countless little ones that scurried around like hyperactive children. If he turned slightly, he could look out to the open sea. He wished he'd thought to bring a spyglass; perhaps he'd be able to make out some migrating whales. He chuckled to himself. He'd have been better off bringing a gun, really—lions were common here, and he probably looked like a tasty meal.

The water was shifting greens and grays, colors that made him think of the word "home" and the word "trapped," and he wasn't sure why.

He was tempted to stay up and watch the sunset, but he didn't have a light and didn't much care for the idea of finding his way back in the dark, so he slowly descended. The guard had set up a tent a few yards from the pier and started a fire. Ennek could smell coffee brewing and meat over the flames.

He didn't talk to the guard as he ate. He didn't even know the man's name, actually. But they chewed companionably together, Ennek shared his bottle of wine, and they gazed into the flickering flames for hours, listening to owls cry and, somewhere close by, a coyote bark and howl.

Finally Ennek clambered to his feet. "Going to call it a night," he said.

"Sleep well, sir," said the guard, still not quite cracking a smile.

The tent was cozy, with pillows and warm blankets piled atop a thick pad. A small wooden stool held a lantern, and Ennek liked the way its warm glow bathed the small space. As per his usual orders, there was also a fresh bottle of whiskey and a green glass tumbler. Ennek considered the amber liquid for a few moments and then shook his head. No, not tonight. He stripped off all his clothes—it pleased him to sleep naked when he was outside like this—and climbed beneath the layers of soft wool. He leaned over and turned out the lamp and then, with a heavy sigh, closed his eyes.

THE DREAM started as it always did. He was very small, and he was descending an endless stairway that circled and twisted like an insane snake. He didn't want to go, but his feet wouldn't stop, and he knew that if he didn't walk, he'd tumble down the stairs instead. At the bottom of the stairway was a long corridor in which pale spiders lurked in enormous webs. He was frightened of the spiders and tried to hurry past them. And then there was a door, tall and so narrow he could barely slip inside.

The wizard was in the shadows at the edge of the room. He was gray—gray hair, gray shirt and trousers, a long gray coat, gray skin. His face was as bloodless as death, and his lips were peeled back to expose long, yellowed teeth. His hands had too many fingers, each multijointed and much too long. One of the hands rested on the shoulder of the boy beside him, a youth with hair like tasseled silk and a face that might have been smirking or caught in a rictus of fear. The boy's mouth was smeared with sticky scarlet, and more of the stuff coated his outstretched palm. "Sleeping potion," he whispered. "Just what a restless sleeper needs."

At the center of the floor was a hole. If he looked into it—and Ennek always did; he couldn't help it—he saw empty space and, beneath that, the sea. The waves boiled and tumbled, and Ennek could tell they were rising and would soon enter the room, filling it.

At this point in the dream, Ennek would whirl around and try to find the door, but it would be gone. The shape of the room itself would shift, like lungs moving in and out, and Ennek would realize he was actually inside the Chief, and the Chief *was* the keep. Thelius and the boy would watch silently as Ennek ran around, trying desperately to find his way out, until he began screaming. He'd awake hopelessly tangled in the bedsheets, sweaty and feverish. If he tried to speak, his voice would be hoarse.

Tonight, though, there was a difference.

He still looked down into the hole, and the waters were still getting nearer, but now he could see a hand—a pale human hand—sticking up through the waves. It was attached to a skinny arm. Another arm breached the surface, and then so did a head, bald as an egg. The head turned and looked upward. The man's eyes were the exact color of the sea around him, as if the ocean was inside him too. He blinked with lashless lids and choked a little on a wave that washed into his mouth. "Help me," he said, not a shout but a quiet plea. "Help me, please."

Ennek woke up then. And when he did, he remembered.

chapter three

USUALLY THE things a person remembers as being very large when he was a child turn out to be quite small when he visits them again as an adult. When Ennek was eight, for example, his mother took him along when she called on a friend who had a daughter close to his age. The father was a member of the Council, and the family lived in a grand house at the top of a hill. The house had seemed incredibly warm and comfortable to Ennek, who was used to the angular stone confines of the keep. And it had a large grassy lawn in back, trimmed short by bond-slaves and surrounded by colorful flowerbeds. On one edge of the lawn was the daughter's playhouse, cunningly built to mimic the main house in miniature, with child-size furnishings. Ennek and the girl had spent a pleasant afternoon inside, drinking tea and reading books and making forts out of building blocks. The playhouse had seemed like perfection itself, and he remembered wishing he could live there. Two years ago he'd gone there again, this time to discuss port business with the father. Of course the girl was grown and now a mother herself, and her daughter had smilingly led Ennek to the playhouse. Ennek had had to stoop and turn awkwardly to fit through the door, and inside he stood with his head bowed under the low ceiling, afraid to move lest he damage the tiny, delicate furniture.

When Ennek walked down the stairs that led Under, though, they were every bit as steep and long as he remembered, the gaslights flickered just as eerily, and the sound of pounding surf was just as loud. At least it had been easier to gain access as an adult. He had his own keys now, and the guard recognized him and stepped aside without asking for explanations. No need for drugged candies this time.

It felt as though it took him weeks to make it to the bottom, but eventually he was there, and he carefully locked the door behind him. He thought what it would be like to run into Thelius here and he shivered, even though he knew the wizard was at a Council meeting right now, along with the Chief and Larkin.

Although he was fairly certain of the correct general area of the corridor, he couldn't remember exactly which door. The first cell he unlocked was empty except for the ropes. There was a prisoner in the second, though a quick glance told Ennek this was not the one he was searching for. This man's skin was very dark, like that of some of the sailors who came from far away. Still, Ennek couldn't resist stepping in for a closer look.

When he did, his gorge rose. Patches of skin were missing from the man's chest and upper thighs, precise squares that revealed red masses of muscle. The edges of the cuts were regular and sharp, except for one that seemed to have begun to heal a little, the sides of which were ragged and a light tan.

There were burns as well. Six circles in two even rows across the man's hollow belly, each about the size of a coin. The burned skin was blistered and charred.

The worst, though, was the part that Ennek's mind had refused to register at first. An opening had been cut near the center of the man's chest, and silvery clamps held the flaps of skin and muscle aside so that Ennek was looking straight into the prisoner's ribcage and at his bluish, unbeating heart. A long metal skewer protruded from the heart itself.

Ennek backed away and turned around, then leaned his forehead against the cold, damp wall. He squeezed his eyes tightly shut, as if that would somehow erase the image of what he had just seen. His breaths were ragged and coarse, his mouth tasted bitter, and his heart seemed to be trying to escape his body.

He didn't know how long it took to get himself under control, but eventually he crept out of the room, carefully keeping his back to the inhabitant. He heaved a sigh of relief when the door was locked behind him. For several moments he looked longingly at the end of the corridor and considered going back up. He knew if he did, though, his dreams would be even more haunting, and he wasn't certain he could force himself to come Under again.

The next cell was the one he'd been searching for. He recognized the man at once, even though the memories had been buried for so long. Ennek realized with a slight start that the prisoner, who'd seemed infinitely old when Ennek was twelve, had probably been in his midtwenties—a few years younger than Ennek—when he was put in Stasis.

Ennek stood very close to the man and hesitantly stroked one of the ropes that held him. It was silky, like human hair, and he drew his fingers away in distaste. The man wasn't moving, every bit as lifeless as a person in Stasis ought to be, and Ennek began to wonder if he'd imagined the whole thing all those years ago. Boys are excitable and could easily spook themselves, and he'd been overtired and jumpy in any case. Maybe Gory had jostled the man a little. They'd both been standing very near him, and the rope web wasn't completely stable.

This prisoner was a traitor. Long before Ennek was born—perhaps very long before—he had committed some perfidious act against one of Ennek's forebears. Against the polis itself. His punishment was humane and just, considering the nature of his crime. Had he been in another polis, he would certainly be dust in an unmarked grave. He was—

The man opened his eyes.

They were as sea-colored as Ennek recalled, and deeply tortured. They focused straight on Ennek's face, and the prisoner's legs spasmed as if he were trying kick his way free. His mouth opened and a thin, dry croak emerged from his lungs. He struggled for a breath and his shoulders twitched. Then his eyes rolled back in his head, his lids fell shut, and he was once again motionless.

Ennek had been frozen in place, his mouth hanging open, and only now did it occur to him to talk with the man. "I don't know if you can hear me," he said. Despite the eternally pounding waves, his voice sounded very loud. "I'm... I was here before, once. A long time ago. My name is Ennek."

The prisoner didn't respond.

Ennek set his hand on the cold, smooth skin of the man's shoulder, wondering if somehow the prisoner could sense the heat of his body, and if so, whether it comforted him. "If you're... aware, that's not right. It's not supposed to be like that." And then he did something very foolish— he made a promise. "I'm going to look into it. I'll help."

What kind of answer did he expect? Tears of gratitude? Singing angels? The furious fire of retribution? None of those happened, of course. In fact, nothing happened at all, except that his own heart counted away another few seconds of his life.

PACING THE length of his bedchamber didn't help. Nor did climbing on a horse and galloping through the streets past startled pedestrians. A long sail around the choppy waters of the bay, followed by a vigorous hike in the headlands, was of no benefit. And predictably, a bottle of whiskey didn't help either.

He'd never been much for planning. He was bright enough, but he rarely thought about the future, and he tended to take things as they came. He hadn't *needed* to plan; he was the younger son. Even since he'd become portmaster, most of his responsibilities were rather simple routine tasks that hadn't changed much for generations and certainly required little in the way of innovation. Oh, sometimes he had a small bit of fun, like with the *Eclipse*, but mostly he just did what he was supposed to and moved on. It had been enough, all these years. But it wasn't enough now.

A week after Ennek went Under for the third time in his life, the Chief was hosting a state dinner. The chiefs from a half-dozen other polises would be there, and the entire Council, and all the spouses as well. Of course Ennek was expected to appear, sit at the Chief's left side, and look sober and well-bred. He had to wear his uniform—the whole thing, not just the stupid coat—and he swore as he buckled the uncomfortable long black boots over tight navy trousers with more gold braid down the sides.

His hair had grown a bit longer than he generally permitted, and the curls were starting to have their way with him. He oiled them in place, pleased that at least he wouldn't have to wear the ridiculous hat. Then he buckled a scabbard around his hips and let his hand rest for a moment on the finely made hilt. The sword was ceremonial, of course, a vestige of days when the office of portmaster involved less bureaucracy and more swashbuckling. He knew how to use it, though—he'd had several years of lessons when he was younger—and he liked the feel of the weapon at his side.

With a last glance at the mirror to ensure he was presentable, Ennek left his chambers. The keep was unusually noisy tonight as guests, guards, servants, and bond-slaves scurried here and there. Ennek nodded to a tall woman in a turquoise silk dress who was waiting for someone outside an open door as he made his way to the broad main stairway.

The Chief stood outside the entrance to the dining hall, his back very straight, seeming much taller than he really was. For once, his lips twitched in an almost smile when he saw his younger son.

"Good evening, sir," Ennek said.

"Good evening to you. You look very fine in that uniform. You ought to wear it more often."

"Thank you, sir," Ennek said, and then stepped inside to make room for the couple behind him.

Because Ennek had procrastinated about getting ready, most of the guests had already arrived. The huge room was awash in color from the women's dresses, and quiet conversations and polite laughter echoed off the walls. Ennek caught sight of Larkin talking to the chief of Vinovia while Larkin's pretty wife, Velison, clapped her hands at something the chief's husband had said. Larkin gave Ennek a little wave, but Ennek wandered in the other direction, where he'd caught sight of a councilman named Hils. Hils was younger than most of his colleagues and less grim, and besides, Ennek had been meaning to speak to him about a possible expansion of the piers that the small fishing boats used. Hils's family conducted the majority of the maritime construction in Praesidium.

On the way across the room, Ennek managed to snag a glass of wine from a servant's tray. It was quite good, probably some of Vinovia's best. He sipped at it appreciatively and grinned at Hils, who was swathed in an unwieldy-looking ceremonial robe himself.

"Nice outfit," Ennek said.

"Yeah." Hils looked miserable. He'd inherited his Council seat from his father, of course, but Ennek had the idea he hadn't really wanted it, that he'd much rather be standing on a half-built dock in sweat-stained clothes, swinging a hammer and yelling orders at his crew. "You're pretty spiffy yourself."

"I feel like a trained pony."

"Well, just make sure and step lively, then." Hils gestured across the room to where the Chief was making his way to the table. "Put on a good show."

Ennek sighed. "Yeah, yeah. Hey, we need to talk. I've been thinking about the piscarium piers. If we were to expand them, I'll bet we could convince some people to spend their gold earnings on larger fishing fleets, and if Nodosus improves the road as it plans, the inland markets would probably—"

Hils laughed and clapped him on the shoulder. "Hey, show ponies don't need to talk business. Looks like the Chief is ready for us to settle down. How about you join me for dinner… um… two nights past New Year? I'd very much like to discuss it then."

New Year was in less than a week. With his other concerns, Ennek had nearly forgotten.

"That sounds good," he said. "I'll probably be ready to eat again two days after."

"We can always have something light. Fish broth and greens, perhaps."

"And dry crackers, no butter."

With a small chuckle, they walked together toward the table. Hils patted him once more before they went their separate ways, Hils toward one end of the table and Ennek the other. Ennek had always had the hunch that if things had been different, he and Hils—well, it didn't bear thinking about.

The Chief was already seated and looking expectantly at Ennek. But Ennek couldn't help a scowl when he saw who would be sitting on his left. It was perfectly appropriate for the wizard to attend functions like this, but he rarely did. He rarely left the confines of his laboratory, actually, preferring the company of his potions and charms to that of other humans. Thelius was in gray as always, but tonight he was wearing fine wool trousers, a silk shirt, and a coat made of knobby raw silk with patterns sewn in silver threads—strange symbols that made Ennek feel a little dizzy when he looked closely at them. The wizard's face was ageless; if he had changed at all over the years, Ennek couldn't see it.

The Chief nodded at Ennek when he sat, but he didn't pause in his conversation with the person across from him, a tall, striking woman with white-streaked black hair and a long, slender neck. They were talking about horses, the one subject besides Praesidium itself that the Chief could grow passionate about. The man across from Ennek was a councilman whose name Ennek couldn't recall, and he ignored Ennek completely as he stared rapturously at the woman beside him.

On Ennek's left, Thelius made a small, raspy sound that might have been a throat clearing. "It's pleasant to see you," he said when Ennek turned his head to look at him. "It's been some time."

Ennek mumbled something in reply, but his mind was teetering on the brink of panic. The wizard was giving him a knowing sort of look, a little half smile of sorts. Did he know Ennek had been Under again?

A servant came from behind and filled Ennek's wineglass. He had to restrain himself from draining the thing without waiting for the Chief to give the opening toast. Luckily, the Chief stood just a moment later, his own glass held high.

"Ladies and gentlemen, friends and honored guests, thank you for joining us this evening. I know the chefs have prepared a wonderful dinner for us tonight, and our generous friends from Vinovia have graciously provided the excellent wine." A few seats down, the chief of Vinovia nodded magisterially. "Please join me in drinking to the health of the heir and his wife, who are expecting their fourth child next year."

Fourth. Wonderful. Soon the keep would be overrun by Larkin's spawn. But Ennek raised his glass along with everyone else, took a small, polite sip, and then drank the rest in one long draught. As soon as the crowd put down their glasses, a bevy of servants appeared as if by magic, bearing robin's-egg blue bowls of steaming soup.

Ennek wasn't particularly hungry, not with Thelius's steady gaze aimed at him, but he picked up his spoon anyway and dipped it into the bowl, then brought the fragrant broth to his mouth. It was good stuff, salty and meaty, perfect to fill a belly on a cold winter night. He ate three or four more spoonfuls before setting down the silverware. He regretted doing so, though, because Thelius seemed to take that as an opportunity to engage in conversation.

"How are you enjoying your duties as portmaster, Ennek?"

"It's interesting," he replied shortly.

"A lot of activity, I'll wager. Always something to pique a man's curiosity."

"Yes, I suppose so."

"You are a man with an inquisitive mind, are you not?"

Ennek shifted uncomfortably in his seat. "Um, sure, I guess."

"I thought so. Even when you were a child, you struck me that way."

Ennek tried not to think about why the wizard had been contemplating him when he was a child. A servant whisked away his still-full soup bowl and replaced it a moment later with a plate of shelled crab and a small crock of drawn butter. Ennek attacked this with more relish—Dungeness season had only recently begun, and it was one of his favorite foods. He carefully avoided watching the way the small morsels of white meat slipped between Thelius's thin, dry lips. The wineglass now held a crisp white that Ennek actually managed to savor rather than gulp.

As soon as Thelius finished the crab, however, he addressed Ennek again. "I hear you've managed to reduce the magnitude of the gold smuggling problem."

"I hope so." Ennek dabbed at his lips with his navy linen napkin.

"If you'll allow me, I have something that might aid you. I've not yet mentioned it to the Chief."

Ennek glanced the other way, but the Chief was still deep in his discussion with the woman. "Aid me how?"

"It's a magical device for detecting contraband. If you'd be so kind as to come by my laboratory, I'd be pleased to demonstrate it for you."

Ennek did not want to go to the laboratory. But he had the feeling that if he refused, the Chief would hear about it, and then Ennek would have to explain himself, which he wanted to do even less. "All right," he said, probably not very graciously.

But the wizard smiled anyway. "Wonderful! Tomorrow evening, perhaps? Eight o'clock?"

"Fine." The next course arrived—rare beef baked inside a golden pastry and covered with a spicy sauce. Ennek's fickle appetite had deserted him again, but as he picked at the course, he enjoyed the red wine that accompanied it. He was relieved when Thelius began chatting about herbs with the middle-aged woman across from him. The man opposite Ennek remained entranced by the Chief's conversation partner, so Ennek toyed with his cutlery and looked around the room, admiring how the flickering candles threw shadows onto the tapestried walls. Someone had hung over the doorways great boughs of fragrant fir with sprigs of bright red pepperberries entwined, and the effect was warm and festive.

Ennek didn't eat the next course at all—lightly steamed carrots, broccoli, and fresh winter greens—but he picked at it with his fork so maybe nobody would notice. Finally, a servant gave him a plate containing candied walnuts and spiced almonds, and a tiny pear tart that smelled of cinnamon. Ennek ate a few of the nuts.

When the last dishes were cleared away, the Chief stood, signaling the end of the meal. The guests stood as well and began to gather in small clusters in the dining hall and in the reception room next door, most of them holding glasses of sweet wine. Ennek went to leave, but before he managed to escape, a bony hand clutched at his arm.

"Don't forget: eight o'clock," said Thelius, grinning like a death's head.

"Eight o'clock," agreed Ennek. When the wizard released him, Ennek found the Chief surrounded by a group of men and women. He bowed his head slightly, and the Chief gave a small frown but then waved him away. The younger son was excused.

ENNEK SLEPT very little that night. He took off his clothes and bathed and got into bed, but then he tossed and turned until the sheets were in a hopeless knot and his skin felt bruised and tender. He got up and stood at his window, looking out over the sea. The moon was full, and it made the water sparkle like precious jewels. Despite the cold and his nudity, he opened the glass and listened to a sea lion calling loudly, as if it meant him to answer. He suddenly remembered a story his mother had told him when he was very young, about a young chief who'd heard a sea lion calling to her every evening and had been unable to sleep. She'd finally ordered it killed, and only when it was dead did the corpse morph back into her lover, who'd been enchanted by an evil wizard. His mother had claimed it was a true tale, something that had really happened long ago to one of his ancestors. He had told her then that he'd never have the animal killed, because he liked the raucous barking. He still did.

He wasn't sure how long he stood there, ignoring the chill on his skin, but at some point an idea began to form. It wasn't a very good idea, but it was something, and perhaps it would grow into something good.

By the time the sky had begun to lighten, he had climbed back into bed and fallen asleep. The sea lion was still calling.

chapter four

ENNEK HAD been in the laboratory once before, when he was ten. His mother needed something from the wizard. He didn't know what; she'd only instructed him to go fetch it for her. Even then, he wondered why she didn't have a servant do it, or one of the miserable bond-slaves who toted garbage or scrubbed toilets. But he didn't ask her—she had a wicked temper when questioned—and instead trotted off to the laboratory, which was in an odd little corner of the keep.

He had been uncomfortable around Thelius. But if the wizard hadn't been there, Ennek would have liked to explore the laboratory. It was fascinating. Everywhere his eyes fell were jars full of mysterious objects or multihued liquids. Dried bits and pieces of... things... were stacked on shelves: bones and hides and plant materials, and other things he couldn't identify. A shelving unit near the door held a collection of stones, some tiny and some very large. Some were dull and rough, while others sparkled and gleamed, and a few, he thought, might be precious jewels. Several tables were scattered around the large space, but the one in the center was huge, covered with books and manuscripts and glass beakers boiling away over flames. Books were everywhere, actually. On shelves and tables, on most of the chairs, even piled on the floor. A narrow winding staircase led upward, and if Ennek craned his neck, he could glimpse the tower room above, bathed in bright light from many windows.

Thelius had stood near the door, silently permitting the boy to look around for a while. But then Ennek remembered the purpose of his visit and politely asked for the thing his mother wanted. The wizard handed him a small wooden box closed with a tiny padlock and then, with a thin smile, ushered him out the door.

Ennek had always wondered what was in that box. Medicines, perhaps? The wizard was a skilled healer. His mother had died only a week or so later, and he'd never found out. He'd never seen the box again either.

Now Thelius greeted him happily and waved him into the room. Just as when he was a child, Ennek couldn't help but stare around for several minutes, trying to mentally catalog the room's wonders, and Thelius let him. Finally Ennek turned to him. "You had something to show me?"

"Yes, certainly. Follow me, please, Ennek."

They made their way across the chamber, skirting towers of books and a small table topped with a wooden crate full of seashells. They came to a halt by a larger table up against one wall, its surface empty except for a tube made of a dull-colored metal. It was about the size of a wine bottle and had what appeared to be a cap on one end, made of purplish wood with a dark grain.

Thelius picked up the tube. "This is something I've invented myself," he said proudly. "It works on the principle that like calls to like. A very important principle indeed." He gave Ennek what seemed to be a significant look, but Ennek didn't understand why and chose to ignore it.

The wizard continued. "It is quite simple to use. You put a small amount of the sought-after substance inside, and it will lead you to more. It can detect within approximately a twenty-foot radius." He held the tube out in one hand and stroked it slightly with the other, which Ennek found disturbing.

"What kinds of things can it find?" he asked, just to be saying something.

"Anything you like. Here, allow me to demonstrate its operation."

Ennek watched as Thelius strode across the room to the shelf that contained the rocks. He took something from a box there and returned, cupping a small red stone in his palm. "Watch." He carefully pulled off the wooden part and dropped the stone inside, then replaced the cap. Immediately the tube began making a high-pitched hum. "Here, take it," Thelius said and pressed it into Ennek's not particularly willing grip.

The metal was surprisingly warm—almost hot—and it was vibrating slightly. "What am I supposed to do?" he asked.

"Just hold it, but walk toward the door."

Doubtfully, Ennek complied. But as he approached his destination, the tube began to vibrate more urgently, requiring a firmer grip.

"Wave it around a bit, Ennek."

When he did, the movement became more agitated as it got closer to the shelf and calmed a little as he drew it farther away. Using the object to guide him, Ennek found himself standing in front of the shelf, holding the tube close to an octagonal metal box.

"See?" the wizard said from right behind his shoulder, making him jump a little. He hadn't noticed Thelius's approach. Thelius reached over and opened the box. Inside were six or seven stones identical to the one in the tube.

Thelius gently took the tube from Ennek's hands, unstoppered it, and poured the stone out. He placed it with the others and closed the metal box. Then he handed the tube back to Ennek.

"You can use it for anything, organic or inorganic. It's fairly discerning, but not completely. If I put a bit of silk fabric inside, for example, it would find anything made of moth's silk but not, say, spider's."

Ennek had a quick memory of a web of ropes, and he shivered a little. Thelius didn't notice or at least chose not to remark on it. Instead he continued his lecture. "But if I placed an owl's bone inside, it would find anything from an owl—other bones, feathers, blood. In your case, I imagine you'll be searching primarily for gold, and it will easily lead you to any gold nearby, whether or not it's hidden."

"That's... amazing," Ennek said, because it was.

Thelius looked pleased. "I'm quite proud of it. As I said, I invented it myself, and I've showed it to nobody but you. In fact, Ennek, I made it especially *for* you."

That wasn't anything Ennek wanted to hear. "Why?" he asked.

"Because I thought you might appreciate it. And, honestly? Because I hoped it might persuade you to listen to me."

"Listen to you about what?" Ennek realized he'd been backing toward the door, Thelius following step by slow step, like a strange little dance. Or like a predator stalking its prey. Ennek stopped moving altogether and clutched the tube so tightly that his knuckles were white.

"Would you like to sit? I can get you some tea, if you like, or perhaps some wine." He raised an eyebrow as if to acknowledge Ennek's fondness for alcohol.

"No. Uh, no thanks. Just... what do you want from me?"

"Look around, Ennek." He swept his arm to indicate the room in general. "What you see is the product of a lifetime's work. No, more than that, because my own labors have merely built on those of my predecessors. This chamber represents several centuries of study."

Ennek looked around obediently, but he still had no idea what the man was getting at.

"Do you know how new wizards are chosen, son? It's not like Chiefs, you know. We rarely procreate, so the office is not inherited."

"No, I don't." He'd never once thought about it.

"Each wizard chooses his own successor. He finds a likely young man or woman and invites that person to join him, to learn from him. I was a member of the guard when the previous wizard discovered me. Did you know that?"

Ennek shook his head.

"I was part of the covert unit, charged with finding traitors and spies, that sort of thing. I enjoyed it very much—was quite good at it, if I say so myself—but the wizard took notice of me when I brought him prisoners for Stasis. He thought I might have a knack for magic, an interest in the work wizards do, and he was correct. As soon as I saw this laboratory, I agreed to become his… apprentice, I suppose, although I was rather old for the title. I was about your age, actually. I assisted him for several years and he taught me everything he knew, and when he died, I succeeded him."

Thelius came very close and his voice dropped until it was barely over a whisper. "I'd like you to fulfill that role for me, Ennek. I see in you the same things my mentor saw in me. You have the potential to become a great wizard, son. And a great wizard can, in his own way, wield as much power as the Chief."

Ennek felt as if he'd been punched in the gut. Not because of the near-sedition of Thelius's words about power, but because of the rest. The implication that he was anything like this man. The realization that Thelius *wanted* him. The knowledge that his own circumstances prohibited him from simply punching the wizard in the face and storming out.

But then a thought struck him, and it wasn't an unwelcome one. He'd rather drown in the bay than become like Thelius. But if Ennek were truly going to keep his promise to the prisoner Under, then being in Thelius's good graces could be a very good thing.

He took a deep breath and let it out. "This is quite a surprise," he said. "I, uh, hadn't any idea you even noticed me, really, let alone…." He let his voice drift away.

"Oh, I noticed you, son, of course I did. How could I not?"

Was that a small leer on the old man's face?

"The… um, the Chief, I don't know what he'll say. I mean, there's the port, and—"

"He can find someone else to manage the port, I'm sure. I believe he will be very pleased to have his younger son in such an important role." He said *will*, not *would*, Ennek noticed. "It's been done before, you know. The Chief's younger child becoming wizard. I'm sure it was in your lessons, but perhaps you weren't listening to Bavella that day."

Thelius's voice was almost playful as he said that, which for some reason disturbed Ennek more than anything else had. But he simply replied, "I don't remember."

"Well, I am certain the Chief does remember, and I can assure you that he will be delighted with this development."

Off in one corner of the room, something rustled. An animal in a cage, perhaps. It made Ennek's skin crawl.

He looked into the wizard's gray eyes, the color of heavy fog, and did his best to muster a smile. "I need some time to think about this."

Thelius smiled broadly, as if he'd scored a great victory. "Of course, of course. You mull it over. In the meantime, please, take the finding device and use it. Perhaps it will help you appreciate the benefits of a wizard's toils."

"Perhaps it will," Ennek said, and then, with a feeling of relief, he slipped through the door. He hoped he had a full bottle of good whiskey in his chambers.

IT DIDN'T surprise him at all when he dreamed that night of going Under. It would have surprised him more, in fact, if he had not. This dream was different, though. For one thing, even as he slept, he was aware that he was dreaming, and the entire thing felt more like a vision of things to come than a nightmare.

When he walked down the long stairway this time, he was confident, ebullient almost. Instead of trudging downward as if to his own execution, he leapt nimbly from step to step, so quickly as to be almost running.

When he reached the corridor, he hurried to one of the doors with no doubt whatsoever that it was the one he sought. Inside, the prisoner hung in his web of ropes, twitching slightly, as Thelius looked up at Ennek and smiled. "I've been waiting for you, son," he said and gestured at a small wooden cart beside him. The cart bore small metal tools of several kinds—scalpels and scissors and drills—as well as an iron cylinder whose end would make small circular burns if it were heated in a flame.

Ennek entered the room and stood between Thelius and the cart. He picked up a knife with a thin, razor-sharp blade and a smooth wooden hilt that seemed made to fit his hand exactly. "Where shall I begin?" he asked.

"Oh, the heart, of course. One must always begin with the heart."

Ennek pressed the very tip of the knife against that marble-white chest. He watched as the skin indented just a bit before giving way, and then a bead of blood welled up, thick and purple. The prisoner's eyes flew open and he looked right at Ennek, pleading silently. But Ennek only pushed the blade a little harder and drew it down, opening a deep gash over the man's still heart.

The man opened his mouth and emitted a horrible keen. Thelius laughed delightedly, and so did Ennek. It was the thrill of power, a thrill even the Chief would never know. Yes, the Chief could order people about; he could even issue commands that would result in the deaths of others. But he would never do this, would never have complete dominion over another being the way Ennek did now.

A fat tear slipped from the prisoner's eye, and Ennek caught it with his fingertip before it could trickle away. He brought his finger to his mouth. It tasted like the sea.

Thelius came close and placed a hand on Ennek's shoulder in a familiar manner, as if he did it all the time. His skin felt cold even through the fabric of Ennek's shirt. "He belongs to you, doesn't he?" he said, sibilant as a snake. "He always will. Under, you are not a younger son. You are a god."

Dream-Ennek's heart sang with these words. He was a god. He *was*.

With a savage cry, he plunged the knife directly into the prisoner's anguished eye.

chapter five

THE DAYS leading up to New Year were extremely busy at the port, as everyone hurried to load and unload cargo before the holiday shut things down for a number of days. The festival market had been set up nearby, and the citizens of Praesidium came in droves to wander among stalls and carts piled high with fabrics and spices and jewelry and exotic trinkets from around the globe. Musicians played, mouthwatering scents drifted from portable braziers and ovens, and children darted here and there. And everywhere, guards stood, watching closely to make sure taxes were paid, the crowds remained orderly, and pockets stayed unpicked.

In short, the entire atmosphere was one of controlled chaos, and nothing could have pleased Ennek more. He dashed from pier to pier, counting this and negotiating that, making sure port business ran smoothly. Mila gave him long sideways looks more than once—he didn't really need to do quite so much of the work himself—but he ignored her and continued on, so that each night when he retired to his chambers, he was too exhausted to do more than drink himself to sleep.

He didn't dream at all, which was an enormous relief.

Most people went home at noon on the eve of New Year, but he stayed at the port until dark to make sure everything was closed up properly and the guards were deployed to keep a close eye on unattended ships. When the last papers were piled carefully on his desk, he locked the office behind him and trudged home through empty streets. The whole city seemed to be waiting with bated breath for the moment when the celebrations could officially begin.

The halls of the keep were largely deserted as well, with most of the servants having the evening off. Only the bond-slaves still toiled away, slinking unhappily near the walls with loads of food or garments in their arms.

Someone had left a small meal for him outside his chambers—some bread, fruit, and cheese—and he took a few bites before setting the plate atop his chest of drawers. Ennek had laid out his costume on the bed before he left that morning, and now he scowled at it angrily. Yes, it would likely serve his desired purpose, yet the image of himself wearing it made him decidedly uncomfortable. Tired of the costume just lying there and mocking him, he pulled off his clothing and left it in an untidy pile on the floor.

It was almost physically painful to pull on the trousers, although they were made of very fine, smooth wool, and his frown deepened as he fastened the mother-of-pearl buttons on the silk shirt. When he shrugged on the long coat, it felt as heavy as lead, and he nearly wondered if he'd be able to walk at all. He made it into his bathroom, though, and took a moment to stare morosely at himself in the mirror before he upended the small container of ashes over his newly shorn hair and rubbed them in, quickly turning his stubble gray.

It wasn't quite time yet, although boisterous voices became audible in the streets below, and the noises in the corridor outside his door had grown louder and more urgent. He wanted to wait until most people had moved on to whatever parties they were attending. Most of the denizens of the keep would be gathering in the reception room for light snacks and warming drinks before they moved to the gardens, where fires were roaring and a space to dance had been cleared.

An hour before midnight, a great shout arose outside as every citizen of the polis celebrated the burning of Malus Jack. That was Ennek's cue. He left his chambers and strode confidently down the halls, seeing nobody but a few unfortunate guards, until he came to the entrance to Under.

The guard there, antsy because his shift was almost over, smiled at Ennek. "That's a fine costume, sir, although you've a bit more muscle to you than the wizard."

"Yes, and Thelius never had brown eyes either, but there's only so much I can do for the sake of a disguise."

"Well, the clothes are spot-on, sir."

"Thank you. I need a few props as well." He gestured toward the door.

"Ah, well, I'm sorry I won't see the result. I'm due to be relieved any moment now."

"A prosperous year to you, then."

"And to you, sir."

The route Under was becoming disturbingly familiar. At least he knew the proper cell to unlock this time, and he did so, half expecting to see the prisoner with a gash in his chest and one burst eye. He let out a long sigh of relief when he saw that the man looked the same as last time, his skin pale and unmarred. Ennek touched him briefly on the arm, but this time the man was as still as someone in Stasis ought to be.

Ennek had brought a knife. It was nothing like the one in his dream, he'd made certain of that. This one was heavy and thick, the handle ugly and scarred from use. It had been Uncle Sopher's, used for skinning the deer he shot. Sopher had taken good care of the blade, and it was still very sharp—well suited for cutting through heavy things. Ennek hoped that the ropes weren't enchanted in some way.

They weren't. The smooth fibers parted easily under his knife, and very soon Ennek was left with another problem: how to disentangle the man without allowing him to fall heavily to the floor. In the end Ennek didn't solve that predicament very well, and the man's feet slammed onto the ground as his torso tipped upward. At least it wasn't his head, Ennek thought as he cradled the body and freed it from the web. He gently laid the man on the floor.

He needed a few of the ropes to make the disguise more authentic, so he cut suitable lengths and wound them around the man's body. Then, lest he offend anyone's delicate sensibilities, he pulled a strip of flesh-colored cotton cloth from his pocket and wrapped it around the man's groin. He had to bite his lip when the back of his hand brushed against the genitals, but soon enough his task was complete. He hoisted the prisoner into his arms. He weighed very little, more like a child than a grown man, and that was lucky, as Ennek was going to have to carry him a long way.

As he locked the cell behind him—awkwardly, due to his burden—it occurred to him this was probably the first time in decades that the man had left that tiny room. Not that the man was aware of it, and for that Ennek was momentarily thankful. He just hoped he remained properly Stasis-like until Ennek could get him to his chambers.

As he'd expected, a different guard was now on duty at the top of the stairs, glowering fiercely at having to be on duty this night. Ah, but he'd been at the parties already; Ennek could smell alcohol on his breath from many paces away. The guard's frown turned to confusion when he saw what Ennek carried.

"But... but... sir...," he stammered, completely uncertain how to deal with this turn of events.

"Great costume, innit?" Ennek slurred his words, knowing his reputation for imbibing would benefit him now. "Had it made months ago. Looks like a real traitor, doesn't it?"

"It's… it's not?"

Ennek sneered. "Course not! Pretty good fake, right? Sailor from Emesa made it. Even feels real. Wanna touch?" He thrust the prisoner slightly toward the guard, who backed away unsteadily.

"No, uh, no thank you, sir."

Ennek shrugged as best as he could with his arms full. "Suit y'rself. Had to get the ropes myself, though. More authentic that way, innit?"

"Yes, sir." The guard did not look convinced.

"A prosperous year," Ennek shouted, pretending to stumble a bit as he made his way down the corridor.

"You too, sir."

Ennek passed only two more guards as he made his way to his rooms, and they lifted their eyebrows but said nothing. A bond-slave dragging a heavy load of bottles toward the doors to the gardens gasped and cowered when he saw Ennek, and Ennek wondered if he had once been Under himself. He smiled encouragingly at the man.

By the time he had locked himself in his chambers and set the prisoner on his bed, Ennek's arms and back were aching. The man looked strange atop the blue coverlet, out of place. Ennek frowned and pulled away the pieces of rope and then, with a defiant look that was wasted without an audience, tugged away the makeshift loincloth as well. Now the man looked especially vulnerable.

With a muffled growl, Ennek ripped off his own clothing, not caring if it tore. He wouldn't be wearing it again anyway. But the ashes were still in his hair, and the very thought of that made him itch. So after another long look at the man on his bed, he headed for the shower. The hot water sluicing over him felt so very good, as if it could wash away all his problems. He scrubbed thoroughly, using a rich citrus soap that was resupplied every time the *Phoenix* came into port.

When he felt as clean as he was going to get, he pulled on a pair of soft, loose trousers and a warm shirt he'd had for years. He wasn't planning on leaving his rooms again tonight. He ate the remains of his earlier meal and, for the first time since he could remember, washed it down with water instead of wine. He wished he had some tea, actually. He might have had some aromatic leaves tucked away somewhere, but he had no kettle to heat over his fire and no desire to go tromping through the keep to fetch one.

The man hadn't moved at all, of course, and Ennek had no idea what to do with him. He didn't know how to pull him from Stasis. Or push him further in—that would at least give him some peace.

All right. There was *something* he could do.

Ennek went into the bathroom again, but this time he filled the tub with steaming water and drizzled in a little scented oil. He wasn't sure what it smelled of—the sailor he'd bought it from hadn't known the word in the mother tongue—but Ennek liked it. It was spicy and warm and a little sweet. It made him feel comfortable and content, like eating bread hot out of the oven or basking in the sun on the first truly warm day of summer.

Ignoring the residual soreness of his muscles, he scooped the man up and carried him into the bathroom, then let him down into the tub. The man flopped bonelessly, with no evident signs of life, and Ennek was careful to keep his head above water—even though it wouldn't particularly matter, given that the man didn't breathe. He rubbed gently at flesh and bone until the man's body warmed. Ennek knew the heat was stolen from the bathwater and wouldn't last, but he still found it somehow satisfying.

Only when the water began to cool did Ennek pull the plug. He dried his prisoner, although long-ago memories of Thelius's intimate stroking of the man's skin caused him to hurry. Finally, he carried the man back into the bedroom and tucked him, naked, into the big bed.

The bath hadn't been a bad idea, but in the interim, no brilliant ideas about what to do next had leaped into Ennek's head. Not even any mediocre ideas, actually. If he was honest with himself, he'd have to admit he'd never expected to get this far. He'd thought that either he'd remain too much a coward to carry out the rescue, or else his simple plan would fail. But here he was, with the prisoner, and now—

Bang! Bang bang bang!

Ennek startled violently before his rational mind registered that it must be midnight. He took a few calming breaths, willing his racing heart to quiet, and he glanced out the window, where colored lights sparkled and popped. Usually the fireworks were one of his favorite parts of the holiday, and he loved to watch them reflected in the dark waters of the bay, but this time he only blinked, shook his head, and turned back toward the bed. The man, of course, hadn't reacted to the noise.

Bavella used to mutter under her breath that he was a stupid boy. When they were young, Larkin called him Thick Ennek. The Chief, too, would scowl and shake his head at Ennek's less than stellar schoolwork. Even Ennek's own mother would smooth his curls out of his face and wipe smudges of dirt off his cheeks with her thumb and say, "You're my handsome boy, aren't you? We're lucky you needn't be bright like the heir." So Ennek had always thought of himself that way—pretty but not very smart, a nice ornament, perhaps, but nothing serious. Nothing important. Lately, his work at the port had begun to change that self-image. He'd been doing well as portmaster. He was competent at the challenging position and had caught on quickly to the job's varied demands. As he stood in his bedroom, though, he swore at himself and repeated his brother's old gibe. "All right, Thick Ennek. You have a naked, bespelled man in your bed. Now what?"

When no answer came, he sighed and climbed into bed himself, carefully leaving an empty expanse between himself and the other man. But before he put out the light, he turned on his side and stared at the slack face, slightly amazed. He'd never shared a bed with anyone before. Despite the prisoner's condition, Ennek felt as if he still had a presence of sorts, that his living essence radiated invisibly just a few inches away. It wasn't eerie, as he'd feared it might be.

Ennek was about to roll over and try to sleep when the man moved. Not much, just a slight jerk of his leg, but Ennek felt the mattress shift a little, and he froze. The man's eyelids opened slowly, as if they were enormously heavy, and a tiny mewl snuck between slightly parted lips.

"Are you awake?" Ennek whispered.

The eyes rolled toward him, the whites wide around seascape irises, the pupils small and bright. The man *saw* him.

"Who are you?" Ennek said.

The man opened his mouth, and Ennek saw the blankets rise a little as the man tried to lift his arm. He made another sound, a choked, hissing sort of garble, and then his entire body shook with a tremendous shudder. After which he went completely limp, his eyes closed, and his lungs stopped moving.

And to Ennek's surprise, his own cheeks were wet with tears.

chapter six

HE WAS drowning.

He struggled desperately to rise, to draw a little precious oxygen into his burning lungs, but something was gripping his ankles, dragging him down into water so murky he couldn't see anything but cloudy flashes of green and gray. He tried to kick his legs free, but whatever—whoever?—held them, held them fast. His arms were strong from persistent exercise, they were able to lift great weights, but no matter how he thrashed, he couldn't break the surface of the water, couldn't save himself.

He woke up with a gasp that was nearly a scream. The blankets were twisted around his legs, nearly causing him to crash clumsily onto the floor. Although the room was cold, his body was drenched with sweat, and his clothing clung uncomfortably to his skin. Next to him, the prisoner had been uncovered and lay slightly canted to one side. Ennek wasn't sure whether that was from the drawing away of the bedding or from the man's occasional spastic movements.

It was the first New Year that Ennek could remember when he hadn't awoken with a sore head and queasy stomach, but still he groaned and sank his face into his hands. His daring, stupid act hadn't eliminated his nightmares—it only seemed to replace the old ones with new, improved versions.

Ennek kept a desk in his chamber. It wasn't an enormous affair like the Chief's, nor was it elaborately carved like the one his mother had used. It was rather small actually, and plain, although the grain of the oak made nice ornamentation, and the steel drawer handles had been made from the melted remains of ships' anchors. When the captain of the *Crescent Moon* had brought Ennek into his stateroom to show off his private stock of brandy, Ennek had immediately taken a liking to the captain's desk. The captain had been willing to part with it in exchange for a few small pieces of gold. Sitting near one corner of the desk was a brass clock, slightly pitted from the salt air. It had come off a ship as well, although Ennek wasn't sure which one; a sailor had traded it to him for a warm hat and gloves.

The clock said it wasn't yet eight o'clock. That was good. Everyone else would still be fast asleep after the night's festivities. It would be hours before they staggered out of bed and cleaned themselves up, and hours more before they bathed and arranged their hair and put on their finery. The servants would be awake, though, and the bond-slaves, busily preparing the food, cleaning the rooms, and setting up the banquet hall for tonight's feast.

Quickly Ennek changed into a pair of plain trousers and a drab shirt. He covered the prisoner and stepped into the corridor, carefully closing the door behind him. He had banned everyone from his chambers years ago, preferring to do the occasional light cleaning himself rather than having servants messing with his private things. It wasn't that he had a great many personal belongings, or that what he did have was especially valuable; he just didn't like the idea of others handling them, especially when he wasn't there.

The solitude of the hallways gave way to the noisy bustle of the kitchen. He stood to one side for a moment, watching as chefs inspected vegetables and huge chunks of meat and ordered everyone else about. Servants scuttled back and forth, and chopped and stirred and mixed; and bond-slaves dragged in enormous sacks of potatoes and bags of flour and bins of wood for the stoves. It smelled wonderful already.

One of the servants caught sight of him as she hurried past, did a double-take, and then skidded to a halt in front of him, nearly breathless from her labors. "Sir? May I help you?" She was pretty. Younger than him, slightly plump, with apple-red cheeks and reddish hair escaping from a braid.

"I'm looking… I just want some stuff to take up to my chambers. I have some work to do today and…." He stopped trying to think up an excuse. He didn't need one—he was the younger son—and besides, her slightly raised eyebrow spoke volumes.

"What can I get you, sir?" was all she said.

"Bread. Butter. Fruit. Some meat. Um…." He caught a whiff of a pastry as it was carried past him. "Some of that."

"You want quite a lot of food, sir?"

"Yes."

She gave him a brief quizzical glance—everyone else would be saving their appetites for tonight—and shrugged slightly. "Just a moment, please."

So he waited as she grabbed a basket from somewhere and started to fill it. By the time she handed it to him, it was heavy. He saw that she'd tucked in a bottle of wine and two of ale, and he smiled and gave her a gold coin. Her eyes grew wide, and she quickly tucked it away in the folds of her clothing. "A prosperous New Year," he said.

"Thank you, sir." She dimpled and then scurried away.

Fortified with provisions, he spent the day in his chambers. Mostly he sat and watched the prisoner. He was trying to see if he could discern some pattern in his behavior, but if there was one, Ennek couldn't tell. Sometimes the man was motionless for an hour or more, sometimes he twitched and jerked only slightly, and sometimes his eyes opened and he made small noises, seeming almost awake before falling back into a statue-like state. It seemed to Ennek that the man was slightly more likely to move when Ennek was near him, but he wasn't certain. He did know that there was no reaction if he shouted at the prisoner, or shook him, or blew in his face.

Ennek had plenty of time to study the man. He was pale as milk, of course, and it was impossible to tell what his hair color had been. His nipples were slightly pink. His bones were rather fine, and Ennek thought the man was probably three or four inches taller than him. He had long, slender hands. Ennek touched them; they were cold, which was no surprise, but the pads of the fingers and the flat of the palms were callused, which Ennek hadn't expected. The fingernails were very short and uneven, as if they'd been broken or chewed off. Ennek wondered if they'd been like that when the man was put in Stasis. The man's face was not as delicate as the rest of him. His cheekbones were broad and sharply sculpted, his eyes set at a slight slant. His jawline was square, determined-looking. At one point Ennek snuck a look at the man's teeth, and they were white and straight. So he'd likely come from a little money, despite the fact that his hands felt like they'd done hard work.

When he wasn't just staring, Ennek thought about the man in his bed. About who he was, and what he had done and when, and why Stasis was different for him. About how long it would be before Thelius discovered the prisoner was missing, and what he would do. About whether there was any chance at all of truly saving the man, and if so, what Ennek would do with him then. There were no answers to any of these questions, of course, just speculation that ranged from the unlikely to the unthinkable.

In the middle of the afternoon, when there were signs of stirring elsewhere in the keep, a brief squall blew over. Ennek watched it through his window—he'd always enjoyed storms—and thought about what it would be like to be on a ship far out at sea when the wind blew and the water roiled. You'd never be quite certain whether the next wave would be the one to send you into the deadly depths. The concept was both terrifying and exhilarating.

The food he'd brought up with him was good. The chefs always did their best for this feast, in part because the Chief would soon determine their salary for the next twelve months. A prosperous year—that was what they hoped for. That was what the whole polis hoped for, from the Chief down to the lowliest servant. Everyone except the bond-slaves, who were just thankful for another year gone if their sentence was a finite one, or mourned another year of freedom lost if their sentence was for life. And the prisoners in Stasis, who had no way to mark the passing years. And Ennek himself, who yearned for something gold couldn't buy.

The clouds cleared just in time for Ennek to watch the sun sink into the ocean, staining the sky nearly bloodred. Some of the deep orange hue appeared to leak into the water itself. He glanced again at the man in the bed and then ducked into the corridor.

It took him a few minutes to find a guard since most of them were patrolling the streets today, making sure the celebrations remained under control. He finally found one, a slightly portly man leaning up against a wall as if he were holding up the keep single-handedly. There was a faint greenish cast to his skin.

"Had fun last night?"

The guard jumped—he'd been half dozing and hadn't seen Ennek come around the corner. "Y-yes, sir!" he stammered. He swayed a little as he tried to stand straight, and he pulled nervously at his coat lapels.

"Me too," said Ennek, with the most wolfish grin he could manage. "But now… I'm not feeling so great, you see?"

The guard nodded in enthusiastic empathy.

"Please tell the Chief that I won't be attending tonight. I'm just going to stay in my chambers."

"Yes, sir."

"A prosperous New Year, Sergeant."

"And to you, sir," replied the guard before stumbling quickly away.

Back in his own rooms, Ennek lit a few extra lamps and sat in his most comfortable chair with a book in his lap and an open bottle on the table beside him. He didn't read, though, and only sipped at the wine. His mind had made its errant way back to his childhood and the first time he had been permitted to attend the New Year dinner. He'd just turned ten and was thinking himself rather grown-up. A week or so before the holiday itself, he made his way to his mother's chambers as she was sitting at the big window that overlooked the polis. Her father was the chief of a polis unimaginably far east of here, months and months of travel over plains and deserts and mountains, and her parents had brought her here by sea instead, when she was only a young girl. She told him once how awed she'd been to see the sun set into the sea instead of rising from it, how strange the language and dress seemed here. There had been a formal ceremony in which she was wed to the Chief, who was then only a teenager himself and actually still heir rather than Chief. And then her parents had sailed away.

"Aelia," he'd said, and she'd turned her head, surprised he had addressed her by her title. "I'd like to go to the feast this year. Larkin went when he was only eight. I remember." That was a lie. He'd been only a baby himself then. But Larkin had rubbed it in his face often enough that it felt like he'd known at the time.

His mother's face grew unaccountably sad. "But you're still so young," she said quietly.

"I'm ten. Ten years old. I'm ten and Larkin was only eight and I want to go! I'll be good, I promise." He held his breath in suspense.

After a long pause, the corners of her mouth lifted slightly. "You'll have to wear a fancy suit, you know. Very uncomfortable. And shiny shoes, not those miserable boots you've been wearing everywhere. We'll have to comb the snarls out of that hair." He loved the sound of her voice, with her exotic way of pronouncing everyday words.

The conditions she'd just described sounded like torture, but he set his jaw determinedly. "I want to go, Aelia."

She'd nodded. "All right, then."

It had taken the better part of the day to get ready. He'd been forced to take a bath and then, when his mother decided the results were less than satisfactory, a second one. He hadn't complained, though, for fear of being denied his goal. Then he sat and only grumbled a little as a servant ran a comb through his hair and fastened the zillions of tiny buttons on his scratchy, starched shirt. Finally Aelia allowed him to stand, and he noticed he was nearly as tall as she was. She stroked his cheek fondly. "My handsome boy," she said.

He'd skipped ahead on the way to dinner, impatient with her stately adult pace. He stopped in awe when he came to the dining hall, though. The familiar room had been made glamorous with hanging ornaments of silver and gold and tiny jewels that sparkled in the candlelight. His people had never forgotten that, while Praesidium was blessed with temperate weather year-round, their ancestors had come from colder climates, where the icy wind and snow would be battering at their doors this time of year. Enormous fires roared in the room's four fireplaces, swags of dried fruit and nuts swayed slightly at the top of every doorway, and the tables were covered in acres of bright silk embroidered with shiny thread. The scents of roasting game and spiced wine were so strong he could almost taste them.

He'd felt very proud to be sitting at the head table with the Chief and Aelia and Larkin, and members of the Council had shaken his hand as if he were a man. Normally he ate on the run, just a few hasty bites here and there between lessons and riding and all the other things that occupied his time. But tonight the meal went on for hours, with platter after platter of food. Ennek had no idea what many of the dishes were, but he tried at least a tiny taste of each. Occasionally the guests rested for a while between courses, and then the musicians wandered around the room and played while people milled happily, chatting and laughing, a few even dancing. Small gifts were exchanged here and there, to many delighted exclamations. His mother had smilingly passed him a bundle wrapped in purple fabric. It had turned out to be a dagger—a real, adult's blade—with a carved ivory handle and a red jewel set at the end. It came with a finely made leather scabbard, and he'd felt immensely mature as he buckled it around his waist.

He'd started to feel sleepy, almost drugged with all the food and the small amounts of wine he'd managed to sneak, but then it was near midnight, and the parade of platters ended, and the high spirits of the crowd settled into something more solemn. The Chief stood and Aelia took his arm. They marched across the room and through the reception hall, with Larkin walking just behind and Ennek bringing up the rear. The other guests followed at a respectful distance.

They'd gone through the entry hall and through the great double doors that Ennek rarely used, preferring the less formal side entrances. There was a cobblestoned square in front of the keep, framed by a stone wall on the side that overlooked the sea and by lawns on the others, and with a wide road leading down the hill. Usually the square was empty except for the large central statue in the middle, of Princeps Primus, the first Chief, the man who'd brought law and order to a chaotic and bloody society, thereby laying the foundation to make Praesidium the greatest of all polises. He'd been an ugly man, Ennek had always thought, but he kept it to himself.

That night the square was anything but empty. A stage of rough-hewn redwood had been erected near the seawall, and a vast crowd had gathered, citizens jammed in shoulder to shoulder in their finest clothing. There was a small space roped off near the front for the Council members and the Chief's other guests, and between that area and the stage stood a row of guards, each one straight and tall and staring stone-faced at the throng.

Ennek followed his family up the stairs and onto the stage. His mother gestured to show him where to stand: on her left, near the back of the platform. Larkin stood on her right, and the Chief was at the front, in the exact center. Ennek felt a swell of pride—this was his father, his Chief, the keeper of the law, the leader of the world's foremost polis.

The Chief gave a speech. Ennek wasn't been sure what he was talking about, exactly. Something about morality and might and the majesty of the law, and the ways in which decency and obedience led to wealth. It didn't matter. Ennek just enjoyed listening to him. His deep voice boomed and echoed, and everybody listened raptly.

Finally the crowd clapped and cheered, and the Chief granted them one of his rare smiles. "It is time," he said.

Ennek watched as two huge guards cleared a narrow path through the citizens. Behind them was the wizard, stately in his spare gray robe, holding a heavy chain in one hand. The chain was attached to an iron collar around a man's neck. Behind him was another pair of enormous guards. The little party made its way to the stage, and Ennek fought the urge to hide behind his mother when Thelius's gaze settled on him. The wizard smiled, tight-lipped and somehow triumphant.

The man in the collar was led to a spot next to the Chief and then pressed down to his knees by one of the guards. Thelius handed the chain to the Chief, who gave him a brief nod of thanks, and the guards climbed down to join their brethren in front. Thelius stood at the far end of the stage.

The prisoner was trembling. He was young, Ennek saw, hardly more than a boy, really. Although he was dirty, he was also handsome, with long honey-colored hair and bright blue eyes. His clothing was hardly more than colorless rags, and Ennek had thought that he must be very cold. His hands were bound behind his back and his ankles attached by a short hobble. His feet were bare. Ennek could hear his harsh panting, could see the sweat beaded on his forehead, could almost smell the fear pouring off him in waves.

The Chief's loud voice startled Ennek. "This man has violated our law. In his greed and selfishness, he has undertaken acts that, like all crime, threaten the stability and order of our polis. He has offended us. What say you, Praesidium?"

A huge roar rose from the crowd, as if it was a single, monstrous entity. An entity that hungered for justice and vengeance and blood.

The Chief waited for the noise to die down. "Out of generosity and humanity, our great state has chosen not to execute those who offend us, but instead put them in service to us as bond-slaves, paying back the debts they owe. But on this first day of the New Year, we sacrifice this criminal. We make an example of him, a symbol of what should happen to all who dare to imperil our peace and safety and prosperity."

As the crowd yelled again, the Chief pulled a knife from the scabbard at his hip. The blade glinted dully in the light from the gas lamps. Hardly realizing what he was doing, Ennek patted the knife that hung at his own side, and he watched as the Chief dropped the chain and used that hand to pull the man's head back by his hair. The man shook violently, and a large wet stain appeared at his crotch. Ennek was close enough to see the tears coursing down his cheeks. He wondered why the man didn't cry out, didn't beg for mercy or maybe just damn them all. He wasn't especially surprised when Larkin mentioned, some months later, that the wizard always enchanted the New Year prisoner into silence.

The thousands of people were hushed. Behind Ennek's back, the waves crashed as always, unknowing and uncaring about the human drama above them. The Chief's arm moved swiftly, the blade flashed, and thick crimson blood spurted onto the stage and onto the heads, shoulders, and backs of the guards unfortunate enough to be standing right there.

The prisoner jerked, just once, and when the Chief released him, he sank to his side on the splintery wood, his eyes already glassy and blind.

The people in the crowd let out their breaths all at once, creating a single massive sigh that served as the nameless prisoner's epitaph.

As Ennek followed his mother off the stage, back toward the massive keep and his waiting bed, she'd glanced at him once, her face tight with anxiety. He'd smiled back. No big deal. He was practically a grown-up, wasn't he?

That had been the first New Year feast he spent with Aelia, and the last. She'd flung herself from her high chamber window only weeks later and landed just yards from where the stage had been.

Ennek had attended every feast since, sitting at the Chief's side and eating and drinking all night, so that usually everything was a drunken blur by the time he climbed the stage. He always stood steadily and kept his expression blank as that year's prisoner was led to his death. He couldn't remember any of their faces now, only the young, terrified face of the first one he'd seen. Of course their faces didn't matter any more than their names. They were merely symbols, just like the one who was no doubt cowering miserably somewhere in the keep right now, counting and dreading the minutes until his throat was slit.

Ennek definitely didn't regret missing this year's festivities.

chapter seven

ENNEK BECAME used to sharing his bed, even though his companion was mostly inert and occasionally erupted in small spasms and convulsions. Even so, the man provided a strange companionship of sorts. Sometimes Ennek had to restrain himself from reaching out and touching that pearly skin. He knew this was only a small respite in any case—the situation could not and would not continue like this—but he was enjoying it while it lasted. He didn't know if he'd ever have the opportunity to sleep with another person again.

Nobody commented when he didn't return to work immediately. Many people took a few days off after the holiday, and anyway, he'd spread the word that he was feeling ill. He spent his days watching the prisoner, reading, and exercising in his chamber, leaving only to call for a servant to fetch him some food.

But two days after New Year, he had to visit Hils, as he'd promised. Normally he would have looked forward to the occasion, but now he wished he hadn't made the obligation. He reluctantly pulled on a suit, stole a quick look at the man, and left.

Hils lived in a fine stone mansion on the edge of the polis. Ennek could have taken a carriage, but he chose a horse instead, arriving with slightly gritty eyes and, he could tell, cheeks flushed from the cold night air. A dour servant took his coat and led him into a small salon. The furniture was dainty, the sort that looked as though it might break if he actually dared to sit on it, so he stood instead, gazing at a painting of a bowl of flowers.

"Ugly thing, isn't it?"

Ennek spun around to see Hils grinning at him. Hils entered the salon and they shook hands heartily.

"It's pretty," said Ennek diplomatically.

"No, it's hideous. Mother painted it, though, so…." He shrugged. "I hear you were under the weather. Missed you at the feast."

"Yeah. Just felt kind of logy. I've been sleeping a lot." Which was the truth, actually.

"Well, it's good to see you." Hils clapped him on the shoulder. "How about a drink?"

"I wouldn't say no to that."

Hils led him out of the salon and down a hall, then into a large room with one wall made almost entirely of glass panels. It was difficult to see well in the dark, but Ennek thought that the view was across a wide paved patio and down a gently sloping lawn. The furniture here looked much more comfortable. Hils waved him to a deep, wide chair upholstered in pale green brocade, then wandered over to the side of the room where a long table held various bottles and glasses. "Whiskey's your drink, isn't it?"

"It is."

Hils returned a moment later with two glass tumblers filled with amber liquid. Ennek sipped at his. It was very good. They were silent for a few moments, and then Ennek said, "I like your house." It sounded a little awkward to him, but Hils smiled.

"Thanks. The family's owned it for... I don't know. A long time. It must seem pretty small compared to the keep, though."

"The keep... most of it's not really *home*, you know? It's Praesidium's place, the Chief's maybe. Not mine."

"Have you ever considered getting your own place? Some younger sons do, don't they?"

Ennek nodded.

"Maybe get married, build yourself a nice house up on Vorax Hill? My brother Rufinos builds fine houses. He's usually busy, but he has nearly fifty men working for him. I'm sure he'd give your project priority if I asked."

"Thank you. I've seen his work, and it's beautiful. But I don't think that's what my future holds." His gaze caught Hils's, and they silently exchanged words they could never speak out loud.

A polite knock at the door interrupted them, none too soon, Ennek thought. A different servant poked her head inside. "Dinner is ready, sirs."

The dining room was close by. It was much more intimate than the hall in the keep, of course, but elegant. The tablecloth was the same pale green as the chairs in the other room, the dishes gilded at the edges and hand painted with colorful beetles and butterflies, the crystal wineglasses intricately cut, and the silver cutlery finely wrought.

Only two places were set. Ennek sat across from Hils, and a servant immediately appeared with tiny bowls of consommé. "When I heard you'd been ill, I asked Cook to prepare something light. Is that all right?"

"That's fine." The soup tasted faintly of fennel. He liked it.

Over the course of the meal, they talked of nothing particularly consequential—some port gossip, the weather, the relative merits of two small boats Hils was considering buying. Ennek rarely had the chance to just chat with people like this, and it was pleasant. Would have been more so if he wasn't dually preoccupied over the secret in his bed and the way Hils's mouth dimpled at the corners when he smiled.

After they'd eaten some spiced baked apples, they retired to the solarium and Hils poured sweet wine as a servant set out small bowls of sugared almonds. "So," Hils said, popping a handful of nuts into his mouth. "About the piscarium piers. You had some ideas?"

Ennek sat back in his chair. "One or two...."

It was very late by the time he returned to the keep, weary but pleased that his plans for the port seemed promising. If only everything else could go so smoothly! When he'd left Hils's house, their hands had lingered just a little as they shook good-bye, and a look of deep regret flashed momentarily over Hils's face. "Ennek, I... I'm happy to be working with you." His voice was raspy.

Ennek had nodded and ridden away.

Although he didn't realize it until he walked back into his chambers, he'd half expected to find the prisoner gone. But he wasn't. He was still there, white as the sheets that covered him, his face slack and lifeless. "Hi," Ennek whispered to him. He suddenly wished very badly that he at least knew the man's name.

"WE WERE going to chat, weren't we, son?"

Ennek started slightly and whirled around. He'd been standing at one of the third-story railings, looking down toward the center of the polis, and hadn't heard the wizard approach. "Hello, Thelius," he said as evenly as he could manage.

"A fine afternoon. We're fortunate. Most polises don't enjoy such balmy weather this time of year."

"No, I guess not." Ennek turned away again and leaned on the stone railing. The *Queen's Glory* had arrived in the harbor. He ought to go down soon and see her captain, who'd promised him a casket of fine teas when he next sailed this way.

The wizard stood beside him, following his gaze.

"I heard you had occasion to use my gift before the holiday."

"Yes. Uh, thanks." Ennek knew he sounded ungracious. "I found nearly a pound of gold on board the *Eastern Pearl*."

"But you didn't hand the crew to the guards?"

"No. The gold was in the captain's own quarters, stashed under his mattress, actually. I doubt anyone else on board knew about it. The guards took the captain, though."

"The Chief must be pleased."

Ennek shrugged. "I suppose so. I haven't seen him since New Year."

Thelius chuckled, a dry sound like twigs snapping. "Yes, New Year. I understand you had quite an interesting costume."

The blood froze in Ennek's veins.

"I'm honored that you would choose to emulate me, son. I was hoping it was a sign that you'd reached a decision on the matter we discussed. And then when I discovered you'd taken a prisoner from Under... well, quite amusing, really."

Ennek closed his eyes and wondered what it would feel like to simply fall over the low railing. Would it hurt when he hit the stones below, or would he die instantly as his mother had?

"Would you care to come to my laboratory and discuss it, son?"

Ennek finally turned his head to look at the man. He didn't look angry—he had a tiny smile, in fact—but that didn't mean anything. "How long have you known?" he managed to choke out.

"Oh, since that night, of course. I know everything that happens Under. It is, after all, my domain, is it not?"

"But you haven't said anything—"

"Oh, nobody else knows. I was waiting to see what you'd do with him, actually, but it doesn't appear you've done much at all. Simply tucked him in, all nice and cozy, yes?"

Now Ennek had to bite at his lip. The bastard had been in his chambers, probably while Ennek was with Hils. Or maybe he didn't need to enter at all to see what was inside; perhaps he had an enchantment of some kind that permitted him to spy.

"So? My laboratory?"

Ennek didn't answer. Feeling absurdly like a chastened child, he marched beside the wizard. A few people shot them quick, curious looks as they walked by, but nobody said anything. Ennek wondered whether the guard would be waiting for him in the lab, or perhaps the Chief himself. That didn't make sense, though—why wouldn't Thelius simply have had him arrested as he stood on the walkway?

As it turned out, there was nobody in the lab except the two of them. A kettle whistled over the fire, and Thelius offered Ennek some tea. When Ennek shook his head, the wizard poured some for himself, sank into a plain wooden chair that was very close to the flames, and gestured at Ennek to do the same. Helplessly, Ennek sat.

Thelius sipped at his tea and then looked at Ennek over the top of his cup. It made Ennek feel like an interesting specimen of some sort, like the bugs that were pinned to small cards on one of the wizard's tables.

"So you made an interesting choice, my boy. I'm assuming it wasn't an accident, you taking that particular prisoner?"

What was the point of lying? "No."

"And you saw some of my other work Under as well, I believe."

Ennek shuddered slightly and looked away.

"Well, I believe we can reach an agreement, Ennek."

"Wh-what?"

"A mutually beneficial arrangement. You work with me, learn from me, as we discussed. Prepare to someday become wizard yourself. And I will overlook the fact that you've… borrowed… a prisoner. I'll even show you how to remove him from Stasis, if you like. You might find him more diverting if he were awake."

A strange storm of emotions churned through Ennek at these words. Relief, of course—he hadn't fancied the idea of being put in Stasis as a punishment for his misdeed. But also confusion and anger. And buried deep inside, but still clear enough to be acknowledged, a thrill of desire— accompanied by a bit of shame.

"You mean, I can—he can stay, and—"

"Yes. You may keep him, so long as he remains in your chambers, of course, and nobody else learns of him. At the end of every year, the Chief conducts an inspection Under, and you shall have to return him to Stasis then. Your prisoner is too obvious for his absence to go unnoted. But the rest of the time you may have him." Thelius smiled, his teeth gleaming in the firelight. "Perhaps you might practice some of your lessons on him."

Ennek swallowed. His head spun and he couldn't begin to make sense of his situation. So instead he asked a question, one that had bothered him since he was twelve years old. "Why is he different? Why does he *move*?"

"Your prisoner was placed in Stasis a very long time ago. Three centuries, in fact. I don't know whether the wizard who placed him there was incompetent in some way or whether there is something in the nature of the man himself that makes the enchantment imperfect."

"You could have… fixed him."

"I suppose I might have. But why bother? He's no more trouble than the rest, and I've always found his condition interesting. He's actually managed an entire word, now and then. Quite remarkable."

Thelius sipped patiently, but Ennek couldn't sit any longer. He rose and paced back and forth, avoiding the various piles of things with some difficulty, once knocking into a carved statue of a woman whose marble eyes made him extremely uneasy.

At last Thelius sighed and put his cup on a table. He stood in front of Ennek and grabbed him by the shoulders, forcing him to stand still. "Son, a man is born with talents. Your brother, for example, will make a fine Chief someday—he's an outstanding diplomat with a keen ability to see to the heart of problems and devise solutions. Your grandfather, the previous Chief, could recite the lineage of every member of the Council better than they could, and he knew the detailed history of every polis on the West Coast. *His* father was an exceptional general, won decisive battles that truly cemented the preeminence of this polis and ensured our supremacy over the bay.

"A man is also born with inclinations, and he can't help that any more than your father can change his terrible singing voice. You're fortunate, son, in that you are in the position to indulge your inclinations, to enjoy them. Not another soul in the polis would be able to do as you may.

"All that is required is for you to permit me to engage the talents I know you have.

"Say yes, Ennek."

Ennek looked at him for a long time. Thelius's eyes were nearly colorless in the dim room, and his face seemed as devoid of humanity as the Princeps Primus statue that watched impassively as blood spurted from men's throats.

"Yes."

chapter eight

ENNEK STOOD stiffly, biting his tongue as Thelius ran his hands over the body of the prisoner Ennek already thought of as his. "I'll teach you soon to read energies; it can be quite a useful skill. His energy has always felt odd—more chaotic than the others. Like static electricity sparking on a dry day." Thelius's voice was slightly distracted, as if he weren't quite paying attention to his own words. "Usually one can barely feel those in Stasis at all."

"Why is he different?"

"I don't know." Thelius stroked the chalky chest, and Ennek had to look away. He stared instead at the painting that hung on his wall. It was a seascape he'd found a few years ago at the festival market, and he liked that it depicted a violent storm instead of the usual placid swells. The artist—a tall woman with a tattoo of an eye on the back of her hand and silver streaks in her long, dark hair—had sold it to him. She'd looked him up and down and smiled crookedly. "Strange journeys," she'd said with an accent so thick he wasn't certain he'd understood her correctly. He'd wondered briefly what she meant, and then he dismissed it from his mind. Everyone knew artists were all a little crazy.

Thelius interrupted his thoughts by turning toward him. "We shall have to move the prisoner. The process can be quite messy, and I don't believe you'd fancy that on your bed."

"Um, where to?" He certainly wasn't going to drag the man back Under.

"Your bathtub will do."

Ennek scooped the man into his arms. The man's eyes flew open and focused for a moment on Ennek's before rolling back in his head. Ennek wanted to tell him he'd be free of Stasis soon, but of course he said nothing with the wizard's sharp gaze on him. He brought the man into the bathroom instead and laid him gently inside the empty tub. The man's skin was paler than the marble on which he lay.

"Ennek, fetch me my bag, please."

Ennek almost retorted that he wasn't a servant to be ordered around, but he only sighed and walked back into the main room. The wizard's large valise was made of badly scuffed brown leather, and it smelled very strongly of something like camphor and sage. It had a wide strap and was surprisingly heavy—so much so, in fact, that Ennek grunted slightly when he lifted it. Apparently Thelius was stronger than he looked.

Back in the bathroom, Thelius was filling the tub with cold water. "Salt water is best," he muttered, "but I expect this will work." Ennek watched uneasily as the water rose quickly, soon covering the man completely. He knew the man wasn't breathing, but it still looked terrible to see his face under several inches of water.

When the tub was full, Thelius turned off the tap and frowned critically at the prisoner before rooting around in his bag. "You can still work the spell without submerging them. You need to keep the skin very wet, though. Stasis is water magic, you see."

Ennek didn't see, which was probably quite clear to the wizard, who rolled his eyes a little. "You really know nothing yet, do you? All magic comes from one of the elements: water, earth, fire, air. That metal device I made for detecting contraband, it uses earth, since metals are naturally part of the earth. Every wizard can command one of the elements best and will be most accomplished at magic using his element. Mine is earth, like the stone from which this keep is built. Yours, well, we shall have to see." As he spoke, Thelius was pulling things from his bag, small glass vials and fabric pouches and a round box of badly tarnished silver. He set these things on the wide edge of the tub.

"The process for removing Stasis is nearly identical to that of imposing it. Except when it's imposed, of course, the prisoner must be restrained. The spell will inhibit his movements quite quickly, but you don't want him thrashing about at the beginning." He looked over at Ennek. "You must use very heavy restraints, because prisoners will resist terribly. But not metal, because that interferes with the water magic. Something organic is best, leather perhaps. I prefer silk ropes. They're very strong but tend not to damage the body. Prisoners heal very poorly once they're placed in Stasis, and you probably don't want them spending decades looking all torn up. It displeases the Chief."

Ennek thought of the prisoner he'd seen Under, the one with the missing patches of skin and the skewer in his heart. His face must have given away his thoughts, because Thelius shook his head. "The Chief doesn't need to see every prisoner, son. There are a few who have been Under since long before he was born, and he doesn't even know they exist."

This was treason. Knowingly concealing information from the Chief, hiding prisoners who rightfully belonged to him. To have committed such acts and admitted them to the Chief's own kin, Thelius must have been supremely confident.

Thelius smiled—a little condescendingly, Ennek thought—and peered at his small collection of items. "Let's begin, shall we?" As if to underscore Thelius's words, the man in the tub jerked once, so violently that he splashed some water onto the floor, and raised an arm high enough that his hand surfaced. It clutched and grasped at nothing, and Ennek was sorely tempted to grab it with his own to help lift the man up. But Thelius pushed irritably at the dripping fist until it sank below the water again and the man's body went slack.

"Does this hurt?" Ennek asked. "Being brought out?"

"I have no idea. I expect it might be painful at the end, as they're waking up, but I'm not certain. They always scream quite a bit, but that could be simply from the shock of it, you see."

Ennek preferred not to think of himself as weak or timid, but his knees felt a little rubbery, so he sat on the closed lid of the toilet.

Thelius unstoppered one of the tiny glass bottles and poured the contents into the tub. It was oily and dark and made thin swirls on the surface of the water. "Essence of kelp," he said. "It must be collected at night and distilled three times, and then allowed to sit undisturbed for at least twelve months. After that, it's good indefinitely."

The second little bottle contained another oily liquid, but Ennek didn't need the wizard to tell him what it was—his nose informed him quite plainly. "Fish oil," Ennek said.

"Quite. Sardine, in fact. Nothing particularly special about it; you can buy it from the market if you like. And this"—he opened a red velvet pouch and dumped it over the tub—"is simply sea salt. Also from the market, or you can scrape it off the rocks at low tide if you'd rather. But it must be sea salt—quarried won't do."

"Why not?"

"It's water magic, not earth," Thelius answered impatiently. Then he opened the box and used his fingertips to remove a pinch of something powdery, which he sprinkled into the water. "Crushed pearls. Only requires a small amount."

For a moment Ennek absurdly felt as if he was being given a cooking lesson, perhaps for some kind of exotic soup. He pressed his lips together to keep a hysterical laugh from escaping. As he watched, Thelius added several more ingredients—dried fish scales, tiny bits of seashells, the beak of a gull, slivers of driftwood, a bit of foam Thelius said he'd collected that morning. When all the vials and packets were empty, Thelius tucked them into his bag, then stepped back until he was several feet from the tub.

"The spell itself is quite simple actually but must be cast by an experienced wizard. I was overeager to attempt it the first time, I'm afraid, and the unfortunate prisoner was turned inside out. When I was unable to set him right again, my mentor had me put the fellow out of his misery. The Chief—that was your grandfather, the previous Chief—was quite put out with me." Ennek felt ill, but Thelius was grinning slightly, as if he were fondly remembering an incident of childhood folly. "I suspect that the wizard who placed this prisoner in Stasis was not much more practiced than I was, that time. You're lucky he isn't inside out as well!" He chuckled drily.

Ennek held his breath as Thelius began to chant loudly in some language Ennek didn't recognize. It was very sibilant, and the words crawled over his skin like snakes, sinuous and twisting, making him twitch and shiver. As soon as the wizard was silent, the water in the tub began to churn. It turned suddenly bloodred and opaque, so that Ennek could no longer see the man beneath the surface.

For a time nothing else happened. The water boiled and sloshed and the small room filled with the thick scent of the ocean. Ennek recalled Bavella telling him once that human blood was almost exactly as salty as the sea, that all creatures were once aquatic and many still carried that history with them in their veins. "Your heartbeat, your pulse, these are just like the motions of the waves," she'd said.

Then, as abruptly as the blink of an eye, the water cleared.

The man was moving now, writhing and thrashing weakly. His mouth was open wide in a silent scream; every muscle and sinew in his thin body was taut as a bowstring. His hands were opening and closing almost rhythmically. His chest rippled and seized, as if his lungs were struggling to inflate, or perhaps his heart was trying to beat again. He reached up—this time with both arms—and flailed about, trying desperately to find a purchase on something, it seemed.

"It's about time now," Thelius muttered. He stepped forward and yanked hard at the chain fastened to the plug. Water began to swirl and gurgle down the pipes.

As the tub drained, Ennek saw that the prisoner's skin glistened as if covered in a thick ointment. The thrashing grew more pronounced, and then, as the man's face was finally exposed to the air, he froze for a moment. He took in a thin breath and began coughing up great gouts of thick greenish liquid, which splattered onto his chest and dripped down his face. When his lungs were relatively clear, he sucked in a huge amount of air and let it out slowly. Right before Ennek's eyes, his skin pinkened up a little, a slight flush that began on his chest and gradually spread outward until it reached his fingers and toes and the top of his bald head.

Then the screaming began.

It echoed horribly against the hard surfaces of the room, so that soon Ennek couldn't tell where one shriek ended and the next began, and he had to shut his eyes tight and hold his hands to his ears, trying to block out the din. He wanted to leave the room altogether but didn't want Thelius to think him a coward, so he hunched on the toilet and waited for it to end.

By the time the yelling stopped, the man's voice had nearly given out and he was emitting only hoarse, raspy cries interspersed with moans and whimpers. The man was on his side now, as tight in a fetal ball as he could manage in the confines of the tub, and he was trembling violently.

Thelius brushed his hands together briskly and stooped a little to lift his bag over his shoulder. "That's done, then," he announced.

Ennek looked doubtfully at the miserable figure. "But he's not awake."

"Oh, it takes some time for them to come to their senses. Hours at least, sometimes days, especially if they've been Under a long time. I have no idea how long it will be with him."

"But... what should I do with him?"

Thelius shrugged. "Whatever you want. You'll want to keep him restrained, of course, until he understands his situation. You can use metal chains now if you like; the magic is over. I'd recommend keeping him in the tub for a while, or you'll have messes to clean. He'll be pissing and shitting and, most likely, vomiting, and it'll be some time before he can control himself. Oh, and he'll need to eat and drink now. Start with simple things like clear broth—he hasn't eaten in three hundred years! I usually have servants take care of feeding them, but you'll have to manage by yourself." He frowned thoughtfully. "You might try an infant's bottle at first, before graduating to dishes and spoons."

Ennek nodded, overwhelmed.

"Oh, and his collar! I nearly forgot. I'll put it on him tonight, after dinner. I have a few other matters to attend to right now."

Collar. Of course. Now that he was no longer in Stasis, the prisoner would spend the rest of his life as a slave. Lovely. Well, it was a small improvement. Perhaps. Ennek was still staring numbly at the man in the tub when the wizard left, shutting the chamber door firmly behind him.

"I suppose I ought to get you cleaned up," Ennek said, aware that he was perilously close to talking to himself. The man certainly didn't seem to register anything he said. And he didn't react as Ennek turned the tap on again, this time to a warm trickle and without putting the stopper in the drain. Keeping his voice low and soothing, Ennek kept a running commentary as he wetted a soft towel and used it to scrub off the goo. It was much harder to bathe the prisoner this time, mostly because he kept trying to contract into a ball whenever Ennek attempted to pull his limbs free to wash him better. But also because this time it was patently obvious that he was cleansing a living, breathing being, a human being of warming flesh and flowing blood, and not simply a mostly inert manikin.

Ennek found himself blushing furiously when he had to wipe the man's groin and bottom.

When he was finished, he considered the man, who still curled himself into a tight ball. He was still very pale, of course—three centuries underground would do that—but now his lips were quite red, and his nipples a dark rose, as were his genitals. Ennek couldn't see his face very well, but there seemed to be hectic little circles of red high on his wide cheekbones, as if he had a fever. And he was cold, Ennek realized, swearing softly at himself. He trotted into his bedchamber and grabbed a thick blanket from a carved chest, then brought it back and draped it over the huddled form.

He had to think for a while about how to get some food into the man. The broth part was easy—the cooks had made it for him before, on days when he was too hungover for anything more substantial. But a bottle?

It occurred to him at last that surely one of the servants must have a baby or at least know where a bottle could be found. So he made his way to a part of the keep where he'd ventured only rarely before, and not for years. The servants' quarters were mostly deserted this time of day, but a small boy darted past him, and Ennek grabbed him firmly. The boy gaped up at him.

"Where's your mother?" Ennek asked.

The boy's hair was a tangled mess, and he had some sort of food smeared across his chin and down his shirt. He held out a grubby hand and pointed mutely down the narrow hall. Ennek let him go and the boy dashed away.

A few of the doors were half-open, and Ennek peeked inside as he passed. The rooms were tiny, crowded with battered furniture and hanging clothes. This part of the keep was built into the hill and there were no windows, so the air was close and smoky. If the servants lived here, what kind of conditions were the bond-slaves kept in, he wondered. He'd never thought of that before.

But then he saw a young woman sitting in a rocking chair in one of the rooms, a tiny baby nursing at her breast, and she was singing a little song to it and smiling and brushing at its sparse sprigs of hair. Ennek's heart ached at the sight. He didn't remember his mother fussing over him. Of course, as Aelia, she had other duties, and he'd been brought up mostly by wet nurses and nannies until he was old enough for the tutors' firm hands.

The woman was startled to see him. As she began to rise, he hastily gestured at her to stay where she was. "I'm sorry," he said. "I didn't mean to interrupt."

"Can… can I help you, sir?"

"I was looking… I have this project, you see, and I need…." Belatedly, he realized he hadn't come up with a good story. Well, he was the younger son; he didn't need an excuse. "I need a baby's bottle. Would you have one, by any chance?"

She blinked at him for a moment. "A bottle, sir? Like… for milk?"

"Yes. Exactly."

"I don't… I don't have any, sir." She glanced down at where her infant was still feeding happily, clearly in no need of a bottle. Ennek blushed. "But my sister used them with her Raisa, because Raisa was born with teeth, and she'd bite so…." Her voice trailed off as Ennek's face turned an even brighter red.

"Could I have one from her?"

"Of course, sir, if she still has them. Raisa's been weaned for months now. My sister's in the laundry, but I can look if you'd like."

"Yes, please."

The woman readjusted the baby somehow. Ennek heard a slurping sort of popping noise and saw a brief flash of nipple before the woman's breasts were again covered and the baby was balanced against her shoulder. It didn't cry over having its meal interrupted but only looked around in slight astonishment, as if it had never occurred to it that such a thing might happen. It had wide brown eyes and a wet rosebud mouth.

Ennek followed the woman into the chamber next door. It was as crammed full of things as hers, and it looked as if a half-dozen people slept in the tiny room. The woman rooted around in a cupboard for a moment and then, with a small noise of triumph, pulled out a curved bottle of clear glass, topped at one end by a rubber teat and at the other by a small valve. "Here it is, sir!"

He took the bottle from her. "Thank you. Here… for you and your sister, and an extra for the baby." He handed her three gold coins from his pocket, each worth nearly a month's wages to a servant like her.

"Thank you, sir! You're very generous." She slipped the coins into her pocket, and he smiled, tucked the bottle into his coat, and left.

It was slightly past midday. He walked through the scullery—where servants busily scrubbed mountains of dishes, cutlery, and pots and pans—and into the kitchen proper. The three chefs on duty were sitting at a huge scarred table, eating their own meal while their assistants chopped and kneaded in preparation for dinner. Two servants rushed in carrying an enormous halibut between them, already gutted and cleaned. They plopped it onto a work surface, and three other servants descended to cut it into steaks. Ennek licked his lips. He liked halibut.

"Can I get you something, sir?" That was one of the chefs, a large woman with a slight cast to one eye.

"Yes. I'd like some broth, please. Something very plain, like for an invalid. Could you make me some?"

"I've some already," she replied, bustling toward a stove. "The Chief was feeling a bit poorly today, so I've been keeping it for him. Plenty to spare, though. Would you like it in a bowl?"

"Um, how about something with a lid?"

She nodded and grabbed a large pottery bowl from a shelf. She poured several ladlefuls of the broth inside, then covered it with an ornate blue-handled lid. As he took it from her, he remembered that he hadn't eaten anything and was suddenly ravenous.

"Could you make me up a plate of something too? Something more substantial, I mean."

It took her only a few minutes to pile a dish with a hunk of warm brown bread covered in butter and honey; several slices of cold roast beef, pink and juicy; and some soft orange squash with a spicy sauce. She covered the plate with a cloth and placed it and his bowl onto a tray. "Anything else, sir?"

"No. That's good."

"Would you like someone to carry it for you?"

He shook his head. "I think I can manage. Thank you."

The heavenly scent of the food filled his nostrils as he walked back to his chambers. He peeked into the bathroom and saw the man exactly as he'd left him, huddled under the blanket in the bathtub. Ennek wolfed down his own meal, then managed to spoon some broth into the bottle until it was half full. He took it into the bathroom with him.

Ennek had never in his life fed anything from a bottle. Not even himself, he was pretty sure. Certainly not a naked, mostly unconscious man. So it took him some time to figure out how he was going to manage it, and in the meantime he dripped some of the lukewarm broth on himself, the floor, and the blanket. Finally he sighed in resignation and climbed into the tub himself. He positioned the man with his head slightly raised against Ennek's torso, and his legs—which kept wanting to contract and pull the man into a ball again—pinned in place by Ennek's own. It was awkward. But Ennek was able to get the teat between those plump red lips, and once he did, the man sucked weakly and swallowed.

"I guess you like it okay," Ennek mused softly. The man's eyes were still shut, the lids thin and delicate, the faint blue traceries of veins visible through the skin. His breathing was nice and even, although a slight rattle bothered Ennek. The man was fully warm now, like a human ought to be, but his bones still seemed sharp enough to tear through his flesh.

The man didn't resist when Ennek pulled the bottle away and didn't react when Ennek brushed a drop of broth from the corner of the man's mouth with his thumb. "I'll give you more soon," he said. "Don't want to overdo it."

And then he just lay there with his back against the cold marble and the man in his lap, because it wasn't exactly uncomfortable and because he so rarely had physical contact with anybody else. He'd been telling himself for years that he didn't need it. For a while Larkin had tried to convince him to find a wife, probably because he was so happily immersed in married, breeding bliss that he couldn't understand why everyone else wouldn't be. Ennek had been slightly tempted, actually, thinking that perhaps some companionship was better than none, and surely there must be one girl in the polis whom he could take as a partner of sorts. In the end, though, he'd decided it wouldn't be fair to the girl, and he'd rather deny himself altogether than spend his life pretending to be something he wasn't. And mostly he'd considered that a good decision. But there were nights—prior to his recent activities, of course—when he lay in his big empty bed and he ached, actually physically ached, for someone to touch him.

Foolish, he'd thought then.

But now he wasn't so sure. He'd done several things considerably more imprudent lately than longing for human contact, as the weight of the present body atop him most vigorously proved. But that weight felt good, and his body drank it in like fine wine so that he almost felt a little intoxicated with it.

It was perhaps fortunate that these musings were interrupted when warm liquid suddenly soaked his legs and the sharp smell of urine hit his nose. Damn it. Thelius had warned him.

Ennek sighed and carefully extricated himself from under the man, who immediately turned onto his side and curled up. Ennek carefully pulled the blanket away and set it aside, happy to discover that it wasn't soiled. Ignoring his own wet trousers for the moment, he knelt on the floor and ran the tub until the urine washed down the drain. He cleaned the area around the man's groin, then used a thick towel to dry the man and the bottom of the tub. Finally he tucked the blanket back around him. Only then did he remove his own trousers and wipe off his legs.

He was just buttoning himself into clean clothes when he heard a knock at the door. He opened it slightly and discovered Thelius, once again carrying his heavy bag. Wordlessly, Ennek ushered him in.

"I trust all went well today?" Thelius asked.

"Yeah. Fine."

Thelius smirked when he saw the man wrapped in the blanket. "You're going to spoil him."

"He was cold."

"So? It's not as if he's going to complain now, is he?"

"He's… he's naked."

"And he has been for three hundred years, son. I am aware that we have some rather prudish laws here concerning nudity, but there will be nobody to see him but you, Ennek, and you own him. You may see whatever parts of him you wish." *And use them as well* remained unspoken. But when Ennek didn't respond, Thelius only shrugged. "Yes, well, I'm sure you'll get past your inhibitions soon enough. One does, you know."

Ennek remained silent, even as the wizard pulled an iron collar from his bag. It was black and perhaps an inch wide. It looked heavy. Ennek couldn't make out how it would go on, because it appeared to be a solid ring, with a loop in one spot through which a lock or chain could be threaded. But then the wizard tapped it with one finger, spoke a few words, and pulled the collar apart as if it were taffy. "Earth magic," he explained.

Thelius had to kneel to put the collar on the prisoner. He slid the metal around the man's neck, said a few more words, and the collar joined back up into a closed circle. The darkness of it was stark against the man's skin.

"It's a bit loose now," said Thelius, standing again, "but he'll be putting on some weight and muscle soon, I imagine. And that collar's not coming off him again."

"Never?" Ennek asked, although he knew the answer.

"Never. Only I can remove it."

No use protesting, Ennek thought. He had bigger problems anyway. He trailed the wizard to the door, eager to lock him and the rest of the world out, but Thelius stopped and turned before they'd quite reached it.

"I expect you'll be busy for a bit, nursing your slave and wrapping things up at the port. But I'd like to begin our work together very soon. Let's say one week, shall we?" His eyes were bright and avid as a bird's.

Ennek took a deep breath and nodded.

FOR THE next several days, Ennek nursed the man, carefully feeding him first clear broth and then slightly richer stuff. He never gave the man much at once, but he fed him often, and it seemed that the bony frame was beginning to fill out a little. Eventually he was able to supplement with a little soft pap spooned between slack lips. The chefs had looked at him strangely over that request but of course hadn't questioned him. The man's eyes had begun to flutter open a bit as he fed or as he swallowed water, but they hadn't yet focused on anything.

Ennek had to clean the man several times a day, but to his surprise, he didn't mind, and the bodily fluids didn't disgust him. It was almost meditative, slowly swiping a cloth over the man's skin. He thought perhaps the man relaxed somewhat while Ennek bathed him, his usually tense limbs loosening a little and his face settling into more peaceful planes. Ennek noticed that sores were developing where sharp bones jutted against hard marble, so he lined the bottom of the tub with towels, and that seemed to help.

Although the man didn't exactly wake, at times he was clearly asleep and dreaming. He'd twitch then, and whimper and groan. Sometimes he'd scream. The worst, though, was when he cried. Fat tears would course down his cheeks, and he'd curl even more tightly against himself as he sobbed. Ennek would soothe him by rubbing his back and crooning tunelessly—he'd inherited the Chief's inability to sing. It seemed to help; at least the man would quiet and slip back into his usual catatonia.

One morning Ennek rode down to the port, where he found Mila sitting at his desk, a huge pile of papers in front of her. She leaped to her feet when she saw him and walked away from the desk, smiling apologetically.

"I'm sorry, sir. I wasn't certain when you'd be back, and—"

"Don't worry about it. Thank you for carrying on in my absence."

"Of course! But now that you're back, maybe—"

"I'm not really back, not for good. I've had some… complications, I guess. I'm having to take on a new role at the keep."

Her face fell. "You won't be continuing as portmaster, then? You've been doing such a fine job, sir."

He wanted to bask a little in the praise, which he heard so rarely, but he only shook his head. "Thank you, but I'm afraid not. It's… I didn't have a lot of choice, really, or I'd have stayed here. But I know you'll do fine without me. In fact, I'll ask that you be promoted to portmaster immediately."

Mila was clearly pleased that she might be promoted, but still she seemed to view his departure with genuine regret. He gave her Thelius's searching device before he left and then shook her hand and rode back up toward the keep with a heart as heavy as stone.

Back in his chambers, Ennek moved the man to his bed and went to shower. When he was clean, he wrapped himself in warm, comfortable clothing and went to move the man back to the tub. But the man looked so much more comfortable there that he hadn't the heart to do it right away, and instead he decided to feed him there. So he propped some pillows behind himself and pulled the man's head into his lap, then slowly spooned bits of beef and grain gruel into his mouth.

He was wiping a few drops off of the man's cheek when the prisoner's lids slowly opened, and this time the green eyes focused on Ennek's face.

Ennek looked solemnly down at him. "Are you awake?" he asked.

It wasn't the first time he'd asked it. But it was the first time he received a response. In a voice as thin and rusty as an ancient nail, the man said, "Yes."

chapter nine

AT A conservative estimate, Ennek wanted a thousand questions answered. And he supposed the man might have one or two of his own. But the man looked so weak, his grip on consciousness so tenuous, that Ennek knew he'd be lucky if they managed to exchange more than a few words. So he began with the simplest: "What's your name?"

The man's eyes went wide and his brow furrowed. His lips moved a little, as if he wasn't certain how to use them or had to try out several possible responses. He blinked rapidly and his breathing sped up, became harsh and shallow. He made a tiny sound of distress.

Ennek decided to try another tack. "I'm Ennek," he said, slowly and carefully. "Ennek. And… you're safe, okay?"

The man blinked again and his eyes rolled a little as he tried to take in his surroundings. He couldn't have seen much. Ennek's face looming over him, the navy and gold cloth of the bed curtains above him and to the sides, perhaps the paler blue blankets on which he lay. Then he looked back up at Ennek imploringly and licked his lips. "Real?" he rasped.

"Yes. This is real."

He began to cry. He was silent about it, but his eyes flooded with tears that slid down his cheeks and onto Ennek's lap, where Ennek could feel his flannel trousers dampen slightly. Ennek considered moving, sliding out from underneath the man's head and shoulders; but that would be awkward, and besides, he had the notion that the physical contact might actually be a little comforting to the man right now. At any rate, the man didn't try to move away.

On impulse, Ennek lifted one hand and stroked lightly at the man's scalp. He was pleased to note that it was now a little stubbly. At least this was one thing taken from the prisoner that he could now have back.

The man let out a long sigh and moved his head a fraction of an inch, into Ennek's caresses.

"I'd really like to know your name," Ennek said mildly.

A few more tears slipped out and the man sniffled a little. "M-Miner," he whispered.

"Miner." It was an odd name. Perhaps it had been common three hundred years ago. But Ennek repeating it seemed to tear something loose in Miner, and his body was wracked with an enormous shudder before he twisted and curled on his side and sobbed and sobbed.

Ennek felt helpless. He'd never comforted anyone before—not anyone who was aware, anyhow—and he had no idea what to do. He couldn't recall anybody comforting him, either. Surely someone must have, at some point. When he was very young, at least. If not his mother, then at least a servant. But he couldn't remember. He did recollect being six or seven and deciding to take one of the guards' horses for a ride. The enormous beast had been much too spirited for him, and he'd fallen or been thrown—he wasn't sure which—onto the unforgiving cobblestones. He'd knocked his head very hard and his wrist shrieked with agony, and he sat and cried until one of the guards fetched his tutor.

Bavella hauled him to his feet and half dragged him into the keep, berating him the whole way. She took him to his chamber and plopped him on a chair and told him to stay put in a voice that brooked no argument. An eternity later she'd returned with his mother and the wizard. All these years later, he wasn't sure whether he'd expected his mother to take him in her arms and soothe his crying. In any case, she didn't. She and Bavella watched while Thelius poked painfully at his head and hand. Thelius had rubbed something stinky over both injuries—making them hurt even more—and then wrapped the wrist tightly in a splint. He pronounced the bones broken and said a few words that made Ennek's arm tingle strangely. And then Ennek had been sent to bed, where he cried himself to sleep. Two days later, his mother watched while one of the guards thrashed him soundly for his misdeed.

No, he couldn't remember being comforted.

So now he patted clumsily at Miner's back and mumbled nonsense at him about how it would all be okay. Maybe it worked, or maybe Miner was just exhausted. After a while, his sobs receded and he fell into a deep sleep. Ennek made sure he was well covered by the blankets and went to the window, where he spent hours thinking nothing, staring at the shifting sea.

HE KNEW Miner was awake was when he heard the thump behind him. He spun around to see the man scuttling backward across the floor, his eyes wide with terror. When Miner made his way to the corner of the room, he moaned and bent himself into a tight ball with his back pressed hard against the stone walls. He was shivering, and Ennek didn't know whether from fear or the cold.

Stepping slowly so as not to panic him any further, Ennek approached. He kept his hands in front of him, the palms flat, hoping he looked relatively harmless. "Hey, it's all right. You're okay. I'm Ennek, remember?" Miner didn't respond, so Ennek practically tiptoed until he was very near, and then he sank to his knees. The floor was cold even through the fabric of his trousers—it must have been terrible against Miner's bare skin.

Ennek carefully placed a calming hand on Miner's shoulder. "You can't be comfortable here. Let's get you back into that warm bed, okay?"

Miner uncurled just enough to peer up at him. "Who—who are you?"

"Told you. Name's Ennek." He suspected his lineage wouldn't be very reassuring to the man right then. "C'mon. How about some food, huh? Maybe something a little more solid than gruel."

Miner blinked as though the words didn't make any sense, but he allowed Ennek to gently raise him to his feet. He couldn't hold his own weight, though, and Ennek ended up carrying him to the bed, then tucking the blankets around him. Miner looked defeated and bewildered. Then Ennek had a sudden thought. "Um… do you need to use the bathroom?"

"B-bath?"

"No, I meant… do you have to piss?"

Miner frowned and looked down at himself. "Yes?" he said uncertainly.

"Want me to carry you to the toilet?"

Miner just looked confused at the question, so Ennek uncovered him and picked him up—the man still weighed alarmingly little—and brought him into the bathroom. He set him carefully on the open toilet but had to hold Miner's shoulders steady to keep him from toppling over.

Nothing happened.

"Um, you can go ahead now." He could feel himself blushing furiously.

"Where's… chamber pot?" Miner looked around, puzzled, and it occurred to Ennek that there had been no toilets when Miner was placed in Stasis, no indoor plumbing at all, actually.

"This thing you're on, it's called a toilet. It's sort of a… self-cleaning chamber pot. You can piss in it or… whatever. That's what it's for."

More blinking, and then Miner let out a sigh of resignation. A moment later the sound of liquid hitting liquid filled the small room. Even though Ennek had been cleaning Miner's waste for days now, his face flushed even hotter and he stared carefully at the ceiling until Miner was finished. Miner watched blankly as Ennek reached for the chain, but when the toilet began to flush, he cried out in alarm and wrenched himself out of Ennek's grip. He fell hard and scooted away, his eyes wide and glassy.

"No, please," Miner whimpered. "Please."

"What's the matter? It's only a toilet. It can't hurt you."

"No… no more water, please, no more." His voice was breaking, and he was trying to squeeze himself backward in the small space between the tub and the wall.

Ennek didn't understand. But Miner looked to be at the end of his rope, and he was still naked and once again shivering on the stone floor. So Ennek coaxed him out a bit, murmuring promises that there would be no more water, and he carried him back into bed.

This had clearly been too much exertion for Miner. His thin chest heaved, and his eyes were hazy and unfocused. If Ennek was going to get some food into him, it had better be soon. He dashed to the door and out into the hallway, where he was fortunate to nearly collide with a servant. "Quick!" he demanded to the startled woman. "Go to the kitchen. I need some soft bread, and broth, and uh, some sweet wine, maybe."

She gaped at him for a moment. "Uh, yes, sir!" she said and scurried away.

While Ennek waited impatiently for her to return, he stood beside the bed, looking down at Miner. Miner's gaze skittered nervously around the room, never alighting on Ennek's face for more than a split second.

"Do you know where you are?" Ennek finally asked him.

Miner shook his head warily.

"You're in the keep."

Miner did a sharp intake of breath, and then he closed his eyes. Ennek thought perhaps he'd gone to sleep, or maybe into his coma-like state, but then Miner's right hand appeared from under the blanket, trembling slightly, and felt at the collar around his neck. He opened his eyes—deep pools of despair—and in a tiny voice said, "How long? Master?"

That word did some strange things to Ennek. Things he tried to hide—from himself as well as the other man—by clearing his throat and biting at his lip and gruffly asking, "How long what?"

"Since I... I was...." He swallowed, unable to complete the sentence.

And Ennek was instantly faced with a dilemma. Miner seemed upset enough by a simple toilet. What was going to happen when he found out he'd been Under for three hundred years, that everyone and everything he'd known was long gone? Ennek briefly considered lying. But Miner was going to find out eventually, and after what he'd been through, he deserved a little honesty. "It's been a long time," Ennek finally conceded. "Um... a really long time."

Miner still looked at him expectantly, the way a dog does when it's been kicked all its life and fully assumes it will be kicked again.

"Three hundred years," Ennek said.

Miner moaned and closed his eyes again.

They were both silent and still after that, until a timid knock sounded at the door. Ennek stuck his head out. The bed wasn't easily visible from outside the doorway, but he wanted to make sure nobody got even a glimpse of the prisoner. It was the servant, of course, and she held a tray in her hands. Ennek took it from her without fully opening the door. "Thanks," he said, and she practically ran away.

Miner submissively allowed Ennek to prop him up against the headboard. He chewed and swallowed obediently as Ennek fed him bits of bread soaked in broth, interspersed with sips of watered wine. But his eyes were blank and dull, and his mind, if it was aware at all, was turned deeply inward. There was no more conversation.

When Ennek determined that Miner had eaten enough for now, he took the tray away. He hadn't had any dinner himself, but he wasn't hungry. He gnawed on a bit of bread to settle his stomach and drank the rest of the wine. Then, after checking to make sure Miner was asleep, he

took a shower. As the hot water sluiced over him, he remembered what
Thelius had said about restraints. Should he tie Miner up somehow? If
he didn't, would Miner stay put inside his chambers when Ennek wasn't
there to keep an eye on him? Right now he wouldn't get far—he couldn't
even stand on his own—but any appearance outside these rooms would
be a disaster.

Gods, what kind of existence had Ennek consigned him to?

When the shower was over, Ennek realized he was exhausted. The
whole day had been emotionally draining. And now there was a man in
his bed—not a man in Stasis anymore—aware and afraid and collared.

There was nowhere else to sleep and it was a big bed, so Ennek
crawled in on his side—funny how he was already thinking of it that
way—and turned off the lamp. He couldn't see the other man anymore,
but inches away, Miner's breaths were soft and even.

ENNEK HAD hoped for a few more answers in the morning.

He'd awoken to a pair of gray-green eyes staring at him from less
than a foot away, and he'd been slightly startled until he remembered.
Miner didn't stir at all, just watched as Ennek sat up and stretched and
yawned and glanced at the clock. Ennek had slept in a pair of soft trousers
and no shirt, and now he ambled sleepily into the bathroom and urinated,
shaved, and cleaned his teeth, then shambled back to the bed.

"Toilet?" he asked.

Miner flinched and tensed.

"It's… you have to use it. No more chamber pots. But I can flush it
when you're not in the room, okay?"

Miner nodded slightly. He was a little stronger this morning, and
although Ennek still had to sling Miner's arm over his shoulders and put
his own arm around Miner's thin waist, and although Ennek was still
bearing almost all of the other man's weight, at least he was upright and
able to shuffle along. Ennek stubbornly ignored the way the bare torso
against his made his stomach feel fluttery and his skin too tight.

This time Miner was able to remain sitting without support. When
he was done using the toilet, Ennek kept him there a few moments
longer while he turned on the tap at the sink—only a small trickle, so
as not to alarm Miner—and wetted a hand towel. He cleaned Miner's
face, noting how the fibers of the towel caught a little on the whiskers

that were beginning to grow in. The whiskers, like the stubble on his scalp, were nearly white. Ennek wiped carefully along the edges of the collar as well, looking closely to make sure the skin wasn't chafed beneath the iron. He chose not to think right then of how he would make sure Miner bathed properly—the tub would probably give him apoplexy. Ennek hauled Miner back to the bed and pulled the blankets over him.

He was going to get some breakfast for them both and then engage in a little gentle interrogation, but Miner looked at him and in a soft voice asked, "What do you want with me, Master?"

Again, an unwanted thrill coursed through Ennek's body. He viciously tamped it down. "I don't want anything." He wanted to add that he wasn't Miner's master either, but, well, that would be a lie, wouldn't it? "I saw you and I wanted to help."

Miner looked quizzical. "But… why?"

Ennek shook his head. "I don't know." That really was a lie as well, but the man didn't need to know he'd been haunting Ennek's dreams.

"Please, Master. Who are you?"

Ennek was mulling over an answer to that—and wondering how it was that Miner seemed to be interrogating *him*—when a loud knock sounded at the door. Ennek started a bit and Miner curled protectively into a tight ball.

It turned out to be a guard this time. "Sir, Councilman Hils is here to see you. He says it's quite urgent."

Ennek swore under his breath. "Where is he?"

"In the blue salon, sir."

"Fine. Tell him—I'm not even dressed yet—tell him I'll be down shortly. Make sure he's offered something to eat and drink. In fact, have some tea and a tray of meats and fruits brought into the salon." Having skipped dinner, he was ravenous.

"Yes, sir."

Suddenly shy, Ennek ducked into the bathroom to dress. When he came out, he looked long and thoughtfully at Miner, who was sitting up slightly in bed with his head bowed. "I have to go out for a while. I'll bring you back something to eat. But it's really important that you stay here, okay? Don't leave this room. If someone comes to the door—and nobody should—don't answer it. Just stay put. Rest."

"Yes, Master" was the quiet reply.

HILS WAS standing and waiting for him, dressed in a splendid suit of midnight blue that looked almost as if it were made to be worn in this salon. His face was ruddy and his hair slightly windblown. He must have ridden over rather than taking a carriage. He had a steaming mug of tea in one hand and a chunk of cheese in the other. He set both down on a small side table, and he and Ennek shook heartily.

"Late night last night?" Hils asked congenially.

"No, not really. Just felt like sleeping in." Ennek found the teapot and poured a cupful for himself, then popped a big red grape in his mouth.

"I've heard you haven't been at the gaming house for weeks, or any of the inns."

Ennek lifted an eyebrow. "Are you spying on me?"

"No." He smiled. "I just hear rumors, that's all. Balnius is a constant font of gossip, you know."

Ennek did know. He'd often seen Hils's youngest brother at the gaming house or inns, and the young man always seemed to have his ears out and his mouth open. "So what else does he have to say about me?" he asked, slightly amused. He filled a small plate with a hard roll and bits of cold meat, then sank into one of the plushly upholstered chairs. He gestured Hils to sit as well.

Hils sipped at his tea. "Actually, that's why I'm here. He says you're no longer portmaster. Is that true?"

Ennek shook his head, bemused. "News travels fast. I just told Mila yesterday."

"So the captain of the port guard knows, and Balnius is married to the captain's sister." He put down his cup and, for the first time that morning, lost his expression of light good humor. "Why, Ennek? I thought you were enjoying it. Certainly nobody could fault the work you were doing."

"I was enjoying it. But I've taken another position instead."

"What?" Hils looked almost angry.

Ennek took a deep breath and looked away, as if he found the painting of a grassy landscape suddenly fascinating. "I'm training to be wizard."

Hils sounded like he was choking. "Wizard? Training to be *wizard*? Good gods, Ennek, *why*?"

"Thelius asked me." He still wasn't meeting the other man's eyes.

"Thelius asked you. That's…. Ennek, that spooky old scarecrow snaps his fingers and you come running? That doesn't make any sense."

"It's an honorable position. Powerful."

Hils's expression turned dark. "Is that what you're looking for? Power?"

"No… I… I don't know. It's… I can be something besides just the younger son."

Hils slammed his cup down and a little of the liquid sloshed out onto the table. He jumped to his feet and loomed over Ennek. "You already are something! Portmaster is an important post. The port is the lifeblood of this polis."

"I sign papers. I read lists. Mila does it just as well. Better."

"She does not! You've practically eliminated gold smuggling— nobody's done that before."

"Yeah, with Thelius's magic."

"No, with the way you used Thelius's magic. You have a reputation among the sailors, you know? They like you. They say you're an honest man, and fair."

Ennek hadn't realized that, and it broke his heart a little. He opened his mouth to respond, but Hils wasn't done. "And your plans for the fishing piers? Really good ones. You'll make millions for the polis and the fishermen. They'll probably erect a damned statue to you, Ennek!"

Ennek folded his arms stubbornly. "Someone else can do it. It was just an idea anyway."

Hils bent down, put his hands on the arms of Ennek's chair, and placed his face very close to Ennek's. "I was looking forward to working with *you*, you bastard!"

Finally Ennek couldn't look away any longer. His eyes met Hils's, and maybe Hils saw something there, because his face softened and he dropped to one knee. "You have to do it, don't you? That monster has something over you." His voice was quiet now too, almost a whisper.

Ennek clenched his jaw and tried not to cry like a baby. "You don't understand, Hils. I live in the keep. Nothing I do goes unseen, unnoticed. Nothing the Chief's own son does is overlooked."

"Gods. What have you done, Ennek?" His hand, as he placed it on Ennek's knee, was heavy and hot as an iron. Ennek felt the warm puffs of Hils's breath too, even fancied he could hear his heartbeat, strong and steady like a blacksmith's bellows. Fire, he thought. If Hils were a wizard, his element would be fire.

"I've done the right thing, I think. The only thing I could do. But… but it's against the law, you see." He laughed bitterly. "The inflexible, precious law."

Hils looked at him searchingly. "Are you all right? Are you safe?"

Those stupid tears came unbidden, because Hils cared. Ennek blinked them away and in a hoarse voice replied, "Yes. I am. As long as I work with Thelius."

Hils nodded slowly and then stood, stepping back a little. Ennek was desperate to grab at his hands. But he didn't. He sat frozen as if he were that statue Hils had mentioned.

"I'm sorry, Ennek. You're a good man. I've always thought so. If you need a friend… let me know, okay?"

More tears, and Ennek could only nod his thanks or he'd have broken down completely. Hils gave him a small smile and a tiny wave, and then Ennek's only friend left the salon.

WHEN ENNEK had himself under control, he marched out of the room and through the reception hall, taking the rest of the food with him. He wanted to put the entire encounter out of his mind as soon as possible. But as he stomped through the keep, his thoughts were free to wander elsewhere, and where they wandered was into near panic. What if Miner hadn't obeyed him? What if this very minute he was lurching through the hall, nude and confused, ready to be discovered by the nearest servant or guard? Gods, what if he'd already been discovered?

Ennek practically ran toward his chambers and was immensely relieved to discover no uproar along the way. He threw his door open, and Miner flew off the bed and crawled frantically toward the opposite wall, where he crouched, panting and wide-eyed.

"Sorry," Ennek said, closing the door much more slowly. "Sorry. It's just… it's just me."

Miner didn't look particularly relieved.

So Ennek walked slowly across the floor and set the tray of food on the table beside the bed. Miner watched warily. He reminded Ennek of a young deer he'd once cornered against some tall boulders. He'd already wounded it with his first shot, and it had fallen to its knees, unable to stand any longer. Its labored breaths had been loud, the scarlet of the blood on its flank almost shocking. Ennek had seen himself reflected in its huge eyes and had known himself to be Death. A moment later he'd shot the deer again. It had fallen without a sound.

"You're fine," he said now. "Everything's fine. I didn't mean to startle you. Are you hungry?"

Miner swallowed. "Yes, Master."

"Come here, then."

Miner tried to stand but couldn't make it to his feet. Ennek watched him struggle, unsure whether he ought to help, but then Miner managed to get onto all fours, and he crawled toward the bed, his head hanging low. Ennek ought to have been disgusted at the sight of it.

Ennek helped him up onto the bed, shocked again at how little substance there was to the man, just skin over long bones. He drew the blankets up—they'd been twisted nearly onto the floor when Miner fled—and brought over the food tray. "Think you can manage something a little more substantial this morning?"

Miner eyed the food from under lowered lashes. The tip of his tongue peeked out for just a moment, shockingly pink, and then disappeared. "Yes, please."

So Ennek sat beside him and shared the food. Miner took only tiny bites, but his eyes rolled up in his head and he emitted small sighs as he ate; clearly, he was enjoying his meal. "Thank you, Master," he said when the plates were empty.

"You don't have to call me that."

"What—what shall I call you?"

"Just my name is fine. Ennek."

"Ennek," repeated Miner uncertainly.

Ennek smiled encouragingly at him. "That's it." He stood and took the tray away. Then he began pacing, because he had a question to ask and couldn't think how to word it. Finally he turned and looked at the other man. "You were supposed to be in Stasis for a thousand years. You know that, right?"

Again, Miner looked like that deer. "Yes," he whispered, so quietly Ennek could barely hear him.

"I sort of have special permission to have you now, even though it's early, but… nobody else can know. Nobody but the wizard." When Ennek said that, Miner hunched in on himself. Ennek continued. "That means you can't leave these chambers—ever. You understand? You have to stay in here forever."

"Who are you, Ennek?"

The question startled him a little. "I'm the Chief's younger son," he answered plainly. "I'm the Chief's younger son, and that means I have to obey the law, because...." He couldn't explain it any better than that. Didn't have the energy to go through it again today.

But to his surprise, Miner nodded. "I know," he said.

Ennek frowned slightly and then continued on his original course. "So I can't offer you much of a life. I can't set you free—can't get the damned collar off you. Can't... I just have to keep you in here. So I need to know: Is that what you want? Or do you want to be put back in Stasis?"

Miner scrambled out from under the blankets and dropped onto the floor. To Ennek's horror, he got onto his knees, pressed his forehead to the floor, and stretched his arms out flat, reaching toward Ennek in supplication. "Please. Gods, please, please don't put me back," he cried breathlessly. "Please, Ennek, sir, Master. Please let me stay here."

Ennek had to turn away, to take a moment to get his own breathing under control. "You can stay," he said. His voice sounded choked and guttural to his own ears. "Just don't *do* that."

Behind him, Miner sighed, long and loud. Ennek heard him climb awkwardly back into the bed. "Thank you," Miner said.

And it was all suddenly too much for Ennek. He felt suffocated. Drowning. "Stay here!" he commanded and grabbed his coat from the back of a chair. He needed to get away from the keep.

chapter ten

IT SHOULD have calmed him; it always had before. But as soon as he tied his catboat to the little pier and stepped out of it, he was overcome with another vision of Miner leaving his chambers. He looked back across the bay, the glare of the sparkling water hurting his eyes. It was almost as if he expected to see Miner running from the keep, pursued by guards, maybe pursued by the Chief himself. Of course he saw no such thing, and although he squinted, he couldn't even make out the window to his chambers.

Calling himself names in a wide variety of languages—hanging around the port had been good for that, anyhow—he stomped off the pier and onto his favorite path, fully intending to make his way to the top. If he hurried, he could be back before nightfall. But he made it only a short way before his doubts again overcame him, and he threw himself down on a fallen log. Out in the woods, where nobody but the birds could hear him, he ranted against Thelius, against Miner, against the Chief and the law and fate and Praesidium itself. Mostly, though, he ranted against himself, against his weaknesses and his failures and his blasted indecision, and against the hidden yearnings of his heart.

When he was finished, he felt empty and drained but no more at peace. He trudged slowly back down the hill and to the little boat, then untied it and sailed back to the city.

On dry land again, he rode through the port, but instead of heading directly for the keep, he turned inland. The streets were crowded this time of day, as people came home from the market with their dinner ingredients, and the merchants began to lock up their shops, and children hurried home from school. Some of the smiths were still at their fires, though, and Ennek found one he'd traded with before, Farius, a one-eyed man with scars on his face and as bald a head as a man in Stasis.

"Sir!" the smith called and shook Ennek's hand with a paw as big as a dinner plate and as rough as sandstone. "It's good to see you again. Are you needing a new rudder for your cat?"

"No, no. The last one's still fine."

"I make 'em to last longer than a lifetime, sir. It'll be fine when we're both dust."

"Am I supposed to be glad that my rudder will outlive me?" Ennek grinned.

"The way I figure, sir, that's a good thing. One less thing you'll ever have to worry about."

"You've got a point, Farius. I've enough worries as it is."

"Don't we all, sir?" The smith had been coiling a length of rope as they spoke; now he hung it on a peg not far from his forge. "What can I do for you, then?"

"Nothing fancy. I just need a length of chain, maybe, um, forty feet long. Something quite light, and with a lock on both ends."

Farius nodded and beckoned Ennek into his shop. He looked up at a large section of wall, where metal lengths of all different weights were hung, and selected one. "Will this do?"

Ennek peered at it, took the end from Farius and hefted it in his hand, then tugged at it. It wasn't heavy at all but was certainly too stout for a man to break. "Perfect," he declared.

As he watched, Farius measured a length, letting the loose end collect on the dusty floor as he went. Then the smith brought over a heavy iron bolt cutter and used it to sever the chain. After returning the bolt cutter to its place, he brought the chain to the forge. Within a few minutes, he had fastened each end to a medium-size padlock.

"Thank you," Ennek said, handing over a few coins and taking the chain.

"My pleasure, sir. Hope to see you before that rudder fails."

Ennek smiled and gave a little wave, and then left.

Before Ennek made his way through the keep to his rooms, he stopped in the kitchen and asked that someone bring up a plate of food. Miner had been without food all day, and he must be ravenous. Nobody in the kitchen, nor anyone else he passed, for that matter, commented on the chain Ennek carried wound around one shoulder.

Miner noticed it right away, though. He was on the bed, sitting against the headboard with his legs bent close to his chest and his arms around his shins. He'd draped a blanket around himself. He looked up sharply when Ennek entered, and when he saw the chain, he swallowed and looked away.

Ennek didn't say anything. What could he say to a man he was about to chain up like a dog? He walked into the smaller of his rooms. The window in there had heavy iron bars on the inside, as if someone had once been kept prisoner there. Ennek wrapped the chain around one of the bars and locked it up, then walked back into the bedroom, bringing the other end with him. He grunted in satisfaction when he discovered the chain was long enough to reach the bed—and almost anywhere else in his chambers—but at least a dozen feet too short to get to the door.

Miner didn't move at all as Ennek attached the chain to his collar, shut the padlock, and stuffed the key into his trouser pocket. Miner kept his eyes carefully downcast.

"I'm sorry," Ennek said when it was done. "I can't risk you leaving."

"I wouldn't" was the soft reply.

"Maybe not. But I can't…. It'd be the end of us both."

"I understand the consequences. Sir."

Ennek supposed that was true. He was crafting a reply when the knock came for dinner. He thanked the servant and took the food inside, over to the bed. He and Miner didn't speak as they ate, but at least Miner managed to get a good bit of real food into himself.

When they finished, Ennek went to his chest of drawers and pulled out some clothing—a pair of soft trousers he sometimes slept in and a warm woolen shirt with wooden buttons down the front. He set them on the bed beside Miner. "These probably won't fit you very well, but I can't get you anything better without raising a lot of questions. At least, not right now. I'll try to make it to the shops later this week. Meantime, they'll keep you warm and, uh, covered."

Miner nodded his thanks and started to awkwardly pull on the trousers. Embarrassed, Ennek went into the bathroom, where he cleaned his teeth and decided on a shower. He almost fell asleep standing up, with the warm water washing over him. His legs felt as heavy as lead and his eyes were half-closed when he came out again. Miner was sitting on the bed again, clothed. The sleeves and trouser legs were several inches too short, and both items of clothing, which fit fine over Ennek's muscular frame, hung on him. The collar was still easily visible over the top of the shirt.

Ennek started to climb into bed, but when he did, Miner rolled off and onto the floor, where he curled into a tight ball once again. "What are you doing?" Ennek asked.

"I didn't think…. Your bed…."

"It's the only bed I have, and you can't sleep down there. Come up. It's plenty big enough. We've been sharing already, you know."

Miner crawled back up. He lay down near the edge of the bed, his legs very straight and his arms stiff at his side. "When I was…. Before I was…. Two men together, it was a crime. An abomination."

"It still is."

"It meant life as a slave."

"Still does. But you're already… I mean, that's not an issue for you."

"But for you."

"My guess is that just taking you from Under would be enough to get me put in Stasis. Sharing a bed with you isn't going to get me in any worse trouble than that."

Miner glanced over at him, eyes shining in the one light still on, then looked away. "Is that why I'm here? So you can—"

"No!" Ennek cried, a little too fiercely. "That's not what I want at all!"

"I'm sorry. Didn't mean to imply you're a… deviant, sir." Miner was almost cowering.

"But I'm—I'm not—argh!" Ennek growled in frustration, which didn't calm the other man at all. "I'm not going to do anything to you, okay?" *Other than chain you up in my room forever*, his mind helpfully added. "Just get some sleep. I'm really tired."

Miner might have relaxed a tiny bit. Ennek turned out the light and within minutes was out himself.

PERHAPS IT was the early morning light shining through the window. Perhaps there was just something about waking up, breathing another person's exhalations into your own lungs, that promoted brutal honesty. Whatever the reason, the first thing Ennek said to Miner when they awoke was "I am, you know. A deviant."

Miner blinked at him and whispered back, "Me too." He frowned slightly. "Is that why you…? Are you going to…?"

Ennek moved backward a little, appalled. Not so much at the question as at the part of him that responded eagerly. "No," he said, a little gruffly. "I told you. I saw you, and… it seemed so horrible. I mean, I'd seen others in Stasis, and that was bad, but you…."

"I was drowning." Miner's eyes had grown blank and distant. "All that time I was drowning. Couldn't sink, couldn't break the surface, couldn't—" His voice cracked and his eyes filled again with tears, which he didn't blink away.

Ennek suddenly remembered an incident from when he was a small child. He hadn't thought about it in many years. It had been an uncharacteristically hot day, and he'd pestered until Bavella took him to the long sandy beach on the west side of the polis. She told him to stay out of the water, which was always cruelly cold no matter how warm the sun, but when she became distracted with unpacking lunch, he'd made a run for the surf. For a few moments it had been exhilarating to feel the waves tease at his legs, as if the ocean were a playful friend. But then he lost his footing, and the sea pulled him under and away. The sea *wanted* him—that was what he'd thought as he felt his lungs begin to fill—and for one sharp second he was sure he'd never touch dry land again. Then one of the guards, keener of eye and fleeter of foot than Bavella, fished him out and pressed the brine from his chest, and he'd soon been well enough for a thrashing.

He tried to imagine what it would be like to suffer that moment of drowning for three centuries. He couldn't.

"Gods," he said to Miner. "How could you stand it?"

Miner looked at him, bewildered. "I couldn't."

They were both silent for a time. Miner looked as if he might withdraw even more into himself, so Ennek asked, "Do you know why Stasis was... different... for you?" Perhaps a change of subject would have been better, he thought belatedly.

But Miner's gaze refocused and he nodded. "Yes."

"Tell me—" Ennek stopped himself, softened his voice a little. "Can you tell me what happened?"

"I was a traitor. I betrayed your family, I expect."

"Everyone in Stasis did that. What did you do?"

Miner sat up slowly and turned so his back was to Ennek. He hugged his legs to his chest as if taking up less space might help. "I fell in love. I was a member of the guard, and I had a wife—Eudoxia; we'd known each other our whole lives—and a baby girl, just a few months old. Marsa. But I fell in love with Camens. He was one of the Chief's younger sons."

Ennek's stomach lurched. "Good gods," he muttered.

"I tried to ignore it, I really did. I even asked my captain to transfer me, anywhere but the keep, anywhere but steps away from Camens's chambers. But I couldn't tell him why, and he refused. I saw Camens every day, and he'd smile at me, sometimes even stop to talk to me a little. Gods, he was so beautiful."

He stopped talking then, and Ennek didn't prompt him. Instead, Ennek lay on his side and looked at the thin, slightly bowed back, which was covered in nubby rust-brown fabric. A shaft of sunlight shone directly on the bed, and in its glow Ennek could just make out the faint stubble on the other man's head. The chain trailed away from his collar, over the edge of the bed, and across the floor toward the other room.

"Camens came back to his chambers one evening just as my shift was ending. He was drunk. So drunk he was tottering on his feet, and I had to help him inside, and then he felt sick, so I fetched his chamber pot and held back his hair while he vomited into it. After I helped him clean himself up, he—he grabbed me and kissed me, and *gods*! I'd never had a kiss like that. We became lovers that night, when he was still drunk but I wasn't. I was completely sober. It was my first time with a man, of course." He paused for a moment. "It wasn't his."

Ennek couldn't help but interrupt with a question. "Were you happy?"

Miner's laugh—the first in Ennek's presence—was more of a cheerless bark. "Happy? I had to sneak around, had to act normal when I was home with my family, call him 'sir' and keep my face blank when we passed in the keep. There were others too, other men he took into his rooms. Not many, but… enough. He trusted me to remain silent about it, you see? Even then I suspected that was why he'd brought me to his bed to begin with. I knew he didn't love me. I knew there was no way… well, no future. But when we held each other, yes, I was happy then. I thought those minutes were worth it."

He took a deep breath. "He let me see other things as well. Secrets. The people who came and brought him money and gifts so he would hire them to build roads and bridges—that was his job; he was in charge of land transportation within the polis. His friends who would join with him and… well, sometimes they would abuse slaves, or they'd gamble, or he'd help his friends put their competitors out of business. I asked him once when we were in bed together how he could so flagrantly ignore the law, and he looked at me as if I were a child. 'I am the Chief's son,' he said. 'I *am* the law.'

"Camens told his brothers and the Chief I could be trusted, so sometimes they'd meet in front of me. Once I heard them agree to attack some farmsteads outside Nodosus and make it seem as if the attacks had been committed by soldiers from Horreum, so that Nodosus would side with Praesidium in a trade dispute. Innocent people died in that attack. Children."

Ennek thought Miner might be crying again. Or perhaps his voice was simply hoarse from so many words after so many years of silence.

"I still loved him, though. I thought that was all that was important.

"Camens got careless. He was discovered in bed with another man one afternoon, a shopkeeper's son. More of a boy than a man, I think. The boy's mother found them, and this time it couldn't be covered up. Too many people knew. Camens and the boy were both tried for perversion. The boy was enslaved. Camens... Camens was executed on New Year. His own father slit his throat. His blood splattered on me as I stood there, keeping the crowd away, and I couldn't save him. Was too much a coward to even try."

It was so long ago, Ennek thought, but did it seem that way to Miner?

Miner wasn't finished. "I remained a guard in the keep. What else could I do? I felt dead inside, as if I'd lost everything." Again that bitter croak of a laugh. "I had no idea what it *really* meant to lose everything.

"I think the Chief and Camens's brothers, I think they forgot who had told them to trust me. Or maybe they truly didn't understand. In any case, I was in the room when the heir and the Chief talked about how they'd deliberately set Camens up to be caught. He'd become an embarrassment to them with his wild ways, I expect."

Ennek's blood ran cold. He couldn't imagine Larkin doing something like that to him, but the Chief... yes, that he could imagine. He was expendable, after all. The Chief would sacrifice him if he thought doing so would buttress his own authority, and certainly if he thought it would benefit the polis in some way. "What did you do?" he asked.

"I tried to kill them." It was a simple answer, plainly said.

"How?"

"I had a sword, of course." Of course. No guns back then. "I ran at them. It wasn't something I planned; I didn't think at all. I managed to run the Chief right through. But the Chief and his sons are well trained in fighting, aren't they?"

Ennek nodded, although he knew Miner couldn't see.

"The heir grabbed me. I wounded him as well, a nasty slash to his arm, but by then they'd shouted and more guards came pouring into the room, and… that was the end for me.

"The Chief survived. He had a skilled wizard to heal him: his wife.

"I was tried as soon as he recovered. At trial I had to look at the faces of my wife, my family, my friends, and they had to hear about how I'd slept with Camens. The disgust on Eudoxia's face, and the knowledge that Marsa would never even know my name…." He took a great, shuddering breath.

"So the wizard who put you in Stasis—"

"Was the wife and mother of the men I'd tried to murder, and the mother of the man whom I'd helped to disgrace and ruin."

Ennek sat up, horrified. "She did that to you *deliberately*?"

Miner didn't answer.

It was a lot to take in, all at once. Too much, really. Ennek stood, and Miner didn't look up as Ennek walked around the bed and made his way to the bathroom. Ennek took care of his morning needs in there, absently noting that he'd need to get some toiletries for Miner: a toothbrush, razor, and a comb for when his hair grew in. Perhaps he'd go to the shops this afternoon. These mundane thoughts distracted him from the tale Miner had told. Ennek did not want to think about the parallels with his own life, or the fact that the family that had so devastated Miner was his own, his own direct ancestors. Their portraits were no doubt hanging in the reception room right now—Ennek must have looked at them hundreds of times, and they had looked down at him.

When he came back into the bedchamber, Miner lay huddled on his side in the bed, his eyes closed. But Ennek didn't think he was asleep.

"I'll be back soon with some breakfast," Ennek said. "And then I have some things to do. If you're up to it, there's a shelf full of books over there." He gestured. "Help yourself."

Miner curled up more tightly, at which point it occurred to Ennek that he probably couldn't read. Not many could, when Miner was a youth. Only those whose families could afford tutors, and a member of the guard was probably not one of those. Even today, two generations after Ennek's great-grandfather had established several schools, most servants still couldn't afford the tuition. That was as it should be, Bavella had told him. It kept the lower classes from getting airs and trying to rise above their rightful place.

"Well, anyway, you can do whatever you want. Maybe get some more rest; I don't think you're quite recovered yet." Miner didn't respond, so Ennek nodded stupidly and then left.

ENNEK HADN'T even made it down his own hallway when he came face-to-face with one of his father's guards. "The Chief would like to speak with you, sir," the man said, somehow managing to be condescending while keeping his face blank and his tone appropriately respectful.

Ennek's pulse immediately accelerated. "When?"

"Now, sir, if you please."

They marched at a rapid pace to the Chief's office, which occupied an expansive space on the second floor. It had views of the bay and the polis, but Ennek had to stand with his back to them, facing instead toward the enormous desk behind which the Chief sat, his face as stony as the walls of the room. Larkin was seated on Ennek's side of the desk, his chair angled to see both of the others at once. He looked pale and haggard. The guard had left and nobody else was in the room.

Ennek stood with his hands clasped in front of him, trying very hard not to fidget, not even to lick lips that were suddenly desert-dry. He couldn't read Larkin's face any better than the Chief's; the bastard must have been practicing.

The Chief looked down at the sheet of paper in front of him, signed it in his firm, sure hand, and set it to the side. Then he looked up again at Ennek. "I have heard some news of you from the wizard."

Ennek's breath didn't catch or falter, and he didn't respond.

The Chief waited a brief moment and then went on. "He has told me that you have resigned your position at the port." He waited again.

"Yes, sir, I have. I was hoping you'd consider appointing Mila in my place. She'll do a fine job."

The Chief waved his hand as if that was of no concern to him right now. "I understand you have also agreed to train to become the next wizard."

"Yes, sir."

"Why?"

Ennek had actually been preparing for that question for several days now, although he hadn't quite expected to have to answer it this morning. "As I said, sir, Mila will do very well with the port, as well as I would. But Thelius said he sensed a talent in me, and he has no other successor, so I'd hoped I'd be of more value to the polis that way."

"And you chose not to discuss this matter with me beforehand?"

"Sir, I... I'm nearly thirty years old. I expect it's time I take some responsibility for making decisions about my life." And that was nothing but the truth.

The Chief had heavy, beetling eyebrows. Unlike his hair, which had long ago turned iron gray, his brows were still coal black. Now they drew together so firmly that the brown eyes beneath were barely visible. "And what is your intent if you are to take on this role?"

Ennek straightened his back. "To serve the polis as well as I am able, sir."

The Chief rubbed his fingertips absently on the top of the desk, and then his brow smoothed. "The wizard has told me that he perceives great potential in you." He stood then and walked around the desk until he was close to Ennek. The Chief was an inch or so shorter than Ennek; Ennek had never noticed that before. The Chief put out one large, square hand and his lips almost twitched. "I'm proud of you, son."

Ennek felt numb as he put his own hand out and allowed the Chief to shake it. His father had never spoken such words to him before, had never even called him *son*. "Thank you, sir," he managed.

"You'll do our family proud, will you not?"

"Yes, sir."

The Chief shook his hand once more and then dropped it. He walked stiffly back behind his desk, sat down, and, without another word, pulled a new pile of papers in front of himself. Ennek understood that he was dismissed. Swallowing a sigh of relief, he left the room.

All this time Larkin hadn't said anything, hadn't betrayed any emotion at all, but now he trailed after Ennek. Larkin caught him by the shoulder a few paces down the hall.

"Ennek! Hang on."

Ennek stopped.

"Why are you really doing this?"

"You heard me."

Larkin shook his head. "But... you as wizard. I don't believe it. You've never liked Thelius at all."

"No, I haven't. But he's the only one who can teach me." Ennek felt bad about skimming the edge of the truth. But this wasn't just his big brother he was speaking to, this was the heir.

"Do you really want this, Ennek?"

"I have obligations too, Larkin. And I want... I want to live up to whatever potential I might have." Again, not quite a lie.

Larkin gave him a long look, and Ennek gazed back impassively. Larkin took more after their mother in his appearance; he was taller and slenderer than Ennek, his hair wavy rather than curly and more russet than black, his coloring more fair. Then Larkin shook his head again, not so much in denial as in sorrow, Ennek thought. "All right," Larkin said. "Just... be careful, okay?"

Ennek nodded once and Larkin released the grip on his shoulder. But Larkin looked so distressed that Ennek asked, "Are you all right? Surely you can't be so upset over this matter."

Larkin shut his eyes for a moment as if he were in pain. "No. I mean, I'm not exactly happy about it, but it's your decision, I expect." He sighed. "Velison lost the baby this week."

"Is she okay?"

Larkin nodded. "Yes. The wizard said... he said she'll be fine, she just needs some rest."

It was Ennek's turn to clasp his brother's arm. "I'm sorry, Lark. Please give Velison my condolences."

"Thank you."

For a moment they both stood there a bit awkwardly, unsure what to do with themselves. Ennek would have liked to embrace his brother, but they never had before, and he wasn't sure how Larkin would accept it. In the end, he did nothing but allow his hand to drop away. Larkin gave him a sad little smile.

Ennek turned and went to gather breakfast.

chapter eleven

As THE carriage bumped and jostled, Ennek couldn't help but remember stories about his distant relative Camens, who had once been responsible for roads like this. Perhaps his tendency to take bribes explained the poor condition of the road, or maybe that was too long ago to blame him.

Ennek wasn't sure why he'd had to come on this journey at all, and he certainly would have preferred to travel on horseback, despite the light rain. But Thelius insisted it was necessary to go, and he'd also been adamant that they take the carriage. Ennek hadn't wanted to quarrel on his very first day in his new position, so here he was, gazing out the droplet-streaked windows as they made their way south. He was relieved that the wizard seemed sunk in his own thoughts, his face turned toward his own windows, and that they hadn't exchanged a word for some time.

He didn't know how long they'd be gone. He hadn't been told to take any clothing with him, so he took that as a good sign that they'd return by nightfall. He hoped so; he'd left Miner with a good-sized supply of food, but he didn't feel comfortable leaving Miner alone for too long.

He and Miner hadn't spoken much over the past few days either. Having told his tale, Miner seemed deep in despair. He spent his time sleeping or leafing listlessly through some children's picture books Ennek had brought him just so he'd have something to do. He was afraid to look out the windows, where he'd see the open ocean or the bay, and for once Ennek wished his chambers overlooked the polis instead. At least Miner was eating, and his body had already begun to fill out a little. He'd gained enough strength to care for himself as well. The bathtub was still out of the question, as was flushing the toilet, but he'd use the sink enough to wet a towel and wipe himself down, or to shave or brush his teeth. Ennek hadn't yet figured out how to obtain clothes in Miner's size, so Miner continued to wear Ennek's. He didn't complain about it, of course. Sometimes Ennek thought Miner was about to ask him something, but Miner never did, and he answered Ennek's questions in mumbled monosyllables.

As they'd exited the walls of the polis proper, the terrain flattened out and the road took them over salty flatlands where seabirds called and the air smelled of mud and algae. At times they passed over low stone bridges, many of which predated Camens by generations. Finally the carriage turned inland a bit and passed between fields. The late winter crops were being harvested, greens and a few vegetables. Artichokes would be in season soon. Ennek was very fond of artichokes.

In every field, bond-slaves stooped and shuffled. Ennek saw one young man look up briefly at the carriage as they passed, and their eyes caught for a moment before the man shook the rain out of his hair and bent again. Ennek wondered what the youth had done to be condemned to this fate, and how long he'd be forced to toil.

Ennek had never thought much about slaves. There weren't many in the keep itself; the servants did all but the heaviest or most repellent tasks. At one time—in Miner's time, as a matter of fact—there had been more of them, toting heavy buckets of water, emptying chamber pots, and making sure the lanterns and candles and fires stayed lit. Slaves must have carried in the coal to feed the constantly roaring ovens as well, and laid the cobblestones for the square in front of the keep, and kept the stables mucked out. They still did the latter chore, actually, and made sure the keep was well-scrubbed.

Being a slave in the keep would certainly not be pleasant. It was long days of hard work, and the best one could hope for was to be ignored by the servants, guards, and others who lived and worked there. Slaves weren't permitted off the premises without a pass, they were beaten for small transgressions, and they weren't allowed the luxuries of family or friendships. Running away meant painful executions for slaves and life in bond-slavery for any free person who helped them. Slaves ate scraps and dregs. But at least the slaves in the keep had a roof over their heads, drab but decent clothes on their bodies, and a warm place to sleep at night.

The same could not be said for the majority of the polis's slaves, who worked in the fields to the south or the quarries to the east. They worked from sunup to sundown, seven days a week. They were given miserable rags to wear, and they shivered even as they toiled. Although he'd never seen it himself, Ennek had heard that they were chained in place under meager shelters at night, like dogs, hoping to gain a bit of warmth from one another's bodies. They were expected to work even if they were ill or injured, and if they did not, the overseer was always nearby with a whip in hand.

Even though they spent their days growing and harvesting good food, every slave Ennek saw from the carriage window looked desperately thin.

At a state dinner, Ennek had once sat, bored and getting progressively drunker, as the councilmen near him debated the merits of bond-slavery. The younger one had said it was cruel and inhumane, and people were often condemned for minor offenses or when they were innocent of any wrongdoing. Few slaves survived long enough to serve their sentences, and even when they did, unless they had salable skills or family willing to take them in, they'd be released only to become beggars. And since begging itself was a crime, most were quickly recaptured.

The older man had disagreed strongly. The laws must be strict to gain compliance, he said. Despite the constant influx of sailors and other foreigners, Praesidium was one of the safest, most moral polises in the world, and its harsh punishments were part of the reason for that. Bond-slavery contributed to the polis's remarkable wealth as well. Besides, the councilman argued, conditions for criminals must be kept grim, or else the lower classes would have little incentive to work.

Ennek hadn't had any opinion on the matter. He'd merely swallowed more wine.

Until now, he'd never thought of any slave as an individual, as a human being with a history and thoughts and feelings. Which was a bit ironic, of course, seeing as he'd been sharing a bed with a slave for over a week.

Eventually the road twisted back toward the coastline and the fields transitioned into stands of towering trees. Ennek wasn't even certain they were still inside Praesidium's territory; at some point these lands became Olicana's. He'd rarely traveled in this direction. The few times he'd left the polis had been to visit their neighbors to the north and east. Praesidium had little commerce with the polises to the south, most of which were too tiny to be of consequence. Besides, the landscape became rugged in this direction, the roads often rendered impassable by mudslides and washouts. If goods had to be transported, it usually made more sense to do so by ship. Shipments by land usually went via the great valley to the east, which stretched for hundreds of hot miles.

The wizard finally seemed to become aware again. He rapped sharply on the front of the carriage and it rattled to a halt. "Come on," he ordered, opening his door. He grabbed his bag and climbed out a little stiffly.

Ennek stepped out and looked around. They were on a grassy promontory high over the ocean. It wasn't raining, but the wind was raw, sweeping up and over and then whistling through the trees on the other side of the road. It ruffled Ennek's curls, whipped his cheeks, and chilled his bones. He pulled his heavy coat tighter about himself.

Thelius was wearing only his usual light cloak but seemed impervious to the cold. That would be a handy wizardly trick to learn, Ennek thought. Thelius muttered a few words and then spread some powdery substance in a circle on the ground. Ennek wondered how he managed to keep the stuff from blowing away.

The coachman was still sitting atop the carriage, his shoulders hunched and his cap pulled down low so that, what with the thick scarf around his neck, his face was all but invisible. He was looking away from Thelius and the ocean, staring down the road as if he wished they'd just kept going.

"Come here," Thelius ordered. Ennek did, marching briskly over and then standing awkwardly in the spot where the wizard directed him. The air in this particular location felt odd—tingly, somehow—and there was a scent he couldn't place. Something heavy and old, like one might expect to find at the bottom of an ancient crypt.

"We've come here today to determine your element." Thelius had to raise his voice a little to be heard over the wind. "We had to get away from the influence of the polis for this. You'll learn that it has its own magic, which can be a benefit or an interference. This particular location has qualities that make it perfect for performing various spells. It's been used by wizards for over five hundred years. You'll want to remember how to find it so you can use it yourself someday."

No response seemed necessary, so Ennek merely looked back at Thelius and wondered if the wizard who'd tormented Miner so horribly had once stood in this very spot.

Thelius reached into his bag and pulled out a small leather satchel. From the satchel he removed a series of items, setting each around the edge of the circle in which Ennek stood. Directly in front of Ennek he placed a rock about the size of two fists held together; it looked a little like a lump of coal, but orange lines zigzagged through it like lightning. He stuck the end of a short, stout stick into the soil to Ennek's left. When he muttered a few words, the free end of the stick burst into flame, and the fire burned steady and bright despite the wind and without seeming to consume the wood. The third item was a squat glass bottle filled with a colorless liquid. Thelius placed it to Ennek's right. And finally there was a child's toy, a balloon of bright red rubber. Thelius put it to his thin lips and inflated it, then tied it off. Ennek watched over his shoulder as the wizard placed the balloon on the ground behind him. Again, despite the wind, it did not move.

When everything was in place, Thelius stepped back a few paces and smiled. Ennek didn't like the look of it—the smile of a man who had triumphed in an important contest. But he didn't have time to protest, because the wizard began to chant, and Ennek found himself transfixed.

He might have panicked—this could, after all, be some sort of elaborate trap—but the sensation that rushed through his body and pinned him in place felt *wonderful*. It was a little like sexual arousal, but stronger. Perhaps this was what it felt like to have relations with another person. He didn't know for certain because, at nearly thirty years old, he remained chaste. And then he realized it was more than just arousal, it was something much greater. What coursed through him was power, pure power, like the power of a conflagration roaring through a dry forest, or the power of the wind blowing hard enough to bend and twist living things, or the power of the earth when it shook beneath his feet during the occasional quakes that the polis was prone to. Or the power of the waves, always pounding, never stopping, turning even the most solid rock into gritty sand.

As Ennek thought this, the flask to his right rose into the air and hovered at shoulder height, rocking slightly. Ennek twisted his head to the side to look at it but found himself staring instead over the cliff, down toward the sea. A column of water had erupted from the ocean's surface, and it began stretching toward him like a watery rope.

It should have been a frightening sight. It was certainly nothing he had ever seen before. But he knew deep in the marrow of his bones that something in him was calling that water and that it was his to control. He willed it to twist in fanciful loops as it neared him, and it did, tracing impossible shapes in the air. Ennek laughed with delight.

When the end of the ocean tendril almost touched him, he made it dance and hover very close, like a snake mesmerized by a charmer's flute. It took an enormous amount of energy, but he managed to lift one arm and touch his finger to the very tip of the water. It felt alive. He knew if he wanted to, he could call more of it, could perhaps bring up a wave large enough to encompass the promontory on which he stood, to wash over his shoulders like a cloak and then flood away everything in its path.

And then he felt a sharp *snap* somewhere near his gut. The rope of water pulled away and crashed down, back into the roiling surf. The glass bottle fell too, shattering on the ground. And Ennek collapsed to his knees, suddenly as weak as an infant. He turned his head and retched miserably into the grass.

Thelius was standing in front of him, just outside the circle. His face was startlingly red, as if he'd been undergoing some great exertion, and he was panting loudly. But he was smiling, wide and terrible. "I knew it!" he crowed.

"Knew what?" Ennek mumbled and wiped the back of his hand across his mouth.

"It was water. Nearly every ancestor of yours who has become a wizard has called water. But none has done so as easily, as strongly. Certainly not their very first time, and most couldn't have managed that performance after years of study." The wizard's face twisted irritably. "Hardly seems fair that the Chief's identity is determined through the luck of inheritance rather than ability, does it? Most Chiefs couldn't conjure a rabbit from a hat, let alone do acts of sorcery to aid the polis."

Ennek's mind felt as unsettled as the sea itself. A part of him was exulting in the potential he had just discovered, capering happily at the thought of what he could do with such abilities. Another part of him was shocked and horrified that he was capable of such a thing and was churning with all the possibilities that power like this could bring. And a third part—perhaps the largest part right now—was simply exhausted and ill. "Can we go?" he asked quietly.

"Of course, of course." Thelius began bustling around, repacking the rock and the torch, which had been extinguished at some point, deflating the balloon, and clucking slightly over the broken glass.

With a great deal of effort, Ennek rose and stumbled back toward the carriage, where he thought the coachman was casting sidelong glances in his direction. It felt wonderful to collapse onto the padded seat, despite Thelius climbing in beside him and patting Ennek's knee.

"Magic takes energy, my boy. You're going to need plenty of food and rest after that display." He cackled drily. "You'll learn to control it, son, learn the discipline you need. Someday you will be a great wizard."

He kept talking after that, but the words just buzzed like flies around Ennek's ears, and within minutes he was fast asleep.

ENNEK WOKE with a start when the carriage came to a halt. He looked blearily out the window. They were in front of the keep, and it was dark out. He couldn't be certain, but it felt very late.

Thelius patted his knee again. It felt proprietary, and Ennek didn't like it at all. "Go rest. Come to my laboratory in three days and we'll begin your lessons."

Ennek nodded and practically fell out the door. He reeled to the keep, not bothering to see what became of the wizard or the carriage, glared at a guard who looked like he might want to ask questions, and went toward his chamber. The halls were very nearly deserted, so he was relieved to run into a servant along the way and ordered food for his chambers.

"What would you like, sir?"

"I don't care. If it's edible, I'll take it. Lots of it," he growled and lurched toward the stairs. He didn't know how much of the morning's provisions Miner had left, but it certainly wouldn't be enough for his own hollow stomach, which was insisting it hadn't been filled in weeks.

Miner looked up when Ennek entered the room, his expression slightly fearful. He was sitting cross-legged on the bed with a piece of paper lying on a book in his lap and a charcoal pencil in his hand.

"I'm.... Is it all right that I'm using these? I found them on your desk, and—"

"It's fine." Ennek had been using them to sketch out rough plans for new piscarium piers; he wouldn't need them anymore. "But I thought you couldn't write."

"I'm drawing."

"Oh." Ennek let his coat fall to the floor. He made his way across the room to where a bottle of wine sat on a small table, along with the tray holding the remains of the food he'd brought up that morning. There were some fat red grapes left, and an apple. The bread was stale, but he dunked it in his wineglass and ate it anyway. He spent several minutes stuffing food into his face, and then he sat in the nearest chair, unbuckled his boots, and, with a groan, drew them off his feet.

He sat in the chair for a while with his arms hanging down and his head drooping, lacking the energy to move.

"Are you all right?" Miner had put aside his drawing things and walked over, so that now he looked down at Ennek in concern. "Can I help you?"

Alarmingly, Ennek found himself choking back tears. "Just tired," he muttered. "Had a rough day."

Miner walked away, toward the bathroom. Ennek heard water run briefly into the sink, and then Miner returned with a damp towel and Ennek's comb. "Here," he said, handing Ennek the towel. "It's warm. I thought it might feel nice on your face."

It did. Actually, it made Ennek long for a hot bath, but he knew he'd only fall asleep in the tub, and he'd never have the energy to drag himself out.

Miner held the comb out hesitantly. "Your hair… it's pretty tangled. Would you like me to get the snarls out?"

Ennek looked up at him in surprise. "You don't have to do this."

"I want to. You've been very kind, and I've only taken up space here, doing nothing."

Nobody had combed Ennek's hair since he was a child, and the tangles were certainly an itchy, irritating mess. "All right."

Miner was just reaching for his head when the door rattled. Ennek hauled himself upright and retrieved a tray of food from a servant. Several minutes later Ennek was propped in bed on a pile of pillows as Miner gently worked his way through the windblown chaos of Ennek's hair and popped small bits of food into Ennek's mouth. Ennek felt enormously comfortable and pampered. He pretended not to notice the way Miner had to occasionally shift his chain out of the way.

When his hair was finally in order and his stomach full, Ennek smiled sleepily at Miner. "Thanks."

Miner's return smile was a little shy but warm. It lit his entire face the way a lantern lights a dark room. It made him beautiful.

THE SUN had already begun its descent to the west when Ennek woke. He was still wearing the suit from the day before, and he was grimy and sore. His bladder also felt as full as the bay.

Miner was sitting in a chair not too far from the bed, sketching something on the paper in his lap. He looked slightly startled when he saw that Ennek was awake. "Are… are you ill?" he asked.

"No." Ennek sat up and yawned hugely. "I had a rough day yesterday, that's all." He stood and stretched. "Gods, I need a bath. Did I leave you any food last night?"

"There's plenty," Miner replied, gesturing toward the tray that sat on a table. "The stew's cold, of course, but I could bring you something else."

Ennek eyed the food, then the open door to the bathroom, and then the food again. "Um, if I draw myself a bath, would you be able to help with my meal?" It was a daring idea, but the thought of not having to choose between eating and bathing was too appealing to not suggest it. "I mean, if you wouldn't mind being so close to the tub and, uh, me." He was blushing, damn it.

"I don't mind" was the soft reply.

Ennek fled for the bathroom. While he waited for the tub to fill, he urinated and cleaned his foul-feeling teeth, then stripped off his clothing. His suit smelled the same as the circle had, and he suspected his bedding must as well. He'd have to put clean linens on today.

It felt heavenly to sink into the steaming water. He'd even tipped in a little scent, so now the whole room smelled faintly of spiced oranges. And that made him hungrier. "Miner?" he called. "I'm ready."

He actually considered covering his lap with a towel. He was far from used to being seen without clothes. But it seemed as though the towel would be even more awkward, somehow. Not to mention that he'd had ample opportunity to view Miner nude, so playing coy hardly seemed fair. Besides, he told himself defensively, it wasn't like he had anything to be ashamed of.

When Miner came in with a plate full of fruit and cheese, Ennek thought he saw the shadow of a smile playing around the corners of his mouth. Miner's face grew grimmer, though, when he spied the water in the tub, and Ennek heard the sharp intake of his breath. It was Ennek's turn to ask, "Are you all right?"

Miner nodded. "Yes. I... I have to get used to it sooner or later, I expect." He grimaced slightly, then knelt to set the tray on the floor beside the tub. "It smells nice," he said.

"Feels even better."

"All that hot water arrives with only a twist of the hand?"

"Yes." Ennek leaned his head back against the edge of the tub. "I guess people didn't take baths often when... three hundred years ago."

"No. Well, people with servants did. Or people with slaves." He said the last word sadly and then, perhaps to change the subject, asked, "Are things very different now? I mean, aside from water and the lights. The polis, is it the same?"

Ennek racked his brain to try to remember what he'd learned about Praesidium's history. It had never been his best subject. "I think it's pretty similar. More people now, faster ships, I guess. More ships as well. As portmaster, I...." His voice faltered to a stop.

"You're portmaster? That would be interesting, I expect." Miner wrapped a piece of cheese in a bit of bread. When he saw that Ennek's hands were submerged, he smiled and placed it in Ennek's mouth.

Ennek chewed and swallowed. "I was portmaster. Now...."

He looked over at Miner, who was bent over the food tray. His eyelashes had begun to grow back, and they sparkled a little in the light. Miner popped another bit of food between Ennek's lips, then gave a small smile and shoved a section of orange onto his own tongue.

"Now I'm to become wizard," Ennek said after Miner had swallowed.

Miner went very still. Without looking at Ennek, he asked, "Is that why I'm here?"

"No! Gods, no. I'm not...." The truth was the exact opposite, of course: Ennek was becoming a wizard because Miner was there. But would knowing he'd helped put Ennek in this predicament further damage Miner's already fragile emotional state? Ennek sighed. "I won't harm you, I promise. But if I weren't training to become wizard, I wouldn't be allowed to keep you."

Miner did raise his face then. His expression was unreadable. "How long until you put me back Under?"

Ennek shook his head. "I won't."

Miner's long, delicate throat worked, and Ennek wanted very badly to draw the man into his arms and soothe away his fears. Instead he remembered what Thelius had said about how Miner would have to be back in Stasis for the Chief's annual inspection. He looked at the chain trailing from Miner's neck and out of the room. "I won't," he repeated. "I promise."

chapter twelve

THIS PART of his apprenticeship wasn't too bad. Thelius had given Ennek a book, a thick one with a red leather cover and creamy blank pages. It was Ennek's task to go systematically through every item in the wizard's vast collection, describing it and then listing its uses. He also had to sketch the details of some specific items, such as the many amulets and talismans stashed throughout the laboratory. Ennek had begun his assignment in the northwestern corner of the laboratory, the one closest to the door, and in several weeks had progressed only to the next corner. At this rate he'd be ancient before he was done.

But he didn't mind. The bits and bobs he handled were mostly quite interesting, and he liked learning about what they could do. Some of them seemed very ordinary at first—lengths of string, a few scraps of paper, a small jar of seashells—but he could actually feel the magic when he touched them, a tickling sensation he found very pleasant.

Thelius was in the room as Ennek worked, sometimes messing about with vials and powders, sometimes just sitting by the fire and reading. He'd say a few words now and then, telling Ennek a detail or two about a particular item or instructing him where to find a book that could teach him more. His constant presence grated on Ennek, but at least the wizard wasn't standing over him all the time, watching him. Touching him.

"What's this?" Ennek asked one afternoon, holding up something long and slender and ivory-colored. It felt greasy, and he wanted to wipe his hands.

Thelius glanced up from his book. "Dragon's bone. Very hard to find, but useful for many things. I bought that one from a sailor from, let's see.... Quaretia, I think. He had no idea of the value of the thing and I got it for a song. *Beluae Magicae* has quite a lot on dragon-bone properties." He gestured vaguely at a huge book with a worn leather cover, which took up a good bit of a tabletop. Ennek had been consulting that tome often enough that he hadn't bothered to reshelve it.

Ennek set the bone carefully back on the shelf where he'd found it, in between a bundle of bluish feathers and a black pottery cup that looked as if it had been made by a small child. He scrubbed his hands at the small sink situated under one window, then strolled over to the book. Fortunately, his Latin was very good; Bavella had drummed it into his head thoroughly enough, and he had a bit of a knack for languages. But the writing in this book was crabbed and faded—it looked as though it had been written in blood, actually—and he had to squint to make it out. The spelling was atrocious as well, and he wondered whether the author had been semiliterate, or perhaps just not well versed in the tongue.

By the time he'd puzzled his way through the passage and taken notes in his own neat hand, the hour was getting late. He set down his pen and stretched a little, looking wistfully outside at the polis's evening bustle.

"Had enough for today?" Thelius asked, dry humor tingeing his voice.

"I expect so. My eyes feel squinty and my fingers are cramped."

"Hazards of the trade, I'm afraid."

"Don't you get tired of being cooped up inside?"

"No, not really. I've always fancied the indoors myself." Thelius closed his book and set it aside, then stood. "But I think I'll go find something to eat. You can go now. I expect your slave is waiting for you."

Ennek froze. They hadn't spoken of Miner since Thelius had put the collar on him. Of course Ennek hadn't thought Thelius had forgotten, but he'd hoped that the knowledge of Miner's situation was buried away somewhere deep in the wizard's head.

"Have you been enjoying him, son?" Thelius's voice was oily, insinuating.

Ennek set his jaw and glared at a jar of preserved bats. Good for enchantments to increase land's fertility, he remembered, or for healing minor burns. "He's fine," he growled.

"Because if he's not… satisfactory… we can replace him with another."

"He's *fine.*"

Thelius didn't seem upset by Ennek's tone. "Very well, then. Oh, don't bother coming until ten tomorrow morning. I've an appointment first thing." With that, Ennek was dismissed.

Miner smiled broadly when Ennek entered their chambers. Ennek didn't blame him—after spending months locked up in two rooms, he'd be glad for whatever company he got too. Miner was drawing again, this time the view of the bay, which he'd recently been able to stomach. He'd made real progress in facing his fears; he had even begun to take showers, although baths were still sometime into his future.

Now, Miner brushed a curl from his face. His hair was a nice length now and very thick. He'd told Ennek it used to be yellow as butter, but now it was dazzlingly white, like the snow that Ennek had read about but never seen. He still looked very youthful, though, his face smooth and unlined. Unless you looked into his eyes—they were ancient.

As Miner waited patiently, Ennek gave him a careful assessment. Ennek had finally found him some clothes that fit properly, so his ankles and forearms no longer stuck out past the hems. Miner had put on some weight as well. He was still thin but not skeletal. Sometimes he used Ennek's exercise machine and weights, and now ropy muscles snaked up his forearms, and his pectoral muscles were well defined. Not that Ennek *tried* to see these things, but when two men shared a small space—shared a bathroom and bed as well—some familiarity with one another's bodies was inevitable. Miner didn't appear ashamed to be seen unclothed; perhaps three hundred years of nudity would do that. Ennek was still dealing with his own silly modesty.

"You look tired," Miner said after a lengthy pause.

"Lots more old things to count today."

"As old as me?" Miner grinned.

Ennek couldn't help but smile back. "Some even older."

They sat together at the table and ate the meal Ennek had carried up. He wondered if anyone in the kitchen had noticed he seemed to be eating for two. If so, they hadn't mentioned it. Tonight they had fresh strawberries, which turned out to be a favorite of Miner's. He ate them until his fingers were stained red and his lips looked juicy and crimson. Ennek had to force himself to look away.

"There was a state dinner tonight," Ennek announced.

"And you didn't go?"

"No. They're a horrible bore." And, he didn't add, he'd have to face Hils. "Besides, I have something else planned."

"What?"

"A surprise." Ennek went to the bathroom to wash his hands. Then he walked to his chest of drawers and pulled out a fabric-wrapped bundle that he'd tucked away a few days earlier. Miner watched as he untied the bindings.

"More books? I've been enjoying the drawings in the others."

"These aren't picture books, though. Come here." Ennek set the books on the bed. Miner strode over and peered curiously over Ennek's shoulder. "They're primers. They're for teaching children—or adults, I guess—to read."

He couldn't see Miner's expression, but he could hear his quick intake of breath. "You'll teach me to read? Really?"

Ennek turned around to face him. "Sure. It'll help with the boredom, I think."

"But slaves aren't—"

"Who gives a damn what slaves aren't? It's just the two of us anyhow. Who will ever know?"

Miner put a long, slender hand on Ennek's shoulder. "Thank you," he said earnestly. "Thank you, Ennek."

Ennek almost leaned forward and pressed his lips against Miner's. What would it feel like? He'd taste of strawberries and wine.

Ennek pulled away. "Let's go learn the alphabet."

WHEN ENNEK arrived at the laboratory the next morning, Thelius wasn't there yet and the door was locked. So Ennek leaned against the wall and gazed at his shoes, remembering how Miner had looked when Ennek had left his room: bent studiously over a child's book with his hair still bed-tousled and his chain pooled on the floor beside him. Ennek reminded himself to find more strawberries that evening.

When Thelius finally arrived almost fifteen minutes late, Ennek was startled. The wizard trudged slowly down the hall as if his body weighed twice as much as normal, and he looked awful. His thin face was pasty white, his lips pressed so tightly together as to be nearly invisible, and his shoulders sagged. Thelius must have been in his late sixties at least, but for the first time, Ennek saw him as truly old.

He grunted at Ennek and unlocked the door. "Go catalog those plainar stones," he ordered when they were inside. "Size, color, and number of inclusions. Mark them in that register I showed you the other day."

Ennek stifled a groan. There were probably hundreds of the stupid things. It would take him all day. In fact, that was apparently the idea, because Thelius mumbled a few more instructions and then staggered off to his bedchamber, which was next door to the lab. He didn't tell Ennek what was wrong with him, and Ennek didn't ask.

Ennek was stiff and weary and grouchy by the time he finished his task. It was a little earlier than his usual quitting time, but Thelius hadn't reappeared with new directions and Ennek had no desire to disturb him to ask for them. He left a brief note by Thelius's favorite chair, informing him that the cataloging was complete, and then he left.

He went down to the kitchens, where he asked to have a platter delivered to his chambers in three hours—roasted spring lamb and tiny vegetables in a buttery sauce, and lots of berries. Then, because he couldn't stand more time indoors, he headed for the stables and waited impatiently for a stableboy to saddle a horse. He rode down to the waterfront near his old office and watched the ships for a while, then turned around and looked up at the keep. Was Miner standing at the window right now, looking his way? Was Miner aching for just a few minutes under the open sky?

Ennek had returned the horse to the stables and was about to walk back into the keep when a large party came crowding out. Some of them were guards dressed in the yellow and red colors of Nodosus, and a few were well-dressed men, probably high ministers by the look of them. In the center of the group was a tall man with corn-silk hair. He was walking slowly, as if he were in pain, but he stopped when he saw Ennek.

"Ennek?" he called.

"Gory! I'm sorry—I mean Chief," Ennek said and shook the other man's hand. Gory had become chief of Nodosus three years earlier when his father died of some wasting sickness, but it had been much longer than that since Ennek had seen him.

Gory grinned. He was still very tan and handsome, but now there were thin lines of tension across his forehead and at the corners of his eyes. "It can still be Gory to you, Ennek. You already have a Chief."

"It's good to see you. I hadn't known you were visiting."

Gory shook his head. "If it had been a normal visit, I would have been sure to find you. But this was more of an emergency. My horse threw me yesterday morning." He frowned. "I haven't been thrown since I was a child. I was badly hurt, and our own wizard, well, she's good, but she's visiting family out of town. There's nobody else in Nodosus I trust my life with."

"So you came here?"

"Yes. We sent some runners ahead yesterday to say I'd be here by morning. We rode all night." He leaned closer and nearly whispered, "I almost died."

"Gods! But you're walking now."

"Your wizard did the trick. Spent half the morning working his magic over me, and bad as I look now, I assure you it's much better than I was this morning. I'm going back home to finish recuperating."

"I'll let you go now." Actually, Gory looked like he might collapse if he stood much longer, and the men around him were getting anxious. "Come visit when you're better, though."

"I will. And you can tell me then how you ended up apprenticing to a wizard."

They shook hands again, and Gory and his entourage made their way to a waiting carriage.

When Ennek entered his rooms, Miner looked as happy as always to see him. "You've been for a ride," he observed.

"Yes. How can you tell? Do I smell like horses?"

Miner laughed. "No, not especially. But your cheeks are all flushed and your hair's wild."

Ennek turned an even brighter red to find himself under such careful inspection and patted self-consciously at his curls. That made Miner laugh even more.

Seeing Miner so playful—after all he'd been through, after he'd spent weeks confined and with no prospect of freedom, as he stood there with a collar around his pale neck—made something twist in Ennek's heart. Without making a conscious decision to do so, Ennek fished his keys from his pocket, closed the few steps between them, and quickly unlocked the chain. It rang loudly as he dropped it to the floor.

Miner's grin disappeared. "Ennek?" he said. His voice was tiny, plaintive. "Master?"

"Don't call me that!" Ennek snapped, and Miner flinched. Gods, this wasn't what he'd intended at all.

Ennek held Miner's shoulders and took a deep breath. "I'm sorry about the chain. I shouldn't have…. Nobody should be treated like that. I won't use it again."

Miner blinked at him. "You… you're not taking me back Under?"

"No! Gods, no. I promised you, didn't I? I'll never do that to you."

Miner swallowed. "Thank you," he whispered.

Ennek let his hands drop. He walked briskly past the other man and toward the door. "I'm going to go wash off the equine scent, all right? Then maybe we can get in some more lessons before dinner."

"Ennek?"

Ennek stopped and turned around.

"You can trust me. I won't leave."

"I know," he replied, and went to take a shower.

chapter thirteen

"My mother used to sing me that song."

Ennek looked over sharply. "I'm sorry. I didn't mean—"

"No, it's fine. Keep on singing if you like, but don't move, please."

Ennek repositioned his head so he was staring out the window again. He and Miner had thought the view of the bay might distract him enough to keep him still for a while, and it was working, more or less. In fact, he'd been so engrossed in watching a small fleet of smacks cozying up to a pier that he'd begun absently humming a song about boats bobbing buoyantly. His mother had never sung it to him—he didn't recall ever hearing Aelia sing at all, actually—but he'd heard it somewhere, and it must have stuck in his brain.

"I'll be done soon. Maybe ten more minutes."

"Okay. Take your time."

Out of the corner of his eye, he saw Miner bend over his paper.

A few mornings ago, Ennek had awakened early. Miner was still fast asleep; he'd been restless the night before and had stayed up to pore over his primers when Ennek went to bed. As Ennek padded to the bathroom, he saw a corner of a paper peeking out from under the pile of Miner's books on the desk. Mildly curious, Ennek lifted the books, and the drawing beneath took his breath away. It was Ennek, asleep. He was on his back with the blankets pulled down crookedly to reveal one side of his bare chest. His right arm was bent upward, the hand next to his tousled curls, and his left was resting beside his hip. His full lips were slightly parted, the corners curled up just the tiniest bit, as if he were having a nice dream. Miner had emphasized his broad shoulders, his aquiline nose, and the way his long eyelashes brushed against his cheeks.

Miner has made me beautiful, he thought. He tucked the drawing away and went to shower. By the time he came back with breakfast, Miner was awake and there was no sign of the portrait. When Ennek returned from the lab that evening, he offhandedly asked Miner how his sketching was going.

"Oh, all right. It passes the time. I enjoy it."

"Would you draw me? Nobody ever has, except for an ugly portrait that hangs in the reception hall. I look like a frog with curly hair."

Miner had smiled. "It'd take a pretty poor artist to make you look ugly," he said and ducked his head.

"Well, this guy managed. Would you give it a go?"

"I'm not a professional, you know."

"Well, neither am I."

Today Ennek had a day free of Thelius while the wizard went on some obscure errand. As a result, he and Miner slept in, and Miner had insisted on drawing him as he'd looked when he woke up, with his hair a riot and his eyes all bleary.

"Do you miss being portmaster?" Miner asked, still drawing.

"Yes, I do. I mean, it wasn't necessarily very exciting, but it was good work. Valuable."

"Have you spent much time at sea?"

"No. I've puttered around the bay, of course, and once I sailed down south to Lagentium and back, but that's it."

"Would you like to?"

"Yeah, I suppose." Ennek knew he sounded a little wistful. "I've always wondered what it would be like to be on the other side of the ocean. I've read of some of the wonders there, and of course the ships bring little bits of things over, but that's not the same as seeing it yourself."

"I had a brother who became a sailor." Miner never spoke of his family, never since the one time when he told how he'd come to be put in Stasis. Ennek listened carefully. "His name was Mahlon, and he was two years older than me. My father was furious with him. In my family, you joined the guard. All the men had, for generations. But Mahlon wanted to see the world."

"What happened?"

"He sailed away. He came back again a year later with all these exotic gifts, and these stories… well, we didn't believe half of what he said. He told us he had a wife too, and none of us could even pronounce her name. He left again a few days later, and we didn't hear from him again."

"I'm sorry."

"Don't be. It was a very long time ago. For all I know, he reappeared later, after I… after I was gone."

Ennek thought for a moment. "I could probably dig around in the records, if you like. Find out what happened to your family, whether—"

"No. Please."

Ennek resisted the urge to look at him again. "Okay," he said.

"It's only… I know what happened to them. They died. Centuries ago. And by the time they did, I'm sure they'd forgotten me, or maybe still cursed my name, the disgrace I'd brought them."

"But they loved you."

Miner sighed. "Yes, they did." Then Ennek heard him stand. "I'm finished. You can move now."

Ennek strode over to look at the drawing, which Miner was holding out nervously. He'd done more than catch the planes and angles of Ennek's face and body, the sculpted muscles of his chest and arms; he'd also managed to capture an expression of yearning in Ennek's eyes that exactly fit the feeling in his heart. It wasn't just his old job he longed for.

"That's wonderful," Ennek breathed.

Miner blushed. "Thank you. I didn't make you look like a frog."

"No, you definitely didn't. Thank you, Miner."

And Miner smiled the way that made his face light up like the sun. It nearly broke Ennek's heart.

IT FELT like stretching muscles that had long been unused. Ennek willed the glass of water to rise, and he stuttered through the strange words in the text Thelius gave him, and the glass rose. It hovered a few inches over the table, swaying drunkenly, before slamming back down hard enough to splatter some drops onto the worn wood surface.

"I thought this would be easier!" he exclaimed. "Before, I moved half the ocean."

Thelius chuckled and patted his shoulder. It felt like someone had tapped him with a tree branch. "It takes practice, son. Previously, your natural powers were amplified by my assistance and by the magic of the location itself. If it were always that easy, wizards would rule the world."

"Levitating drinking glasses isn't exactly useful," Ennek said sourly.

"No. But this is." Thelius said a few words—not quite the same spell Ennek had used, but close—and the entire table lifted up, glass and all. It floated almost all the way to the high ceiling and then danced around the room, somehow managing not to dislodge the water. After a few seconds, it settled back into place as gently as an autumn leaf drifting to the ground.

Thelius smiled. "Well, perhaps that was not terribly useful either. But I could lift a man just as well, or a heavy load. One of my predecessors used almost the same skill to unbury the victims of a landslide one hundred forty years ago."

"It doesn't make you ill?"

"Not just a table, no. Moving several boulders, well, I expect that would upset my stomach a bit."

"I can't imagine being able to do so much so easily."

"You will. You didn't build these fine muscles in one day, did you?" He gave a hard squeeze to the area between Ennek's neck and shoulder. With some difficulty, Ennek resisted the urge to shake his hand away. "But you've exercised enough for one day, my boy. I've some matters to attend to in my chamber. Continue cataloging the items on the shelf." He pointed and then marched away.

Ennek had spent an hour or so picking desultorily through bunches of dried herbs when someone knocked on the door. Thankful for the interruption, he rose to answer it.

"Velison!" He hadn't seen the heir's wife in months.

"Hi, Ennek. May I speak with the wizard?"

"He's in his chamber now. I can fetch him for you if you like."

"Well, perhaps you can help me. He has this bit of magic—it can determine whether a woman is expecting." She half whispered the last words, leaning toward him confidentially.

"Oh! But... well, congratulations!"

"Not yet, Ennek. I'm not certain."

"Um, I'll go ask. Just a moment, please." He left her sitting on a chair with a floral needlepoint seat, smiling serenely. She certainly did look better now than when he'd last seen her, only a week or two after she'd lost the baby. Maybe she liked being pregnant. That would be a good thing, since she so frequently was.

Ennek knocked on the door that led to the wizard's private room. Thelius looked irritated and preoccupied when he answered. "What?" he demanded.

"Velison's here. She'd like to borrow something to find out whether she's expecting."

Thelius huffed with irritation. "Damn woman's worse than a rabbit," he muttered. "I'm right in the middle.... There's a small box. It's in the chest under the window, the one with the black leather straps and the dent in the front. It's the only box in there. Just hand it to her; she knows what to do with it." He slammed the door in Ennek's face.

Ennek smiled at Velison and went to the window. He hadn't progressed this far in his cataloging yet, but there was the chest as Thelius had described it. When Ennek lifted the top, he saw a draping of thick burgundy velvet, which he drew aside. The contents consisted mostly of additional fabrics of various colors and textures, all folded neatly, and a few pairs of odd, ancient-looking shoes. And the box.

It wasn't much larger than one of his palms, it was perfectly square, and it was made of a wood so dark it was almost black. A symbol was carved into the top, or perhaps it was only a decorative shape: three circles, each overlapping the others slightly so as to form a sort of triangle. The box was fastened by a tiny gold padlock.

It had been twenty years since he had seen this box, but he recognized it immediately. He remembered tracing those circles with his fingertip as he walked back to Aelia's rooms and trying to see if he could open the lock, which was embossed with a matching pattern of circles. The weight of it, the slight graininess of the wood against his skin—these were exactly as he recalled.

He steeled himself to keep his face neutral as he handed the box to Velison. "Thank you," she said.

"Best of luck." He supposed that was the sort of thing one should say under such circumstances. She patted his arm and then left.

"A MAN is on the bat."

"Boat. See? These two letters together make the 'oh' sound."

"Oh."

Ennek chuckled. "Yes, like that."

"I'm not very good at this."

"Sure you are. You've only begun. It takes practice, you know." He laughed without much humor. "Just like magic."

Miner tilted his head. "Lessons not going well?"

"No, it's… it's not really what I want to be doing."

"Why are you, then? Why not just tell the wizard to stuff it?" Miner looked at him earnestly, a tiny frown creasing his brow. Ennek wished he could lift his hand and smooth it out.

"I can't. I… I discovered a mystery today." He hadn't really intended to talk about it, but he wanted to change the subject, and it was the first thing that came to mind.

"A mystery? What sort?" Miner leaned back in his chair. In the gaslight, his hair sparkled like starshine. He reached over and picked up a cherry from the white bowl on the table. Ennek watched, mesmerized, while Miner's tongue and teeth worked around the pit, which he then spit delicately into red-stained fingers. He put the pit back in the bowl.

Ennek shook his head a bit to clear it. "It was this box. My mother borrowed it from Thelius two decades ago, and today I found out it has magic in it to test for pregnancy."

"So was she pregnant?"

Sometimes Ennek forgot how little Miner knew of Ennek's life. "I don't know. She died a few days later. She jumped out her window."

Miner leaned forward and set his hand on Ennek's shoulder, his face a mask of concern. His hand felt so much nicer there than Thelius's had. "I'm sorry, Ennek."

Ennek shrugged. "We weren't very close…. The Chief's family, it's not like a normal family, you know?"

"I do know," Miner said, and Ennek felt bad. He hadn't meant to remind Miner of his own troubled past.

"Yes."

Miner didn't move away. "Do you think her death was related to her expecting a child?"

"I don't know. That's the mystery. She wasn't a very happy person in general, I don't think. She came from far away, and she didn't want to be here. But I don't believe she was bothered about having children. Larkin and I were raised mostly by servants in any case. Once I saw her holding a councilman's baby, a little girl. I think my mother would have fancied a daughter."

"Perhaps she killed herself because she wasn't pregnant."

"Perhaps. I guess I'll never know." And then, without planning to do it, without any conscious volition at all, he turned his head and kissed Miner's pale knuckles.

He wasn't sure which of them was more surprised. Miner's eyes widened almost comically, and Ennek forgot how to breathe. For an immeasurable time, neither of them moved. Ennek could feel the warmth from Miner's hand still on his lips, the slight pressure of Miner's smooth skin.

Ennek lurched to his feet and staggered back a few steps. "I'm sorry. Gods, I'm so sorry. I didn't mean…."

Miner looked dazed, but he shook his head slightly. "It's all right. You can… you know you can…."

"No. No, I can't." Ennek backed away. "I don't want—"

"You don't want me?"

"Not when…. Miner, you're a prisoner. A *slave*!"

Miner's eyes shut and his head and shoulders drooped. Ennek grabbed his coat and fled.

chapter fourteen

"GODS, ENNEK, these are so good!"

Ennek smiled and popped one of the tiny tomatoes into his own mouth. They were good. He'd needed a few small things at the shops today and had strolled by the market on his way back. He couldn't resist buying some tomatoes and a small, fragrant melon. Now Miner was laughing, swiping ineffectually at the juices dripping down his chin and onto his bare chest.

"You're going to need a lot of towels to clean that up," Ennek observed.

"No problem. I'm going to take a bath today." Miner said it proudly, maybe a little defiantly.

"Yes? Because I have to go to the laboratory, you know, and if you need rescuing again—"

"I can manage, thank you."

In the weeks that had passed since Ennek kissed him, they'd both rather successfully pretended it never happened. But just a few days ago, Miner had insisted on trying to take a bath instead of a shower. He'd filled the tub but then panicked as he was getting into the water, and he'd fallen trying to get out again. Ennek had heard the thump of his body and come running in, and then cradled a wet and naked Miner in his arms as the man cried and shook. That had been awkward.

Still, they'd moved past that as well and had been able to share the chambers—and the bed—amicably. And if Ennek was half-mad with desire to lick Miner clean, well, he didn't have to let Miner know.

"I almost forgot!" Ennek said, rerouting his thoughts with some effort. "I got you something else today."

Miner watched with interest as Ennek strode to the door and picked up the green cloth bag he'd deposited when he entered. He brought it over to Miner and dumped the contents on the table in front of him, carefully avoiding their messy plates.

"More books? Thank you!" Miner eyed them greedily but didn't touch because his hands were sticky.

"These are more advanced. They're intended for much older children than those primers. They'll be a bit more of a challenge for you, but you're certainly ready. Oh, and this one"—he held up a thick red book—"is a dictionary. So you can look up the words you don't know. Think these'll keep you busy for a while?"

"Oh, a minute or two, anyhow. I'm going to go get cleaned up so I can dive in."

"Have fun. I'll envy you while Thelius has me toiling away."

The cataloging still wasn't finished. It was going considerably slower now, actually, as Thelius had Ennek spend more time practicing magic. Ennek still couldn't do very much and often ended up feeling exhausted and sick to his stomach by the end of the day, but the wizard seemed pleased with his progress. For the past few days, though, Thelius had left Ennek to organize and inventory the contents of some of his bookshelves while Thelius was busy with something in his private chamber. And the previous day, the wizard told Ennek not to bother coming in at all the next morning.

When Ennek reached the laboratory in the early afternoon, Thelius was waiting for him, standing at one of his many tables, leafing through a small book and rubbing his chin. "Finally!" he snapped when Ennek entered. "You've been dallying too long with that slave, my boy."

"I haven't—" Ennek shut his mouth. What was the point of arguing about it?

Thelius snapped the book shut and tucked it into his hand. "Well, come along. I haven't all day, you know."

To Ennek's surprise, Thelius led him out of the laboratory and locked the door carefully behind them. Ennek followed as they marched briskly through the corridors. He wondered where they were heading but didn't want to ask. And then, with a sinking feeling, he realized exactly where they were going. As they went down a few stairs and turned a corner, Ennek found himself in a hallway he'd last entered on the eve of New Year.

The guard in front of the doorway stepped aside, not meeting their eyes. Then Ennek was descending again, his footsteps and Thelius's echoing down the stairway that had featured prominently in so many of his nightmares.

Ennek knew which cell had been Miner's, but Thelius continued past that one. He went all the way to the end, in fact, and opened a door that was a little wider than the rest. Ennek braced himself for whatever horrors waited inside.

But there weren't any. Nothing obvious, in any case. He saw an odd sort of chair made of solid stone. It looked as if it had been hewn straight out of the material of the wall itself, or perhaps as if it had grown from the floor like some strange plant. Against another wall was a tub of sorts, also made of stone. It was long enough to hold a reclining man, and its water was cloudy and smelled of salt and decay. Thelius's valise was next to it. And that was all.

Ennek hesitated before entering the room completely, but Thelius grabbed his arm, yanked him inside, and shut the door. Before Ennek could complain, Thelius waved a hand at him. "Undress," he ordered.

"Wh-what?" Ennek's heart began to race.

"You heard me. Strip. Unless you want your clothes soaking wet."

"No!" Ennek started toward the door, but Thelius stepped in and blocked his way.

"I won't debate this with you. It's tiresome and I haven't the time for it. Take your clothing off and get in the water. Quickly."

Ennek licked his lips. "Why?"

"It's a simple little procedure. I must do it so we can make proper use of your talents. It will be quite brief if you hurry up."

"And if I refuse?"

Thelius shrugged. "Then you'll be of no use to me. You can go back to being portmaster, I expect, but I shall have to demand the return of the prisoner."

"Bastard!"

"That's no way for an apprentice to speak, son." Thelius didn't seem alarmed by Ennek's rage, only slightly perturbed at the delay.

If there was some way out of this predicament, Ennek couldn't see it. Swearing, he began to unbutton his shirt. Soon he was completely bare and pretending not to notice the avaricious way in which Thelius stared at him.

"Very good, Ennek. Now get in the water. You needn't lie down all the way; sitting will do quite nicely."

"You're not going to—" Ennek swallowed convulsively. "You're not going to put me in Stasis." That he couldn't allow, not even for Miner's sake.

Thelius rolled his eyes. "Of course not! Why on earth should I do such a thing? Besides, eventually the Chief and the heir would notice, I think."

"Then what—"

"Just get in already! I'll explain as we go."

With enormous trepidation but no other clear options, Ennek climbed into the tub, then sat in the water. He immediately began to shiver violently—the water was cold, as cold as the sea itself. He wrapped his arms around himself as if that might help.

Thelius opened a book and began chanting. Ennek didn't understand the words, but he recognized the sound of the sibilant language—it was the same one Thelius had used to bring Miner out of Stasis. Within moments he started to feel numb, which could have been a relief because it meant the cold was no longer so biting, but it actually scared him terribly. At the same time, his entire body was overtaken by a strange sort of lassitude. He could move, but even the tiniest motion required Herculean effort, as if a single finger weighed as much as a mountain. He lolled against the side of the tub, wanting to protest but unable to gather the strength. It was even difficult to move air in and out of his lungs.

Just as a terrible, sharp pain began in Ennek's head, making him cry out weakly, Thelius stopped chanting, closed the book, and stuck it in a pocket of his cloak. He tilted his head and peered at Ennek the way a man might look at a horse he was considering for purchase. The pain faded, but Ennek was still nearly immobile. "That was the Stasis spell, as you might have guessed. If I'd continued, you would have been completely enchanted, just like the prisoners. Well, it would have hurt a good bit first, and *then* you'd have gone under. But we needn't go that far today. I only needed you compliant for the next bit. Besides, it takes much magic to put someone completely in Stasis, and I don't care to exhaust myself right now."

"Stop," Ennek managed to croak with enormous difficulty.

"Don't worry. If the spell's not completed, it wears off in an hour or so. So we'd best get moving, hadn't we?"

Ennek couldn't protest. The wizard intoned another spell, this time one that was familiar to Ennek and that didn't require Thelius to refer to his book. Ennek felt as if a giant hand was cradling him. He was lifted out of the tub, limp and dripping, then moved slowly through the air to the stone seat before being placed down on it quite gently. He could just barely feel the rough rock beneath him, scratching his skin.

"See? I told you that was a handy little talent." Thelius gave his death's-head grin. Ennek rolled his eyes to watch as Thelius stepped over to his valise and pulled out a wooden box. This one was larger than the one Ennek's mother and Velison had borrowed, and it was of a very light wood stained with splotches of various colors of ink or paint. Thelius opened the box and set it on one broad edge of the chair, alongside Ennek's right arm. There were several small glass bottles inside as well as some sort of metal apparatus with a sharp needle at one end. Ennek didn't like the look of it but couldn't shift his arm enough to nudge the box onto the floor.

Thelius pulled out the device and one of the jars. Frowning in concentration, he poured some of the contents of the jar into the metal thing, then placed the jar back in the box. He poked the needle tip against one of his fingers and then nodded with satisfaction.

"So, we've established that you possess impressive powers. Stronger than my own, I suspect. But as you've seen, it takes considerable time to learn to use those powers. It will be years before you're a capable wizard. And that's fine, because of course the polis already has a very capable wizard, and I don't intend to die for a long time. In the meantime, though, I'd like to be able to harness what you have. Your own magic can act as sort of an engine in tandem with mine. But I can control it, you see, just as I control my own."

"No," Ennek rasped.

"Don't be ridiculous. It's a simple thing." He held the apparatus in his fingers as if it were a giant pen, then pressed the needle against Ennek's bicep. Ennek could faintly feel the bite of it into his skin. Thelius said some more words in a foreign tongue, and the device began to vibrate faintly, the needle working quickly in and out.

"It's a binding charm. The ink has several special ingredients— I'll show you the recipe later, if you like—including a few drops of my blood." He was moving the thing around as he spoke, obviously producing some design, but Ennek couldn't move his head to see what. "I'm putting my own mark on you, so as long as I live, your magic is bound to me."

Ennek made an alarmed noise that sounded to his own ears like a distressed horse.

"Don't worry. It doesn't subvert your will—that requires much stronger magic than this—and you won't be my slave, held captive by me the way your prisoner is held by you. Not that I'm not a bit tempted." He laughed softly and used his free hand to stroke Ennek's chest. This time Ennek's noise was one of rage. Thelius laughed again. "But no, I'll only hold the reins to your magic. I can even loan you the reins when I choose to do so."

For a time he was silent, concentrating on his task. Ennek listened to the waves pounding against the keep—felt them like the pulse in his body.

And then, suddenly, Thelius was finished. He stood up and pulled a small cloth from the box. He used it to wipe the needle clean, then tucked the device away. He brought the cloth over to the tub, dipped it in the water, and returned to Ennek's side, using the cloth to wipe Ennek's arm free of residual blood.

"There we are! Not a half-bad job, if I say so myself."

Soon the box was back in the valise, which Thelius slung over his shoulder. He let his hand rest on Ennek's forearm. "Now, don't be tempted to deface it or remove it, son. It's not the mark itself that binds us but the making of it, and that's done. I've some work to do, so I'll leave you to recover. Shouldn't take long. You can even have tomorrow off, if you like. I'll see you the following morning at eight."

He walked away. Ennek had a horrifying vision of Thelius closing and locking the door behind him, leaving Ennek imprisoned. But the door remained open.

Ennek waited until he was able to move again.

"GODS, WHAT'S happened to you?"

As soon as Ennek staggered into the room, Miner sprang from his seat by the window and raced to him. He caught Ennek before he fell and quickly closed the door with his foot. Then he half dragged Ennek to the bed and set him down on the rumpled blankets. "You're cold as ice and look like death. What happened?"

Ennek shook his head. He had neither the energy nor the desire to explain.

Miner frowned with concern. "How can I help?"

"Bath. Very hot." He badly needed to get the feel of the Stasis water off of him, as well as the ghostly feel of the wizard's long, dry fingers.

"All right." Miner bit his lip, then folded the blankets over Ennek's shivering form before hurrying to the bathroom. A moment later Ennek heard the pipes emptying into the marble tub.

Miner returned and pulled off the blankets and then Ennek's boots. Ennek allowed himself to be moved around slightly as Miner loosened his clothing without actually removing it. "Do you want help with bathing?"

Ennek couldn't imagine mustering the strength to do it himself. "Please."

"All right." Miner helped him to his feet. With Ennek's arm around Miner's shoulders and with Miner's arm around Ennek's waist, they moved slowly into the bathroom. Miner had to prop Ennek up a little as he helped remove his shirt and trousers. It was only after Ennek was in the tub, his limbs flopping bonelessly, that Miner gasped.

"What's this?" he asked, almost but not quite touching Ennek's arm.

Ennek hadn't had the courage to actually look at it before he'd pulled on his clothes and risen from Under. Now he rolled his head to the side and twisted the arm slightly.

It was a tattoo. Ennek had seen tattoos before. They were forbidden to citizens of the polis, but some of the sailors had them, often the names of loved ones or colorful monsters or charm shapes meant to deter evil and bring smooth sailing. This one, though, was a shape that looked like an eight-pointed star. Ennek had recently learned that that was the symbol for the earth element, just as two parallel squiggly lines were the symbol for water. Inside the star, the letter T had been inscribed in a fancy, fussy way, with much in the way of flourishes. The ink was black and the skin around it red and slightly puffy.

"Ennek?" Miner's voice was hesitant.

Ennek didn't want to talk about it. What he wanted, actually, was to slip down into the lovely warm water, which Miner had scented with the citrus oil, until only his nose and eyes were sticking out. Maybe not even them.

But Miner was right there, kneeling on the little blue rug Ennek kept beside the tub, and his white brows were drawn together with worry, his bottom lip just barely caught between his teeth. Ennek realized he was all the other man had, the pathetic center of Miner's little world. His only hope of… of hope.

And so Ennek told him everything, from the very beginning. A boy who made his first visit Under and had seen Miner. The years of nightmares and denial. The agreement Ennek had made in order to be allowed to keep Miner with him. And finally, the events of the morning, in which Ennek had experienced his own small taste of Stasis and had been bound to Thelius. By the time he finished speaking, the water had cooled and Miner's face was drawn and gray.

But Miner didn't say anything as he pulled the plug and helped Ennek out of the tub. He wrapped a big towel around Ennek's shoulders and led him to the bed. Ennek climbed between the sheets without bothering to put on any clothes, too exhausted to even think about it. Miner got into the bed beside him.

"I didn't bring you any food," Ennek said. "I'm sorry."

"I had enough this morning. I can wait."

"I'll call for some soon. I just—" He yawned hugely. "Need a nap."

"It's okay, Ennek. Just rest."

Ennek tried. But as soon as he shut his eyes, he saw the damp stone walls of the cell Under. He felt the touch of Thelius's hand, the prick of the needle, the icy cold of the Stasis bath. He opened his eyes, choking back a scream.

Miner wrapped his long arms around him. The fabric of his shirt was soft, and Miner smelled of fruit. And he was warm, so warm. Ennek burrowed against him, and for the first time since he was a very young child, he sobbed himself to sleep.

MINER WAS still holding him when he awoke. Ennek's eyes felt gritty and sore and his nose was stuffed up, but it felt so wonderful to be held that for a while he pretended he was still asleep. That is, until he woke up enough to notice the way Miner's lean muscles were pressed against him, the other man's heart beating against his chest. That felt a bit too wonderful, and Ennek had to roll away to avoid embarrassing himself.

"Thanks," he sniffed at Miner, who was looking at him intently.

"Are you all right?"

"Yes, I'm… I'm feeling better. Rested." In a minute he was going to get up, put some clothes on, and find some food for both of them. In a minute.

"Ennek? Why have you…. Why did you let him do that to you, do all of it, when you don't want me? I mean, I understand doing a good deed and all, but you've gone well past that. He could have kept you Under! Why didn't you just let him have me?"

"I promised you, didn't I?"

"Yes. But a promise isn't worth risking Stasis yourself, is it?"

Ennek sat up and pulled the blankets tightly around himself. "I've never been much of anything, you know. Just the younger son. Expendable. The pretty one, my mother used to say, not the smart one." Instead of looking at Miner as he spoke, he focused on a small slightly frayed area of the blanket. "You don't know—you couldn't—but I mostly used to drink and gamble and drink some more. Take up space. Even when I was portmaster… well, that was good. I was good at it, but others were just as good. I've never been *important*, Miner, not to anyone. Except you."

Ennek looked up then and met Miner's eyes. Pretty eyes. The color changeable as the sea.

"You're my god, Ennek. You hold my existence in your hands. You're important to me."

Ennek shook his head and blinked back more tears. Gods, now that he'd opened the floodgates, maybe they'd never stop. "It's not right. I shouldn't…. Nobody should have that kind of power over another person."

"No, nobody should. But here we are. And I still don't understand why you would sacrifice yourself for a slave."

"I wouldn't! I'd sacrifice myself for you." Ennek wanted to take back the words as soon as he said them. They were too much; he was laying too great a burden on Miner's already laden shoulders.

Miner opened his mouth, then closed it. He swallowed and opened it again. "But you said you didn't want me. Didn't want a slave. When… after you kissed my hand, you said that."

"I meant… good gods, I don't know how to do this!" Ennek buried his face in his hands and took several calming breaths, trying to gain some composure and bring order to his mind. Then he lowered his hands and said, "I meant, it's not right. I won't take advantage of you." His emotions surged and he shouted, "I'm not Thelius!"

"You'll never be like him, Ennek," Miner responded quietly.

Ennek wished he could believe him.

chapter fifteen

A DAY off was a luxury, especially because Ennek wasn't certain he'd be able to keep his temper if he had to face Thelius right away. He and Miner spent the day reading, and Miner sketched him for a time while Ennek watched the fog roll into the bay. He had always liked fog: the way it smelled, the way it muffled sounds and turned familiar landscapes alien. He didn't much care for the way it made his hair curl even more tightly, but he could live with that if it meant being able to watch exquisite drops gather on tree branches and fall softly to the ground.

He and Miner were just discussing the possibilities for their evening meal when someone knocked loudly at the door. They exchanged quick, alarmed glances. Ennek wasn't expecting anyone. "Get into the bathroom," he hissed. "Shut the door. And don't come out until I tell you it's safe!"

Miner nodded and scuttled away.

Ennek checked the room quickly to see if there was anything to give away Miner's presence. Not really, at least not to the unwary eye, and that was a bit sad. Miner had lived in these rooms for nine months now, and it was almost like he'd never been there at all.

There was another knock, even louder this time, before Ennek managed to get the door open. "Larkin!" he exclaimed in surprise.

"Hello. May I come in?"

"Of course."

Larkin entered and looked around the chamber curiously. He hadn't been there in many years. "I was wondering where you've been spending so much time. We rarely see you anymore at dinners, and I heard you've disappeared from the inns and gambling house. You haven't even been out on the bay."

"I've no time for it anymore. By the time I finish my work, I'm exhausted."

"I'd thought the wizard might be a harsh taskmaster."

Ennek kept his face neutral. "Magic is hard work. Can I get you some wine?"

"No, no, I can't stay. I actually came to let you know I'll be gone a few weeks."

That surprised Ennek. Larkin rarely left the polis. "Where are you going?"

"Not far. Velison's tired of the cold. She can never get warm enough when she's expecting. Her family has a ranch a few hours south of here, where, she says, the sun is always shining this time of year. After she lost the baby last time, well, I don't feel comfortable having her go without me."

"Is she doing well?"

Larkin smiled. "Very. We're going to make a holiday of it, the two of us and the children. They've never been out of the polis at all, you know. The Chief has permitted the holiday, of course, but I thought I'd tell you. If there were some sort of emergency in my absence, you'd be his right-hand man."

Ennek laughed. "There hasn't been an emergency in the polis for decades, Lark. The Chief has it running like a machine."

Larkin shrugged. "Perhaps. But you never know."

"All right. I'll keep suitably vigilant. You have a good holiday, and wish Velison good health from me."

"Thank you." Larkin patted his arm, not knowing the tattoo was right under his hand. Ennek kept a smile on his face. "Don't work yourself too hard, En."

Ennek waited a minute or two after Larkin was gone before he let Miner know it was safe to come out. "That was the heir?" Miner asked.

"Yes. You heard?"

Miner nodded. "It sounds like he cares for you."

"I expect he does."

"But you can't tell him about the wizard? About what he did to you?"

Ennek shook his head. "No. Because he's still the heir, isn't he? He couldn't allow me to release a prisoner early, couldn't allow you to remain out of Stasis before your sentence is over. It's against the law. No, I can't tell him."

Miner nodded sadly.

"Come on," Ennek said. "Let's see about dinner."

AS IT turned out, facing Thelius was easier than Ennek had feared. When Ennek showed up at the lab, his jaw set so tightly that it hurt, the wizard simply motioned him toward a stack of books precariously piled on one table. "Index the spells in those books," he ordered and, without another word, marched off to his private room.

So Ennek spent the entire day sitting on an uncomfortable straight-backed chair, squinting at faded squiggles in a variety of archaic hands, and trying to make some sense of them as he wrote. Rather than calming him, the slow-paced activity made him feel restless and uneasy, as if he had an itch he couldn't scratch. When it was nearly six o'clock and Thelius hadn't made another appearance, Ennek put down the pen and frowned at his ink-stained fingers, then stretched thoroughly.

The kitchen servants had long since learned what to do when Ennek appeared. Without any instructions from him, they piled a tray with fresh bread and some nice stuffed salmon, as well as some sweet, crispy grapes and tiny carrots. "Chef made some pear tarts today," one servant said.

Ennek grinned. "I'll take two, please."

As he carried the tray to his chambers, he came upon a lone slave on his hands and knees, scrubbing the floor. Ennek had probably passed the man many times before, but this time he actually saw him. He was in his midforties, perhaps, with a face as gray and worn as his clothing. His hair was shorn to a bare stubble, and it was gray as well. He kept his head bowed over his task as Ennek scrutinized him.

"What's your name?" Ennek asked.

The man winced a bit, as if Ennek's words were physical blows. "Selnest, Master." He had the mere ghost of a voice.

"How long is your sentence?"

"Forty years, Master."

"For what crime?"

"Theft, Master."

"What happened?"

"I was just a boy, Master. I stole a horse. I only…. She was a beauty, Master. I meant only to have a ride on her."

Gods. "How much longer?"

The slave looked up at him finally, his face devoid of anything but despair. "I've no idea, Master."

Ennek broke off a stem of grapes and handed them to Selnest, who took them, frowning in confusion. "Here," Ennek said awkwardly and hurried away.

He'd found some lovely colored pencils at a shop a few days earlier, and Miner had spent the day working on a detailed seascape of the bay. It was a beautiful view, with wisps of fog and splashes of bright color from the ships' sails. The whole scene was framed by stone, the freedom of air and water enclosed by the walls of the artist's prison.

"Dinner!" Ennek sang with false cheer. He set the food down on his table.

But they'd lived too close to each other these months for Miner to be fooled. "What did he do to you?" he demanded, grasping Ennek's right bicep and looking searchingly into his eyes.

"Nothing, nothing. I hardly saw him."

"Then what?"

Ennek sighed. He felt as much a prisoner as Miner, a captive in his own flesh and bones. "It's nothing. Just a mood. Let's eat, all right?"

So they did, although Ennek's appetite was meager. "I never ate so well, before," Miner said. "We didn't go hungry, but I have to tell you, I used to eye the state dinners with envy."

"Camens didn't share with you?"

Miner laughed dryly. "No. We didn't eat together. We... we weren't friends, Ennek. Not like—well, not friends. I loved him, but I was only a convenience to him. He never gave me the tiniest fraction of what you have."

Ennek shook his head. "But you were free."

"Yes. I suppose I was."

Ennek avoided Miner's eyes for the rest of the meal.

FOR THE better part of a week, Ennek barely saw Thelius. He was given tasks to do—more indexing, painstaking preparation of some healing salves, and one day, fetching some specific plants. He enjoyed the last bit because it required him to sail across to the headlands and hike up his neglected path. The weather was warm and dry that day, as it sometimes was in early autumn, and he was sweaty by the time he descended to his little catboat. He dumped the things he'd collected into the boat and stripped off his clothes for a brisk, cooling swim. It felt wonderful; he'd never dared to swim nude before. A sea lion watched from the end of the pier, nonplussed, probably wishing the man had gone fishing instead. Ennek was still damp when he dressed again, but as he returned to the polis, he felt happier than he had in a long time.

At least, he felt happy until he caught sight of the keep and thought about Miner locked up inside, never able to share the simple joys Ennek had experienced that afternoon.

The next day Thelius once again disappeared into his own chamber after waving Ennek off to a tedious job—counting tiny precious gems and sorting them by color and weight. Ennek worked sullenly, his mind far away, until he grew dizzy and his head began to ache. He wasn't meant for this sort of work, he thought, and he considered just leaving and spending the rest of the afternoon in bed with a cool cloth on his head. Suddenly the small bowl of jewels in front of him skittered and bobbled on the tabletop, shifting the careful little stacks of stones he'd made.

Ennek frowned in confusion for a second before he realized what was happening. Quake. The floor swayed slightly under his feet and a few items fell off the shelves. A jar shattered, filling the laboratory with the scent of alcohol. Ennek immediately thought of Miner and what might happen to him if the keep were damaged. He began to make his way to the door but was overcome with a wave of vertigo and nausea so strong that he fell to his hands and knees and retched onto the stone floor.

The keep stopped shaking. It had been just a small tremor, then, nothing unusual. But Ennek still crouched over his mess, unsure whether he could manage to make it to his feet.

The door to Thelius's room banged open and the wizard staggered out. He looked as awful as Ennek felt, his face tinged almost green and his usually neat hair arrayed like a storm cloud around his head. He looked around the room for a moment before he caught sight of Ennek. "What's wrong with you?" he demanded. His voice was thinner than usual.

"Sick," Ennek replied before vomiting up the small bit of lunch that still remained in his stomach.

Thelius collapsed into a chair. "Get out. Take tomorrow off."

Ennek used a table to pull himself upright. He almost fell again but stumbled his way to the door and out into the corridor. As he made his way to his rooms, he lurched unsteadily, leaning against the wall for support whenever he could. Twice more he fell, and the second time he was sorely tempted to just lie there, curled in a miserable ball. But he forced himself to totter onward. Luckily, most of the people in the keep were preoccupied with assessing the minor damage from the quake or cleaning up things that had broken, so nobody paid him any mind. Knowing his history, they probably assumed he was drunk.

Miner must have been very close to the door, because once again he caught Ennek as he reeled into his chambers. "Are you hurt?" Miner asked, poking a little at Ennek's body as if to check for injuries.

"No," Ennek groaned. "I'm... please, just help me to bed."

Miner pulled off Ennek's clothing and wrapped him in sheets that felt blessedly cool against his skin, then fussed with the pillows until they were arranged just so. He padded off to the bathroom, then returned a moment later with a cup of cold water and a small empty bowl so that Ennek could rinse the foul taste from his mouth. Miner also brought damp cloths, one to wipe Ennek's face and the other folded and applied to his forehead—which felt even better than he'd imagined.

"The quake.... You're all right?" Ennek rasped.

Miner smoothed a curl away from Ennek's face. "I'm fine. We had them back in my day too, you know. But why are you so ill? Did that bastard do something to you again?"

"No, he...." Ennek tried to focus his fuzzy brain. "It feels like this when I do big magic, but I didn't, I was only—oh." The realization, which would have been obvious had his mind been clearer, hit him like a bucket of cold water. "Thelius must have used me."

"Gods, Ennek! He's going to kill you!"

"I feel like shit, but it's not exactly fatal."

"Not this time," Miner said grimly.

Ennek closed his eyes. He was too weary even to think about it.

"All right, then," Miner said, again moving the recalcitrant lock of hair. "Rest now."

Ennek fell asleep with Miner still sitting beside him, holding his hand.

THE KNOCK on the door was loud and urgent. Ennek shot out of bed and wrapped a blanket around himself as Miner rushed to hide in the bathroom. "What!" Ennek demanded of the grim-looking guard.

"The Chief requires your presence at once."

Gods, what now? Ennek nodded slightly. "Fine. A moment while I get dressed."

He threw on some clothing, pausing only to tell Miner what was happening. "Why does he want you?" Miner asked anxiously.

"I haven't any idea. I'll… I'll be back as soon as I can, all right?"

Miner set his hand on Ennek's shoulder for a moment, and once again Ennek wanted very badly to feel those lips against his. But he only smiled wanly and then darted away.

The first thing Ennek noticed was that the Chief looked uncharacteristically out of sorts. He wasn't as bad as Ennek—his shirt was buttoned correctly and his hair was all in place—but it still appeared as if he'd dressed quickly. His face was stony as always, but the lines in it seemed deeper this morning, like fissures appearing in a boulder.

But the Chief looked positively wonderful compared to Larkin, who was slumped in his usual chair in front of the Chief's desk. Larkin's clothing was filthy and torn, his hair was a wild mess, and his face was covered in several scratches. His eyes were wide open, like a man transfixed in horror, as he stared at a spot on the office wall.

"The earthquake was centered to the south," the Chief said without preface. "It completely destroyed Velison's house. She and the children were killed."

For a moment Ennek felt so unsteady that he almost thought there'd been another quake. He clutched for support at the nearest piece of furniture—an ugly, ornate chair. "Gods, no," he whispered. It wasn't that he was that close to them, but still, they were his family. And they were Larkin's world.

"I should have been there too," Larkin said. His voice was quiet and emotionless. "I was feeling housebound and I went for a ride. I should have been there."

"It wouldn't have made a difference," the Chief snapped. "Then you'd have died as well."

Larkin didn't reply, but the look on his face spoke clearly—he'd have preferred that fate to surviving without them.

For a split second, Ennek thought the Chief's face almost softened. But then his jaw worked and his lips thinned, and he turned to Ennek. "I will declare seven days of mourning. I'll expect you at the official dinner a week from tonight."

"Yes, sir."

"I'll be commissioning a memorial statue as well, to be placed near the market square. All the local sculptors will only make a mess of it. Can you give me the name of a reputable ship's captain from Iuenna? The artists there are the most talented in the world, and the captain could be persuaded to find me one and bring him on his next return to Praesidium."

Ennek thought for a moment. "The *New Naantali*, sir. You could trust her captain with that task, and the ship docks here every other month."

"Excellent." The Chief nodded as if he'd accomplished something important. In his own mind, he probably had. He was tying up the loose ends, making sure the polis continued to run smoothly. Doing his job.

Ennek walked the few steps over to Larkin and put out his hand. "What can I do, Lark?"

For the first time, Larkin actually focused his eyes on Ennek. They were as full of anguish as those of Selnest, the slave Ennek had spoken to in the hallway. Larkin extended his hand too, as if to clasp Ennek's. But then something hardened in him, and he let his hand drop. "Nothing. Thank you," he said coldly. He stood and faced the Chief. "I'll go get cleaned up now, sir. If you send your secretary to me in an hour, I can help with the preparations."

The Chief frowned slightly. "You don't have to. You're perfectly entitled to—"

"No, sir. I want to help. And... and tomorrow if you give me a list of eligible women, I'll look it over and choose a bride." Larkin's face was as stony as his father's. More so. "I'll ensure that the line of succession remains unbroken."

He marched out of the room, his movements stiff and unnatural. Ennek was left alone with the Chief, who narrowed his eyes. "I don't expect all your magic can cure this, can it?"

Ennek hid how much the words wounded him. "No, sir."

The Chief nodded. "Very well. I've much to do. You're excused."

It all felt surreal as Ennek walked back to his chambers. He stopped at the kitchens first—he'd kept nothing in his stomach the day before, and despite his shock, he was hungry. Miner must be as well.

A half hour later he sat at the table in his room, wearily rubbing his temples. Miner gazed at him with an odd expression Ennek couldn't read. But then, once again belatedly, realization dawned and he felt all the blood leave his face.

"That son of a *bitch*!" he roared and leapt to his feet.

He would have rushed out the door and found Thelius, and then… well, who knew what might have happened. But Miner caught him around the waist and, with considerable difficulty, wrestled him to the ground. Ennek was stronger and more heavily muscled, but Miner had the advantage of height and formal training as a fighter. Miner pinned Ennek down and straddled him to keep him in place.

"Let me go!" Ennek shouted.

"Ennek! You need to calm down."

"Calm down? Calm *down*? That monster used me, and he killed them, he murdered them, Miner!"

"I know, I know." Miner tried to make his voice soothing, which probably wasn't easy as he struggled to keep Ennek down. "Please, Ennek. Just stop for a minute."

Ennek was still feeling the effects from the previous day's magic and had just suffered dual shocks. As his energy waned, he lay on the stone floor while Miner pressed his hips and shoulders down. "He used me to kill them," he said, his voice not much more than a whimper.

"He did. But if you confront him about it, what will happen?"

"He'll… I don't know. Nothing good," Ennek admitted.

"And if you tell the Chief or the heir what he's done?"

"They'll never forgive me for letting myself be used this way. That is, assuming they even believe me. They'll… gods, eventually they'll find out about you, and then…." He felt so weak. Helpless and stupid. Useless.

Miner must have felt Ennek's muscles go slack, because he climbed off of his body and pulled him upright. They were sitting very close to one another, nearly huddled together. "What can I do?" Ennek asked, forlorn.

"Find out why he did it. Find a way to get yourself out of his clutches. Save yourself, Ennek."

chapter sixteen

THE LAST day of mourning was meant to be a day of public sadness as the polis grieved the loss of the heir's wife and children. But the crowded market had more the air of a festival day as citizens enjoyed the day off work and filled their bags and baskets with provisions for the evening's dinner. Merchants and growers from Praesidium and surrounding polises had taken advantage of the unusual event and set up stalls overflowing with every possible delicacy. Some didn't sell food at all but, knowing the citizens would be opening their pocketbooks wide today, had set out displays of clothing and trinkets and all manner of things that might tempt a shopper.

Ennek was still feeling a little weak; Thelius must have expended an enormous amount of energy to trigger the quake. But that had its good side as well, because Thelius had sent a message that he was ill and that Ennek should not return to the laboratory until after official mourning was over. Ennek was in no hurry to face him, although the intervening days had brought him no closer to finding a solution to his predicament. He'd had nightmares—terrible visions of children buried and screaming—and Miner's warm arms and comforting murmurs were his only solace. But even those gestures brought their own pain, as Ennek's body yearned for more even as his heart reminded him that he mustn't take advantage of Miner's captivity and generosity of spirit.

Ennek had spent the past days napping fitfully or reading while Miner worked his way through his own books or added to his growing pile of drawings. Ennek let Miner draw him, sleeping, sitting, brooding at the windows. Once even as he sat in the bath. He blushed like a schoolboy the whole time, feeling Miner's gaze on him like physical strokes, thinking of Miner's hand recreating his most intimate parts on blank paper. And then when he was dry and dressed and Miner allowed him to see the drawing, Ennek blushed again to see himself depicted that way. He'd seen pornography before—had confiscated it himself from sailors trying to smuggle it into the polis, actually—but none of those tawdry illustrations had been as erotic as this picture of him sprawled in the tub, looking at once timid and inviting. Miner only smiled and put the drawing with the others.

When the last day of mourning dawned, Ennek had grown increasingly restive. Partly this was due to so many days of inactivity indoors, but he was also dreading the evening's dinner. Finally he'd pulled on his coat and boots and announced that he was going out for a while. Miner looked a little relieved. The poor man was probably desperate for some time alone.

Ennek didn't have a real destination in mind as he set out on foot from the keep. But as he meandered toward the center of the city, he was drawn to the clamor of the market, its crowds and stalls and wagons. He wandered here and there, mostly just watching with detached interest as people scurried around and sellers hawked their wares. Nobody recognized him; they were too busy with their own matters, and in any case, he had a scarf covering the lower half of his face and a hat pulled over his distinctive hair.

He caught sight of a pretty young woman selling walnuts and flavored almonds, and thinking how much Miner might like to have some, he bought quite a few of each variety. The woman handed him his laden sack. "Enjoy your nuts, sir," she said with a flirty little smile. He laughed for the first time in many days.

Just a few yards away, a grandmotherly woman had beautiful knitted items for sale. Ennek bought two pairs of thick brown socks to keep the chill of the stone floors from Miner's feet, and a buttery soft wool sweater in a blue-green that matched Miner's eyes almost exactly. Not far from there he found a man with tiny pots of paint and fine little brushes arrayed on a cloth-covered table, and then there was… well, soon his pockets were empty and his arms were full.

He had turned back toward the keep and was almost out of the square when a familiar voice said, "It's nice to see the younger son supporting commerce so vigorously."

Ennek spun around. "Hils! I'd shake your hand, but…." He shrugged awkwardly under his load.

"I'll try not to be too offended." Hils was carrying a single cloth bundle. "I realized this afternoon that I hadn't a shirt suitable for tonight, and I didn't trust the servants to avoid something garish."

Ennek grinned. Hils hated wearing formal clothing; he always seemed most comfortable dressed like a workman. "As long as you don't show up in coveralls and gumboots."

"I'll try to restrain myself. How are you doing, Ennek? I'm so sorry for your loss." He patted Ennek's shoulder.

"Thank you. It's been quite a shock." That was no lie.

"And the heir? How is he?"

Ennek remembered the coldness that had crept into Larkin's eyes like a film of ice. "I don't know. He... he loved them so much, but he's a strong man."

Hils nodded. "Runs in the family, I expect. But even the tallest redwood can topple in a storm."

"And it's very stormy right now," Ennek agreed.

They stood for a moment in silence, Hils's hand still resting comfortably on Ennek's shoulder. Then Hils asked, "And aside from this tragedy, how are you, Ennek? The wizarding's going well?"

Ennek found himself unable to feign contentedness. "It's been... a strain, actually."

"You look pale. Thinner. More than a week of mourning might account for."

"The last several months have been difficult."

"Just tell the wizard to bugger off, then. Go back to the port. Mila wouldn't mind; she's told me herself that she misses you. Or... I don't know. Travel. See a bit of the world."

"I can't, Hils. I have obligations I can't escape."

Hils's face settled into planes of sorrow. "I understand. There are things I have to do, and—well, I understand. But Ennek, if there's any way I can help... I'm a friend, all right?"

Those damned tears threatened again. Ennek blinked a few times. "Thanks," he said gruffly. "Uh, I'd better get back before my arms fall off. I'll see you tonight, yes?"

"Yes, tonight. In my stiff, scratchy clothes."

"Me as well."

With a final small smile, they parted.

Ennek felt rather silly as he deposited his largesse on the bed in front of an astonished Miner. "What's all this for?" Miner asked.

Ennek shrugged and felt his face color. "I was bored."

Miner peered into the bags and poked at the parcels. "Paints! And, mmm." He stuffed a few sugared almonds in his mouth. "Ennek! Gods!" he exclaimed, reverently unfolding the sweater. "This must have cost a fortune!"

"Then it's a good thing I'm the younger son."

Miner ran a hand over the wool. "I've never had anything so nice."

"Put it on."

Ennek realized what an enormous mistake it had been to buy the thing. Miner was stunning. The sweater was high enough on his neck to almost hide the iron collar. He reminded Ennek of ocean waves, white foam over sea green. But Miner was also warm and soft, with a shy little smile and a slight blush on his cheeks. Ennek wanted to drown in him.

He turned away abruptly. "I have to dress for dinner," he announced to the wall. "And I need to shower first."

"Go ahead. I'm going to eat all these nuts you brought." Miner's voice was tinged with amusement.

When Ennek emerged from the bathroom, Miner was sitting at the table, arranging the little paint pots. He looked up and a huge smile spread across his face. "You clean up well."

Ennek scowled down at himself. He was wearing a blue wool suit so dark as to be nearly black. It was free of ornament, in view of the sad occasion as well as the fact that he currently had no official office. His shirt was maroon silk; normally he'd have fancied it, but he couldn't really see much of it due to his waistcoat. His fashionable trousers were too tight, his suit collar scratched his skin, and his black cravat was strangling him. He knew his tailcoat would cause him to overheat in the crowded dining hall.

"I'd like to paint you like that sometime," Miner said. "With the evening light shining on you, just like it is now."

Ennek's frown changed to an embarrassed grin.

LARKIN STOOD stiffly at the door, shaking the hand of everyone who entered. His face had less emotion than the statue of Princeps Primus that stood in front of the keep. He was all in black, with only one small medal on his breast to indicate his status as heir. He remained impassive as Ennek arrived. "Ennek," he said. "Thank you for coming." They might have been distant acquaintances. Even the Chief showed more warmth when he greeted Ennek with a nod and a clap on the bicep.

Ennek took a glass of wine from a passing servant, then stood against the wall as far as possible from the fireplaces, watching. The guests were all in dark clothes, and they stood in small clusters, chatting quietly and with the solemnity demanded by the occasion. Hils looked unhappy, trapped in a corner by three ancient members of the Council. He rolled his eyes at Ennek in exasperation.

Ennek was just thinking of some ruse with which to extricate Hils when a small stir occurred near the main entrance. The wizard had arrived.

He wore gray, of course, but much darker than usual, almost charcoal. His cloak was long and sweeping, and his hair was set carefully in place. He looked dashing, triumphant even. The other guests skittered uneasily away from him, as if they found his mere proximity unsettling. His eyes swept the room and settled on Ennek, and his lips lifted in a bloodless smile. He strutted over.

"It's good to see you, son." The challenge in his face was clear to Ennek but invisible to the rest of the room.

Ennek had to keep his expression neutral. "I've enjoyed my time off."

"But you're feeling better, I take it? You look well."

"I was, but suddenly I'm feeling quite ill again."

The corner of Thelius's mouth twitched. "I'm sure you'll recover soon enough."

"You've not offered condolences for my loss."

"I'm sorry. I hadn't realized you were close with the deceased."

"Close enough."

The wizard nodded sagely. "It's been a terrible blow to the polis. Such a shame, losing the heir's heir. I do hope the line of succession isn't threatened. It's been unbroken for what? Six hundred years?"

"Nearly seven. And I'm certain the line will continue."

Thelius nodded. "Of course. Ah, there's Councilman Brachus. I've some matters to discuss with him. I'll see you in the laboratory in two days, son."

Soon everyone settled down at the tables. The Chief gave a careful, perfect speech in memory of the departed, and everyone drank a toast to them. Then it was Larkin's turn. He betrayed not an iota of emotion as he spoke of the fine qualities of his late wife and the promise that his children had displayed. Everyone drank again. To Ennek's surprise, the Chief turned to him expectantly, so he stood and managed to stutter out a few words. He caught Hils's friendly eyes as he spoke, and that helped him ignore the presence of Thelius beside him.

The food was good, he supposed; he swallowed it, but he didn't taste it. At least Thelius didn't try to speak to him. Nobody did, actually. The woman across the table—some councilman's wife, whose name he couldn't recall—chatted nonstop with the woman seated across from the Chief, while the Chief and the heir spoke in low tones about the details of the memorial statue and whether they ought to name the new state theater after Velison or after Larkin's oldest son.

It was with great relief that Ennek left the dinner as soon as it was politic to do so. He gave a little wave to Hils, who was trapped again, and then hurried upstairs to Miner, who waited anxiously.

"I was worried every time I heard boots in the hall," Miner admitted as Ennek undressed.

"You thought I'd lose my temper around Thelius." Ennek kicked viciously at his dress boot.

"It must have been very difficult not to."

"The smooth bastard," Ennek spat. "Smiling and shaking hands, feigning concern. I saw his eyes, though, whenever Larkin moved across the room. He meant to kill him as well."

"That would leave you as heir."

"And he owns me, doesn't he?" He tugged so hard at his waistcoat that the buttons popped and went rolling across the floor. One of them ended up under the bed. He tossed the ruined garment aside.

Miner strode over and put a calming hand on Ennek's arm as he struggled angrily with his cravat. "Let me," he said.

Ennek allowed his hands to fall to his side. Miner's breath puffed gently against his face as he carefully untied the black fabric. After the knots were undone, Miner continued by unfastening Ennek's shirt and drawing it off his unresisting arms. When Miner's hands went to the belt, Ennek just stood there, his heart beating so hard that surely Miner must have heard. Next came the trousers and then Ennek's drawers, which pooled around his feet and made him feel ridiculous.

But then Miner knelt before him. Ennek had to look away, because the sight of the man bent at his feet was nearly too much. Perhaps Miner didn't notice. In any case, he didn't look up as he lifted one of Ennek's feet—causing Ennek to touch his shoulder for balance—and slipped off the trousers and drawers and sock. Then he did the same on the other side, and Ennek stood before him completely bare.

Miner stood and embraced him, his big hands spread over Ennek's back. Ennek didn't relax, though, but stood stiff as a pillar. "I can't. I don't—"

"Shh," Miner said. "It's nothing. Just a hug. Surely you can do that, at least?"

And Ennek could. Miner was warm. Ennek could press his face into the sweet skin just at the crook of Miner's neck and inhale him, filling his lungs with the other man's scent of smoke and cinnamon almonds. He could pretend nothing else in the world existed. Not the wizard or the ugly mark on his own arm, not the keep or even the polis itself. Just soft fabric against his body and the hardness of Miner beneath, a chest rising and falling with his own, wide palms smoothing over his upper back.

They stayed like that forever.

But it wasn't long enough, because eventually Ennek sighed and pulled slightly away. "Thank you," he said hoarsely.

"Can I draw you a bath?"

"No. I think I'll just go to sleep."

Miner led him by the hand to the bed. Ennek thought about how he was no longer discomfited by his own nudity, how it no longer felt strange being tucked into bed like a small child. And when Miner bent over and kissed him, an almost chaste brush of lips against lips, that seemed perfectly natural as well.

chapter seventeen

"YOU HAVE to tell them, Ennek. He'll try again to murder Larkin, you know he will."

Ennek glared at Miner. "I told you, I can't!"

"They won't punish you, Ennek. It wasn't your fault, it was the wizard's. They'll—"

"It *was* my fault, though, wasn't it? I allowed myself to be put in that position. I should be punished. I don't even care about that anymore. It's you, Miner. They'll put you back in Stasis, they'll—"

"I won't let it happen. I'll kill myself first."

Ennek stopped pacing and sat next to Miner on the bed. "No. There has to be another way." He leaned against Miner for support, and Miner slung an arm around his shoulders. He was doing that a lot lately. It was nice.

For over two months, Ennek had been dancing this dance. Going off to the laboratory so he could seethe under Thelius's watchful, smug stare. Coming back to his chambers and the comfort of Miner's company. And wasn't that odd, the slave comforting the younger son? Sometimes Ennek felt the dizziness and twisting in his gut that told him Thelius was using him, was tugging again on his reins. But it appeared that none of the magic he wrought was too large, and at least no major cataclysms occurred. Larkin continued his duties, barely acknowledging Ennek when they saw each other. It was as if all his emotions had been buried along with his wife and children. But perhaps he'd still make a good Chief, albeit a cold and ruthless one. Much like his father.

And as part of this dance, Ennek and Miner had gone over these steps many times. Ennek had to tell the Chief and Larkin about the wizard's actions and warn them of his evil intent. Ennek couldn't say a word because it would mean disaster for himself and, more importantly, for Miner.

He was at an impasse. Stasis. For a long time they sat there. Ennek listened to Miner's heart beating, like waves crashing against stone. He could hear the real waves outside too, if he concentrated. The noise was always there, of course, but he'd been hearing it since he was in his mother's womb, so he generally paid no more attention to it than the sound of his own rushing blood. He shut his eyes and pictured the water foaming and pounding at unyielding stone, patiently, endlessly, until the stone crumbled.

Suddenly, he sat up straight.

"What is it?" Miner asked.

"Thelius said that this damn tattoo binds me to him. But if I'm tied to him, isn't he tied to me as well? He says my powers are strong. Stronger than his, I suspect. Why couldn't I do to him the same as he's done to me—use his magic?"

"If that's possible, what would you do?"

"Break him," Ennek replied immediately. "Destroy his magic so he can never use it against anyone again."

IT WASN'T a plan to be made lightly or entered into rashly. But the next morning as Ennek entered the laboratory, he felt lighter than he had for some time, as if a great stone had been lifted from his shoulders. It might not work, but at least now he had hope.

In all his toiling for Thelius, he'd gained a good familiarity with the contents of the many books that were stacked on shelves and piled on nearly every horizontal surface. He'd indexed a great many of them, and he knew the spells they contained. One of them, a thin, gilt-edged tome, had a reversal enchantment. It was meant primarily as a defensive weapon for one wizard to use against another, and it would, supposedly, temporarily reverse power flows. Ennek hadn't paid much attention when he'd come across it months ago, but now he waited for the right moment. When Thelius slunk off to his chamber, Ennek slipped the book into his coat pocket.

That night after dinner, he and Miner pored over it. Miner couldn't quite make out the curly handwriting—Ennek made a mental note to teach Miner to read script—but he could help Ennek puzzle over the meaning of it. They concluded that the spell would only work when Thelius tried to use his bond with Ennek; and even then, it would be only as strong as the magic Thelius was attempting to use. If the wizard used only small magic, as he had been doing since the earthquake, Ennek would have only weak control. On the other hand, if the wizard truly exploited all of Ennek's strength, Ennek would be able to master enormous forces.

"I can't just sit around waiting for him to hex Larkin or the Chief," Ennek said. "I'm going to have to lure him somehow."

"Ennek, don't—don't endanger yourself."

Ennek laughed. "I'd say I failed in that goal a long time ago."

Miner looked away. "You should have just left me Under."

"Gods, no!" Ennek caught Miner's arm. "I may have dug my own grave, but bringing you out was the only truly *good* thing I've ever done. The only thing I'm proud of. Besides, the son of a bitch has clearly wanted at me for ages. He'd have found some other way. It's not as if I was such a difficult target. Hell, he could have just waited until I was drunk sometime and dragged me down Under to mark me."

Miner cupped his hand under Ennek's square chin. His touch was tender, but it hurt like fire. "You're a good man, Ennek."

Oh, this kiss was different from the first. Harder. Hungrier. Miner pressed his lips to Ennek's as if he intended to taste every bit of his soul, as if he were drowning and trying to steal Ennek's breath. And Ennek would let him, gladly.

They were both panting when Ennek pulled away.

"Not yet?" Miner asked. "You have to realize by now that I want you as badly as you want me."

Ennek wanted to sing. Nobody had ever wanted him before. Well, nobody except Thelius, but that didn't bear thinking of. But he said, "Not yet."

"Because I'm a slave?"

Ennek shook his head. "No. Because neither of us is free. Because I haven't earned this. But I will, Miner. I promise."

IT WAS only a few days before New Year. As always, the citizens of the polis bustled around making preparations for the festival. Ennek had wondered if the celebration at the keep would be more muted than usual, in light of the events a few months earlier. But the slaves scrubbed seemingly every bit of the keep three times over, and the servants hung decorations and brought in huge amounts of food for the dinner.

Thelius seemed preoccupied. That was good, in that it meant he left Ennek alone most of the time. But it was also troubling. He was planning something, surely, but Ennek had no idea what it was or when it would happen. Ennek had the counterspell ready, though; he'd practiced it diligently. He had no idea whether it would work. It was quite possible that he wouldn't be able to harness any magic at all once Thelius began to invoke the bond. It was also quite possible that Ennek simply lacked the experience to accomplish any magic of his own accord. But he hadn't come up with a better plan, so this small hope was all he had.

Thelius rose from his seat by the fire, where he'd been perusing an ancient scroll of some kind, and came over to where Ennek was silently and painstakingly separating dried pine needles from their branches and grinding them into a fine powder with a mortar and pestle. Ennek pretended to ignore Thelius as he hovered over Ennek's shoulder.

"It's almost New Year," Thelius finally said.

Ennek didn't bother to answer. He was in no mood to chat.

"The Chief will be doing his inspection Under in two days."

Ennek froze. Gods, he'd completely forgotten about that! How could he be so stupid? Trying very hard to keep his response indifferent, he said, "So?"

"So I shall need to return your slave to Stasis, as you know very well."

Ennek put the pestle down. "No."

"Ah, but that was the nature of our agreement, my son."

"Our *agreement*! I never agreed to be bound to you, I certainly never agreed to be used so you could murder Larkin's family, and I never agreed to be a part of whatever plot you're hatching next."

Thelius did a passable imitation of a man deeply offended. "My boy! Don't pretend as if you cared for those people—they were almost strangers to you. If it weren't for me, you'd be nothing. With my help, you can be the most powerful man in the world."

"I don't want that! Power doesn't make you happy. It doesn't bring you love."

Thelius's expression sharpened. "What do you know of love, deviant?"

"More than you do."

For the first time, Ennek saw true anger in the wizard's pale eyes. "A good woman loved me! She didn't care about you brats and she hated your father, but she loved me, and she would have loved our child as well, if she hadn't been so rash."

The words sent Ennek reeling backward. "You... you...."

"Yes, me. She should have had our child. Nobody would have known I was the real father—nobody except the Chief, perhaps, and she was going to poison him. That would have left Larkin in charge, and he was only a boy. Vulnerable. Oh, I would have let him live—let both of you live—until my son was old enough to become Chief himself. But your mother refused to see reason. She wouldn't go through with it."

"You murdered her!"

Thelius shook his head. "No. No, I didn't. I loved her. She leapt from that window of her own free will." He took a step closer, lowering his voice. "You were fortunate, my son. It was shortly after that I realized your... potential."

Praesidium's language held no words foul enough for this man. Ennek felt his lips curling into a feral snarl. "You're despicable."

"Oh, my son, you're not so different from me. You know that; I can see it in your eyes. Soon you'll be glorying in the power I've brought you."

"No."

"Then what? You'll go crying to the Chief about my dastardly deeds? You do and you'll lose that little pet you have upstairs, along with any chance of ever amounting to anything. Ah, perhaps I'll be kind and make sure you're stored in the cell next to his. And for what? It's not as if the Chief cares about you. He'd have been happier if Larkin were an only child, or if you'd been the one to die in that quake. No, Ennek, you're going to do as I tell you. Soon you will be the heir, and soon after you'll do what your mother should have done long ago, and then you'll be Chief."

Again his voice dropped, this time to an insinuating whisper. "As Chief, you can do whatever you want. You'll no longer have to hide your deviant nature. Why, I'm certain you'll have your choice of pretty boys. Once you're Chief, if you fancy anyone, you fabricate a crime and then he becomes your slave, yours to do with as you will."

"Sick bastard!" Ennek hissed.

Thelius chuckled. "Go back to your chambers, son. Go look at your slave and imagine what I can do to him once he's in Stasis. You saw one of my little experiments, did you not? Don't pretend to yourself that you have any choice. I'll see you in the morning to discuss our plans."

Ennek was very nearly out of control. He raised his hand, which was clenched into such a tight fist that his fingernails dug gouges into his palm.

The wizard only moved forward a step. "Did I tell you? With that binding spell, if I die, so do you." He smiled horribly.

It might have been a lie, Ennek thought. Or it might not. He couldn't risk it, not now. With enormous effort, he loosened his fist and let it drop to his side. He wanted to say more to the wizard—no, that wasn't true. He wanted to shred him into bloody little bits with his bare hands. Instead, he pushed past him and out the door.

HE RAVED and paced and raved some more, and Miner consoled him with words and embraces. Ennek wouldn't be placated this time, though. When he turned and punched the wall hard enough to bruise and bloody his knuckles, Miner caught his hand and kissed it, then cradled Ennek's face with his palms. "Stop this, Ennek. Hurting yourself won't help."

"Nothing helps! He's caught me in his web like a damned spider catches a fly." He tore himself from Miner's grip and lurched to the window. What would it feel like to jump, he wondered. For a few brief moments, it would be like flying. Like freedom.

Miner tugged him insistently away, toward his own body. "Lie down with me, En. I can make you feel better."

Oh, he was so badly tempted.

But no. "I have to fix this, Miner. I have to make it right." He pulled away again and made for the door.

"Ennek, don't! Calm down first, please. Please!"

But Ennek only stopped and yanked Miner into a bruising kiss, teeth clacking together, then pushed him gently away and flung himself out the door.

THE GUARD outside Larkin's chamber looked at him with mild curiosity. "The heir has left instructions he not be disturbed, sir. He's feeling a little ill."

Gods, was the wizard already doing something to him?

"I need to talk to him now," Ennek insisted. "It's an emergency."

"But sir—"

Ennek lunged past the unfortunate man, who was only doing his job, and heaved the door open. Larkin was sitting in a plain wooden chair with his back to the doorway, facing his large window. It overlooked the polis, Ennek knew, although he hadn't been in this room in many years. He didn't think much had changed since then. Same furniture. Same paintings hanging on the walls. Same dusty books on the shelves.

"Larkin!" Ennek cried. His brother didn't budge.

Ennek rushed across the room to Larkin's side, and only then did Larkin slowly roll his head to look at him. "Go away," he said flatly.

Ennek was going to argue with him. But then he caught sight of the bottle of whiskey in his brother's lap. No glass, just the bottle, and that nearly empty. A fog of alcohol fumes emanated from him. But his back was perfectly straight, his hair oiled in place, his hands completely steady. "Oh, Lark," he moaned.

"Go away."

And Ennek did, brushing wordlessly past the guard outside.

The Chief was stone-cold sober. He was also in the middle of a Council meeting, three dozen men in somber suits, heads bent over maps and contracts and drafts of laws all marked up in red ink. He looked up irritably and scowled when Ennek entered and then went back to whatever minute detail he'd been worrying over.

"Sir," Ennek said.

The frown was deeper this time. "I'm busy. Come back in two hours."

"But sir, this is very—"

"Two hours!"

Three-dozen pairs of eyes stared at him with barely disguised contempt. All except Hils's; he looked pained and began to move in Ennek's direction. Ennek shook his head and stormed out.

Hils caught up with him a few yards down the corridor, grabbing his shoulder to stop him. "Ennek? What is it? What's wrong?"

He wanted to tell him. He really did. But there was nothing Hils could do about it, and the more he knew, the more danger he'd be in. Ennek shook his head again. "I can't, Hils. Gods, I'm sorry, but I can't."

Hils gave him one of his long, searching gazes. "It's bad, isn't it?" he asked softly.

Ennek didn't reply.

"Oh, Ennek." Hils sighed. "Look, if I can help in any way at all...."

"Thanks. You can't—oh." An idea was percolating somewhere deep in his brain; he just didn't know quite yet what it was. He looked around furtively, but they were the only ones in the hallway. "If I had to leave the polis in a hurry without anybody knowing, maybe by sea...."

Hils tilted his head. "Do you know a ship that would take you?"

"Yes, I think. Maybe. A few, even."

"But you can't go through the port?"

"There are always guards there. They'd see me, recognize me. I don't want that. And…." He paused a moment before charging onward. "I might be traveling with someone."

Hils's eyebrows lifted to his hairline. "Who?"

"A prisoner. A slave."

"Gods, Ennek!"

Ennek said nothing.

Hils looked down at the floor for a moment and then back up. "I keep a little catboat tied up at the new piscarium. There are very few guards down that way at night; who wants anything from a bunch of half-built piers? When the meeting's over, I'm going to stock her with a few of the things a man might need if he were to leave in a hurry. You could sail her around, come up the backside of any of the ships in port. The guards would never see who you were. Or who you're with."

"You don't know how much…. Thank you. Thank you so much." Impulsively, Ennek pulled the other man into a quick embrace.

Hils held him tightly for just a moment before backing off. "Be careful," he said, then turned and walked back to the meeting.

Ennek felt a little better as he returned to his chambers. He had a plan. It might not save Larkin or the Chief, and he wasn't even sure whether the bond would work over the distance of the sea, but at least he might get Miner somewhere safe. There were three hours left until dark. That would give him time to gather a few things, find some of the gold that was stashed in the keep, and write letters to the Chief and Larkin. Oh, and to think of some way to smuggle Miner out of the keep. A scarf would help with that damn collar, and maybe Ennek could dig up a guard uniform or something for him. Wouldn't that be ironic?

He nearly loped through the corridors, up stairs and around corners, until he came to his own familiar door. He threw it open and crashed inside, ready to quickly explain his plan to Miner.

But Miner wasn't there.

chapter eighteen

ENNEK HAD expected to find Miner in one of his usual spots: sitting at the table or in front of the window, or maybe reclining in bed. But he wasn't in the bedchamber at all. A quick glance around the rest of Ennek's chambers told him what his heart already knew. Miner wasn't in the bathroom, nor was he in the spare room, running in place or using Ennek's weights.

Back in the bedchamber, Ennek paused for a moment to catch his breath and gather his thoughts. Had Miner been angry that Ennek insisted on talking to the Chief? Had he run away in fear of being returned Under? But then Ennek's gaze caught on something he should have noticed right away. It was a large piece of paper, and it lay on the floor right next to the table. Several colored pencils were scattered on and around it.

With his heart heavy as stone, Ennek walked over and picked up the paper. It was a drawing of Ennek reclining in bed. His chest was bare and the blankets were pulled up to his waist. His curls were riotous, and he had a sleepy little smile on his lips. Miner had sketched it out a few days earlier, and now it was half colored: Ennek's face and torso were a shade of light tan, his eyes brown like coffee, his lips deep red. But his hair and the bedding were still the off-white of the paper. There was a boot print on it, bigger than his own. And Miner didn't own any boots.

Ennek's stomach plummeted, and he felt so dizzy with fear that he had to collapse into the nearest chair. Gods, if the guards had taken Miner—

No. It wasn't terror or grief that was making him feel ill.

With an inchoate cry of rage, Ennek flung himself to his feet, then across the room and out the door, not bothering to shut it behind him. He tore down the corridors, bumping without apology into a servant, who then dropped a load of carefully folded linens. He flew down stairways and sprinted past surprised functionaries of various types, until finally he was at that out-of-the-way hallway, where a guard stood in front of a narrow door, looking startled at Ennek's abrupt appearance.

"Move!" Ennek demanded as another wave of nausea threatened to make him vomit on the man's shiny boots.

"Sir, you can't—"

"I am the Chief's son, and you will get out of my way or I'll skewer you with your own sword!" Ennek roared.

The guard blanched and scrambled to the side.

Ennek took those cursed stairs three at a time, just barely managing to keep himself from tumbling head over heels onto the hard stone below. It didn't help that his head was whirling and his belly clenching. His footsteps echoed loudly and his breathing was rough, but he thought he could faintly hear a voice at the far end of the dark corridor. It was rhythmic, as if it was chanting.

Although he was running his fastest, it felt like one of those horrible dreams where he was being chased through thick syrup. The dizziness blurred his vision, and his temples pounded with pain at every footfall.

The door at the bottom of the stairs stood open, gaping as if someone had been in too much of a hurry to bother closing it behind himself.

The last cell door, the widest one, was shut. For a brief, horrible moment as he reached for the handle, he was positive it was locked and he'd have to wait helplessly outside. But the knob turned smoothly in his hand and the door swung open easily.

Ennek took in the scene before him very quickly, as if it were one of Miner's drawings. Miner was in the stone basin, lying on his back, only his head and collared neck and the tops of his bare shoulders visible over the cloudy, smelly water. His eyes were wide with terror, and his mouth grimaced in a rictus of pain. The twist of his shoulders suggested that his hands were bound behind him. Thelius stood facing the basin with his right side angled toward Ennek and the door. He held a small open book in his hands and he was reciting a spell. The words he spoke slithered from his lips like so many vipers.

Thelius had turned his face a little at Ennek's noisy entrance, while Miner rolled his eyes from the wizard's face to Ennek's. Thelius smiled viciously. "Ah, you've arrived just in time to see the enchantment completed, son. And aren't you pleased to know it's your own magic that imprisons him?" And then he began chanting again.

Ennek felt the internal lurch as the wizard began to steal his powers. He felt weak, stupid, useless, a witness at his own funeral. And then he remembered the spell he'd learned. His voice was so feeble at first that Thelius probably couldn't hear it over his own; in fact, Ennek could barely hear it himself. But then he found strength and his speech grew in volume.

Thelius abruptly stopped and whirled to face him. His normally gray face was nearly purple with fury. He opened his mouth, perhaps for a counterspell of his own, perhaps just to scream.

But it was too late.

Ennek could feel the force surging within him like a hurricane. The pain and sickness were gone. Thelius's magic was in him, hard and cold and obdurate. It was towering mountains, spinning boulders, and volcanoes spewing ash and molten lava into the sky and across the landscape. But for the first time, Ennek felt the full shape of his own magic. Vast oceans. Raging rivers. Torrential rains. And tiny little trickles of water that would, over time, erode even the hardest rock. His power was also within his veins and in every cell of his body, the true force of life that pounded through every living thing in the polis.

He didn't need spells. He realized that now. The words were only a way to focus and channel magic the way a canal channels water. But the water would flow on regardless, and he had the ability to control that flow.

Ennek pictured an enormous wall of water, akin to the waterspout he'd conjured when he'd traveled to the south, but much wider. It carried with it the entire force of the merciless ocean. He could see it rushing toward land, where it would topple the keep like a child might knock over a pile of blocks, then engulf the polis, washing it clean of buildings and squares and statues, sluicing away citizens and servants and slaves.

It was a very tempting vision.

But then Ennek focused instead on Miner, pale skin and paler hair, collar thick and black, eyes like the sea. Miner shuddered and kicked feebly like a drowning man trying to swim.

Ennek shuddered too.

With a twist of effort, Ennek felt the invisible, sticky strands that meant Stasis. They were everywhere Under, so thick that a part of him wondered how he could manage to breathe. He concentrated and gathered those strands into a single thick cord, which he drew out of Miner, drew out, in fact, from all of the cold, stony cells. Then he twisted that cord and wrapped it around Thelius.

Thelius screamed, but the sound devolved into a strangled gasp as the cord tightened. The spellbook fell from his hands and Thelius toppled like a felled tree. He lay on the floor, unmoving and stiff, his eyes frozen open in horror.

There was a moment of complete and utter silence. Except, of course, for the ever-present crashing of the waves.

Then Miner gasped and stirred. Ennek ran to him and pulled him out of the basin. They collapsed together onto the floor with Ennek cradling Miner in his arms. Water soaked through Ennek's clothing, and tears ran down his face. "Miner, Miner," he sobbed, suddenly as weak as a kitten.

"What did you do?" Miner whispered.

"He won't hurt you anymore. He—"

Just then, ear-shattering cries began to echo from the other cells. Ennek had a moment of confusion but then remembered how much Miner had hurt when Thelius had removed him from Stasis in Ennek's bathtub. The other prisoners were waking up.

"We have to go," Ennek said. "I'm… I don't think I can carry you. Can you stand?"

Miner nodded uncertainly. "I think so."

Ennek untied Miner's wrists, which had been bound with a bit of the silky white cord. He rose, then helped pull Miner to his feet. The two of them stood there, shaking like a pair of ancient, palsied old men. Miner almost collapsed, but Ennek caught him.

In one corner of the room was a pile of clothing that must have been Miner's. The garments were damp, but then so was Miner. As he sagged against the wall, Ennek dressed him. With hardly a glance at the motionless wizard, they walked to the door. But then Ennek remembered the book, and with Miner leaning in the doorway, he went back for it and shoved it into his pocket.

They leaned against the wall as they made their way slowly down the corridor. Ennek stopped and opened each cell as they passed. Some rooms were empty. In others, prisoners moaned and struggled to free themselves from the silken cords. He would have liked to help, but that would have taken time he and Miner didn't have. In one of the cells, he saw the dark-skinned man whose body was still marked by burns and neat incisions. He was moving, and Ennek vehemently hoped the metal skewer was no longer buried in his heart. Ennek even began to step inside to check, but then Miner bleated in distress and fell, and Ennek had to prop him up.

Three times Ennek had to stop and vomit as the aftereffects of all the magic made themselves known.

The stairs were steep and seemingly impossible. But remaining Under certainly wasn't an option, so Ennek put an arm tightly around Miner's waist and, pausing every now and then to retch, pulled them up step by step.

The same guard was standing outside the door. He must have heard some of the screaming below, because he looked enormously distressed. He stared at Ennek and Miner with confusion and dismay. "Sir, I—"

"Shut up. Give me your keys! Now!"

It was fortunate that the man was used to following orders. He reached for his belt and unfastened the metal ring, which he put into Ennek's impatient hand. Ennek set Miner against the wall and carefully helped him slide into a seated position. "Just a second," he murmured. Then he turned and said to the guard, "Sorry about this," right before he shoved him hard through the open doorway. The guard stumbled backward in surprise, his feet dangerously close to the top of the stairs before Ennek slammed the door closed and locked it. The guard began to shout and pound against the heavy barrier.

Ennek was used up. He wanted to curl up on the floor and go to sleep; he couldn't possibly go on. But he did. He yanked Miner up and supported him as they fled.

They passed a few other people as they walked, but those people were too astonished at the sight of them to do more than gape. Eventually Ennek and Miner made it to their chambers. Ennek helped Miner to the bed, which looked entirely too inviting, and glanced out the window. It wasn't quite dusk yet. Too early.

Miner groaned and rolled onto his side. "En?"

"We have to go," Ennek said. "Just let me get ready."

"Stay. Rest. Hold me. So cold."

"We can't. Soon someone's going to discover what's happened Under, and—"

"You didn't do wrong."

"I freed all the prisoners. I put Thelius in Stasis. And there's still you, Miner."

"They won't understand?"

Ennek thought of the Chief's stony face and Larkin's eyes now grown cold as ice. "No."

A wooden wardrobe stood in one corner of the room. Ennek rooted around until he found the large canvas bag he'd used those rare times he'd traveled out of town. It smelled a bit musty, but it would do. He hurried around the chamber, pulling some of his own clothes and some of Miner's out of drawers and throwing them in the bag. He also tossed in their combs and toothbrushes and razors, as well as a few favorite books and some of Miner's drawing pencils. He didn't have much money, but he put all he had into his pocket. He took the few pieces of jewelry that he had—the ring he'd once wagered against a gaudy suit, a fancy pocket watch he never used, a heavy gold chain he was supposed to wear to state dinners but rarely did. He buckled his sword around his hips and stuck into his boot the dagger and leather scabbard his mother once gave him.

Miner had been watching carefully, but he was still shaking and blue with cold. Ennek gathered Miner's warmest trousers and a thick woolen shirt, a pair of cotton drawers, black socks, and the green sweater. "Let's get that wet stuff off you," he said and began to unbutton Miner's shirt.

"Where are you going?" Miner asked quietly.

"*We* are going on a sea voyage, I hope. Didn't you tell me you fancied seeing a bit of the world?"

"But I can't go. I'm a slave, Ennek."

"No, not anymore. We're both going to be free."

"But if you're caught helping—"

"If I'm caught, assisting a runaway is going to be the least of my problems." He leaned closer and kissed Miner's chilly cheek. "And I'm certainly not going anywhere without you."

For a too-short moment, they slumped into each other's arms. Ennek was the first to pull away. He tugged Miner's clothes off, pretending not to notice the way his hands brushed over the other man's body, and then helped Miner get the dry clothing on.

"All right. Just a couple more things to take care of." He walked over to the table, where there was a pile of Miner's drawing paper, and picked up a dark green pencil. Then he scrawled a note to the Chief and Larkin. He didn't tell them everything that had happened. He didn't even mention Miner. But he told about Thelius and Aelia and the murder of

Larkin's family, as well as the wizard's plans for the polis. Ennek didn't know whether they'd believe his tale, but he felt the need to attempt an explanation. When he was done, he signed his name and put the pencil down. And then, on a whim, he grabbed some of Miner's completed artwork from the stack nearby, rolled the papers tightly together, and bound them with a bit of string. He put them in his canvas bag as well.

Miner had neither shoes nor a coat. Ennek frowned at his own small collection of footwear and finally chose his biggest boots. "These are going to be pretty tight on you," he said, tossing them toward the bed. "We'll find new ones later."

As Miner struggled to jam his feet into the boots, Ennek pulled his only other warm coat from the wardrobe. It was the navy one with gold trim that had been part of his portmaster uniform. The arms would be too short for Miner, but the fabric was thick and water-repellent. He added a long scarf of rust-colored wool and a black knitted cap.

Miner's iron collar was invisible with the coat collar turned up and the scarf wound around his neck. "You're pretty presentable like that. That is, you would be, if you didn't look halfway dead." Ennek squeezed Miner's shoulder.

"Don't look so great yourself. Kind of green."

"Yes. My stomach's still… unsettled. Let's just keep our heads down, all right?"

Miner nodded. But Ennek was still worried. Miner could barely stand straight, and Ennek was staggering slightly himself. Then inspiration struck. He darted over to a cupboard and pulled out a half-empty bottle of whiskey. Good whiskey. Expensive. Pity, he thought, as he splashed a good dose of it onto Miner's chest and then onto his own.

"We smell like a distillery," Miner muttered.

"Good."

Without even a last look at his chambers, Ennek wrapped his arm around Miner, and they left.

The corridors were quiet. Most people were getting ready for dinner now. Ennek's stomach pitched at the thought of food. He'd worry about a meal later, when he'd no doubt be ravenous. Nobody spared them more than a passing glance, and soon they were walking out of the keep and into the lamp-lit square. While Miner gaped at his first view of the open sky in three centuries, Ennek scowled at the statue. He wasn't at all certain they'd both make it down to the piers, but if he took a horse, there was a good chance someone would later find it near the pier and deduce where they'd gone. If they took a carriage, he'd probably be recognized. So with a resigned sigh, he gathered Miner to him and they set off down the hill on foot.

Several times as they walked, Ennek was sorely tempted to stop somewhere and rest. Miner was moaning quietly and stumbling at his side, but public drunkenness would soon attract the guards' attention, and he definitely didn't want that. He muttered encouraging words to Miner as they walked and pointed out some of the landmarks. It was a strange sort of tour, but it served to distract his companion a bit from his poor physical condition.

As they passed one narrow, badly lit street, Miner came to a complete halt. "It looks the same," he gasped.

"You know it?"

"I lived on that street. My house was five minutes' walk from here."

"Do you want to see it?" Ennek asked and was relieved when Miner shook his head.

Soon, but not soon enough, they neared the water. They skirted the edge of the piers where the big ships docked. Every slip was full, as was often the case this time of year, but Ennek couldn't make out exactly which ships were there. There were more people over here, most of them carrying loads back and forth, but none seemed interested in the two fugitives. Ennek tried to keep to the darker bits of the street, where neither his face nor the ornaments on Miner's coat would be visible.

The traffic and activity lightened as they approached the piscarium. The fishermen were long since finished for the day, probably all back in their cozy little homes, tucking into their dinners. And the workmen constructing the new piers were gone as well.

Ennek refused to even consider what would happen if Hils's catboat wasn't waiting for them.

The new piers smelled of pitch and fresh-cut wood. They were long and L-shaped, forming a calm little harbor between them. The piles had been set and the planks laid; most of the bollards were piled onshore waiting to be installed. Despite his exhaustion and distraction, Ennek noticed that the project was well done. Scales and cleaning stations were set up along the piers, and only a few steps away, some small open-sided sheds were under construction. It pleased him to see how closely Hils and Mila had followed his initial ideas.

By the time their boots hit the newly hewn planks, Ennek was, for all intents and purposes, carrying Miner. "Sorry," Miner croaked.

"Shh. Almost there. Save your strength."

The trim little boat with the yellow-and-blue sail was the most beautiful sight Ennek had ever seen. But Miner froze when he caught sight of it and dug his feet feebly into the pier. He moaned miserably. "Can't. Water."

Ennek turned his head and kissed Miner's soft hair. "It's all right. I'd never let you drown, I promise."

Miner raised his eyes to meet Ennek's, then sighed deeply and nodded. "All right," he whispered.

Ennek helped Miner into the craft and then unfastened the rope and pushed off. Miner curled in a ball at the bottom of the boat.

It took Ennek only moments to steer out into the bay. The water was placid tonight, lapping gently against the wooden hull, reflecting the crescent moon and the countless stars. It was almost as if the sea itself were trying to aid in their escape.

Ennek suddenly remembered the book tucked in his pocket. He pulled it out, gave it a long look, and then let it drop over the side of the boat. The bay swallowed it without a splash.

A large black leather satchel was tucked under one of the seats. Ennek pulled it out and peered inside, finding clothes, a pair of broad knives, and at the very bottom, two cloth purses heavy with a small fortune in gold coins. "Thank you," Ennek whispered. He found a folded sheet of paper as well, but it was too dark to read it. He tucked it into his coat pocket for later.

The gentle rocking of the boat was almost hypnotic. He could easily fall asleep like this, he thought; it looked like Miner already had.

Sanctuary first, Ennek admonished. He could sleep later.

He kept the boat a fair way out from shore, trying to determine which of the ships might be a good choice. And then he spied a familiar shape anchored away from the port itself, a jaunty three-masted clipper with her sails tightly furled. It was the *Eclipse*. He hoped the captain still remembered Ennek's part in saving him from slave labor.

A launch was tethered next to the *Eclipse*, and a rope ladder hung down the ship's side. Ennek brought the catboat up close to the clipper's hull and craned his neck to see a sailor peering down at him. "Ahoy!" Ennek called. "Permission to board, please."

The sailor stared at him a moment more. Ennek couldn't make out the details of the man's face well enough to see his expression. But then the man gestured, making it clear that Ennek's request had been granted.

Ennek shook Miner awake. "We're here, love. I need you to be strong for just a few more minutes."

Perhaps it was the endearment that did it. Miner blinked a few times and then struggled to his feet. He stood in the bottom of the boat, swaying slightly.

"I need you to climb that ladder," Ennek said. "I'll be right behind you."

Miner nodded. Ennek slung the satchel over one shoulder and the canvas bag over the other and followed Miner up the ropes. He'd been careful not to tie the catboat to anything. He hoped it wouldn't drift so far by morning that Hils wouldn't be able to retrieve it.

It was slow going as they climbed. Miner's hands slipped a few times, but Ennek was able to catch him, and soon the sailor was helping them onto the deck.

Miner immediately collapsed against Ennek's legs, and Ennek himself had to lean against the rail. The sailor, a short, wiry fellow with a curly beard, looked at them doubtfully.

"I need to speak with Captain Eodore. My friend's ill and... just fetch the captain, please."

The sailor cocked an eyebrow at them and then called to a half-grown boy who was gawking from a few yards away. "You heard the man, boy. Go get the captain!"

The boy scurried away. "'E ain't contagious, is 'e?" the sailor asked, looking at Miner. "Don't wanna catch nothin' nasty."

"No. He's not contagious."

The sailor frowned but said nothing else.

It was only a few minutes later that the boy reappeared, scampering excitedly in front of the captain. Eodore squinted at Ennek and Miner, did a double-take, and then said a foreign word that Ennek was positive was a blasphemy. "Sir! What the hell—"

"Uh, could we maybe discuss this privately?" Ennek jerked his head toward the boy, who glared in response.

Eodore bit his lip and then nodded. "All right. Follow me."

Ennek had to help Miner to his feet again, and Miner's eyes were barely open as they walked across the deck and to the stairs leading below. They went into the captain's cabin, a tidy little space full of maps and leather-bound books. Ennek sat in a chair and Miner immediately lay down on the floor, curling up near Ennek's feet.

"Is your friend all right?" the captain asked with concern. He had taken a seat opposite Ennek.

"He's had a rough day. We both have." Ennek sighed deeply.

"Well, can I get you something to drink?"

It was tempting, but Ennek shook his head. "Look, I'm about done in. Let me make this quick. I've… got myself in some trouble. I need to leave the polis right away. People might be looking for me. And Miner, here"—he looked down at the sleeping man—"is an escaped slave." He took a deep breath and let it out slowly.

Captain Eodore sucked on his teeth. He was a florid man, slightly stout, with a deeply lined face and crinkly blue eyes. "What sort of trouble?"

Ennek lifted his chin. "I haven't done anything wrong or immoral. But I've broken some laws. The Chief won't be pleased. And Miner… let's just say he's had more than his share of punishment already."

"Helping you escape, that might be treason. Could get a man put in Stasis."

Ennek smiled wickedly. "I can assure you, Captain, that whatever happens, you will *not* end up in Stasis. Nobody will, ever again."

The captain leaned back in his chair. "That's a relief, I suppose. But there's still bond-slavery."

"There is. And I can't guarantee that as cleanly."

"I expect I'd be a slave already if you'd made a different choice last year."

"I've made a lot of interesting choices in the past several months." Ennek rolled his head wearily. "I can pay our way, if you like. Generously. Or perhaps help out a little. Neither of us is a sailor, but I know a little magic. That can come in handy sometimes."

Eodore nodded. "That it can." He looked down at Miner, then up again at Ennek. "The two of you…."

"Yes." Ennek kept his own gaze steadily on the captain.

"Hmph." It wasn't a judgmental sound, just a thoughtful one. And then the captain nodded to himself as if he'd reached a decision. "We're sailing out in four days. I'd recommend making yourself scarce until we're well out to sea. I've got a good crew, but greed can overcome any man's good sense."

Ennek huffed out a huge breath of relief. "Captain, it feels like I could sleep for just about the whole journey anyhow."

"I have a very small space—it's intended as storage, really, but you could probably squeeze in. I expect it'll be comfortable enough."

Ennek smiled weakly. "I could sleep on hot coals right now."

Eodore grinned and stood. "Then follow me. But I'll be wanting the whole story once you're rested. Something tells me it's a good one."

It was indeed a tiny space and it smelled strongly of spices, but Ennek didn't care. Before the captain bid them good night, he had the boy fetch a mattress from somewhere—a narrow one meant for only one person, but they'd manage. Ennek helped Miner get comfortable and then crammed their bags into a corner of the room. He curled against Miner's back, and it was warm and soft and familiar. He pulled the covers up over both of them and instantly fell asleep.

chapter nineteen

Dear Ennek,

I hardly know what to say. I hope that these provisions are enough for you; they're all I could muster on such short notice. I wish things could have been different between us. I think you know that. But I'm pleased to call myself your friend, and to help you as I can. It's my most sincere hope that wherever your journey takes you, you find the peace and happiness you so richly deserve. And I do hope that someday we shall meet again.

Yours,

H

Ennek smiled, folded the paper, and tucked it away. He'd read it before, of course—probably had it memorized by now, actually—but it still soothed him to see Hils's slightly messy handwriting, to know that Hils was thinking of him fondly.

A moment later Miner stooped through the low doorway. He carried two bowls of fragrant stew and had a long loaf of bread tucked under his arm. "Cook says if you want any more you can come and get it yourself." Miner grinned.

Ennek took the bowls from Miner's hands while Miner sat opposite him on the mattress, his legs crossed in a way that made Ennek's heart beat faster. "I'm too lazy. Besides, I like being waited on."

Miner rolled his eyes and grabbed his bowl back. "It's a beautiful night. You should go up and see. I suppose the stars are the same, but they look different somehow."

"We're only three days out of Praesidium."

Miner shrugged. "Three days farther than I've ever been."

They ate silently. It was good food—the *Eclipse* had a very able cook—and it didn't take them long to finish it off. Miner stared down at his empty bowl. "En? I'm sorry I let the wizard take me. I should have fought—"

"Gods, Miner, don't! He would have zapped you with a spell if you'd refused. He could have killed you."

Miner didn't look up. "I was a coward. He had two guards with him and they had swords, and—"

"And you were unarmed. I'm glad it worked out as it did. If you'd been hurt...." His stomach lurched uneasily at the thought. He wondered, though, what had become of those two guards. Had they told the Chief who they'd found in Ennek's chambers? Well, it didn't matter much anymore, he supposed.

Miner sighed. "I still wish I'd stood up to him."

"You weren't a coward. Look how long it took me to stand up to the bastard."

"What will happen to him?"

"He'll stay in Stasis, I think. Indefinitely. Nobody but me knows how to get him out."

Miner nodded. "Good."

Ennek nodded back and finished his meal, then set the bowl aside. He was getting used to their tiny quarters. It felt like home.

"Do you have plans for when we arrive?" Miner asked.

"Nope. But we have some money, and—" He stopped abruptly. "You don't have to stay with me, you know. You're a free man. I can give you the money and you can do whatever you want. Maybe find a way to get that damned collar off."

"Is that what you want? For me to go my own way?"

Ennek's breath caught, and he shook his head. "No," he whispered. "That's not what I want at all."

Miner's smile lit up the room. "Good. Now that I'm a free man, I'd like to give myself to you. Can I belong to you, Ennek?"

Oh, Ennek felt warm inside, the joy so large he couldn't imagine how his body could contain it all. "And I'll belong to you."

They undressed each other slowly in the flickering lantern light. Although they'd both gone through those motions before—unbuttoning, sliding cloth over skin—those times had been very different. And when they were both naked, that was nothing like previous times either. Ennek blanketed Miner's form with his own and pressed kisses against the flesh at the edge of his collar, against his delicate eyelids, against his trembling chest. Miner grasped Ennek to him as if Miner were drowning and Ennek was his savior, and Ennek clutched Miner back just as fiercely. They murmured softly to each other until they could only gasp and moan.

Long into the night, their bodies rocked together to the rhythm of the ocean beneath them.

Exclusive Excerpt

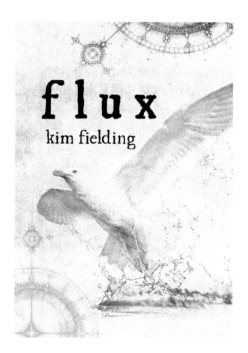

By Kim Fielding
Ennek Trilogy: Book Two

Ennek, the son of Praesidium's Chief, has rescued Miner from a terrible fate: suspension in a dreamless frozen state called Stasis, the punishment for traitors. As the two men flee Praesidium by sea, their adventures are only beginning. Although they may be free from the tyranny of their homeland, new difficulties await them as Miner faces the continuing consequences of his slavery and Ennek struggles with controlling his newfound powers as a wizard.

Now fugitives, Ennek and Miner encounter challenges both human and magical as they explore new lands and their deepening relationship with each other.

chapter one

THERE WAS a pattern in the wood grain on one part of the ceiling: a knothole and some curved lines. The more Miner looked at it, the more it looked like a whirlpool, the sort rumored to swallow entire ships at sea. He tried not to look at it at all, but that was difficult when he chose to spend so many hours confined to the tiny compartment, and when there wasn't really much else to see.

He didn't have to stay inside; he was free to wander the decks as Ennek often did. Like Ennek, he might have found a way to help out, to coil ropes or swab decks or whatever sailors on the *Eclipse* did at sea. He could have kept his slave collar covered in the thick scarf his lover had given him and nobody would have thought anything of it, because the weather remained cold and blustery and clammy in a way that seeped into his bones and made them ache. And really, he should have yearned to go outside, to have open skies above him for the first time in three hundred years.

But he didn't go above deck, at least not often, because then he would inevitably see the water tossing and foaming beneath them. And despite the angry words he muttered to chastise himself, he just couldn't face the ocean without trembling in fear.

Ennek spent hours up above, returning to their small space with hot drinks and spicy stews and hunks of dry bread, his black curls wild and his skin smelling like salt. But he was very understanding of Miner's terror, and he tried to tamp down his enthusiasm over their adventure, instead drawing Miner against his muscular body and telling small tales of the day's occurrences.

And sometimes after the sun had set and only a few other men remained awake, Ennek would persuade Miner to climb the ladder to the top deck, and Miner would stand with his back to the railing—even though it was too dark to see the water well—and he'd breathe in some fresh air and try not to tremble noticeably.

"I won't let anything hurt you," Ennek told him one night in a low voice. "Not again. Thelius is… gone… and this is only water, no more dangerous than a bathtub."

Miner had been afraid of the bathtub too, at first. He didn't remind Ennek of that, but only nodded. "I know. I'm sorry. It's just…."

Ennek set his hand on Miner's shoulder. "I understand. What those bastards did to you, it was hell, and for so long…. You're not going to get over it right away. We'll give it time, all right? And anyway, we'll be on dry land in less than a week, and then I promise you, we can stay far away from the ocean."

"Thank you," Miner replied. He knew Ennek didn't understand his fear—couldn't, really. After all, Ennek had practically grown up on the water, had spent the best times of his life puttering around the bay in his little catboats or stomping about the great sailing ships as portmaster. The sea had been his lifeblood even before he'd learned he was a wizard with the element of water at his command.

"Do you want to walk around a little? I could show you how the steering works, or maybe you want to take a look at the aft rigging? It's just a bunch of strings, really, but it's so ingenious—"

"I think I'd like to return below."

Ennek nodded. "Okay. I'm kind of worn out anyway."

Miner led the way back down the ladder and through the cramped corridor. Their room wasn't meant to be a place where people slept; it was actually a storeroom of sorts, and it smelled strongly of the spices that had been transported during the ship's voyage to Praesidium. The ceiling was low enough that Miner couldn't quite stand up straight. The floor space was barely big enough for a mattress on which they had to squeeze together, but neither of them minded that. There were no portholes—which made Miner happy—and it was a serviceable means of escape and privacy.

As soon as the door to the room was shut, they began to shed their damp clothing, piling it in a heap up against one wall. All that movement in the cramped space was awkward and Miner knocked into the hanging lamp with his elbow, sending shadows careening crazily about. The dancing light revealed Ennek's broad shoulders and the dark curls on his chest.

Ennek reached over to steady the lamp. He smiled shyly at Miner as they stood there in their woolen underpants. He was still timid about nudity and about the way they shared their bodies. Miner found it endearing.

"You must be going crazy locked up in here all the time," Ennek said softly.

"But I'm used to it. Besides, I have my books. My reading's getting much better."

Ennek smiled again. "So why don't you read to me tonight?"

They arranged themselves on the mattress with two or three thick blankets to keep out the chill. Miner reached into the canvas bag that contained all his worldly belongings and pulled out a volume with a slightly battered blue cover. He didn't know whether Ennek had chosen this particular book on purpose when they'd fled the polis, or whether it was simply the closest one at hand, but either way, Miner liked it. It contained a series of morality tales and was clearly meant for children, but Miner was able to puzzle out most of the words himself and there were line drawings to help when he got stuck.

They leaned their backs against the wall, cushioning their skin from the splintery wood with two pillows, and Ennek snuggled in against Miner's chest. Miner wrapped one of his long arms around Ennek and opened the book to the page where he'd left off. He'd marked it with a white-and-gray gull feather that Ennek had brought him a few days before.

"The Tale of the Cat and the M-Mouse," he began, stumbling slightly. "There once was a mouse who lived in a great c… cas…."

"Castle," Ennek prompted.

"Castle. The mouse lived in the scull… scullery?"

"That's it."

"Scullery wall, and he ate the… the crumbs of fine food that the cooks per… pre…."

"Prepared."

"Prepared for the king. And the mouse th…. What's that word, En?"

"That's a tricky one. Thought."

"And the mouse thought he was very fine indeed."

Ennek turned his head and kissed Miner lightly on the cheek. "Your reading really is improving."

Miner blushed a little under the praise. He continued the story, Ennek patiently helping him with a word now and then, until the mouse allowed his pride to make him foolish and the cat, naturally, ate him up.

He was going to continue on into the next story, "The Tale of the Miller's Daughter," but the feel of Ennek's skin against him proved too distracting. He abandoned the book and they made love in their quiet, sweet, still slightly fumbling way, until they fell asleep in one another's arms.

ENNEK LOOKED slightly worried as he brought Miner some lunch the following afternoon. "The weather's looking a little iffy," he said. "Captain Eodore says it's too early to tell if we're in for a bad storm. Could be just a little bit of a blow."

Miner nodded and wondered whether he was going to be able to eat at all with that new worry gnawing at him, making his stomach tighten and roil. But Ennek handed him a cup of grassy-smelling tea. "Drink this. It has some herbs in it that Cook says help with seasickness. Just in case. I think it has some lambs-ease in it, and maybe some spineroot. Thelius had those in his jars, and when I was cataloging I read that they ease nausea. It's relaxing, too. Slightly sedative."

"Thank you." Miner took the mug and warmed his hands around it for a moment. It was thick and gray and not very well made, as if the potter were new at his craft. But it was heavy and sturdy, and he supposed it worked well enough for onboard a ship. He sipped cautiously. It didn't taste much better than it smelled, but someone had added a little sugar to it, and that made it slightly more palatable.

Ennek took a big bite of his own bread, which had been soaking in the cup of meaty-smelling soup. "Look, if we do get a storm, stay in here, all right? You don't want to be underfoot when everyone's rushing around, and things can get pretty… exciting up there."

"The last place I want to be during a storm is above deck."

"Yeah, I know."

Ennek slurped down the last of his food and rose to his feet. "I'm going back up. There's a lot of preparation to be done, just in case. You'll be all right down here?"

"I'm fine. I'm going to find out what sort of trouble the miller's daughter gets into."

Ennek bent down for a quick kiss, which eased Miner's worries more than the tea ever could. It still surprised Miner when Ennek showed these momentary sparks of affection, and it pleased him as well, because he knew that showing how he felt didn't come easily to Ennek.

When Ennek left, Miner read for a while. But the tea made him sleepy and he found it hard to concentrate on the words—the print seemed to squirm and crawl like insects—so eventually he gave up and tucked the book away. He briefly considered bringing out his drawing things, but then his jaw nearly unhinged itself with an enormous yawn and he lay down, inhaling the scents of Ennek and himself as he drifted off to sleep.

Pounding footsteps and rough shouts woke him. It must be the storm, he thought sleepily, not as alarmed as he might have been. Perhaps the effects of the tea still lingered. But then it occurred to him that if they were caught in a storm, he would surely feel it; and now all he felt was the normal pitch and sway of the sea, a more or less gentle motion that seemed to have settled permanently in his body.

Miner scrambled inelegantly to his feet, getting tangled up in the bedclothes as he did, and then simply stood there, rocking slightly, his heart beating so rapidly it was difficult to hear anything but the blood rushing in his ears. But he did hear things: more footsteps, several thundering crashes, frantic yelling, and one piercing scream.

Miner had learned to fight when he was young. His father had taught him basic swordsmanship when Miner was barely old enough to hold a weapon; it was assumed by all that Miner, like his father and his father's father, would join the Guard when he reached adulthood. Of course he had, and although he never became a stellar fighter, he managed well enough with a variety of weapons and even with his bare hands. But that had been so long ago—over thirty decades!—and Miner wasn't the same man he had been then. The last time he had wielded a weapon was when, overcome with rage and stupid grief, he had tried to assassinate the Chief, the father of his dead lover, Camens. The Chief had survived and Miner had been punished, and now he was weak and scared and unarmed.

So he simply crouched in his hiding space uncertainly, much like the mouse in the story he'd read the night before. But the mouse had been eaten by the cat, and now loud voices resounded in the passageway outside Miner's room. The voices were calling to one another in a language he didn't recognize, something guttural and consonant-rich. Miner looked around the small cabin frantically, searching for something he might use to defend himself.

But before he could think coherently, the door crashed open. Two men came crowding through the opening. They were tall and wiry and wild-eyed, with dark beards tied up in knots, and strange, colorful clothing. They carried swords, and they looked surprised to see him.

One of them, the one with the billowy scarlet shirt, shouted something unintelligible at Miner.

Miner stood as straight as the low ceiling permitted and tried not to appear terrified. "I don't understand you," he said. It was the first time he had spoken to anyone but Ennek or Thelius in three hundred years.

The man growled something at his companion, who jabbered excitedly back. They both looked at Miner again, this time more slowly, and their lips curled up into smiles as they focused on Miner's neck above the blue-green sweater he wore: at the heavy slave collar, permanently attached.

"Come here!" demanded the shorter of the two men, whose shirt had broad vertical stripes of emerald and gold. His accent was very thick.

Miner took a step backward, which meant he was pressed up against the wall. "Bugger off," he said. And then, because he felt like he had nothing to lose at this point, and because he was horrified to think about what had become of his lover, he yelled, "Ennek!" But there was no answer. Miner ducked and tried to slip past them, knowing it was hopeless but preferring a quick death to the alternatives. But these men were well practiced at such maneuvers, it seemed. The red-shirted one slashed at Miner's upper arm, not very deeply but enough to hurt, causing Miner to instinctively duck away. And when he did so, the man in the striped shirt was there to catch him, dropping his sword so he could hold Miner's arms behind his body. Miner squirmed and kicked. He had a moment of savage glee when his bare foot connected with Red Shirt's groin and the man grunted in pain and doubled over. But then Stripes locked a strong arm around Miner's neck, choking him, and Red Shirt recovered enough to stick the tip of his blade directly underneath Miner's left eye.

"No move!" said Stripes, letting go of Miner's neck. Miner remained motionless as he listened to Stripes rustling around, out of his line of sight. Then his arms were seized roughly and his wrists were tightly bound behind him with fabric. Red Shirt sheathed his sword and, with a savage grin, brought his knee up between Miner's legs. The pain was so intense that Miner collapsed and then lay on the floor, retching miserably.

The men laughed and hauled him to his feet. With one of them in front and one behind, he was dragged and pushed down the passageway toward the ladder. Additional bearded men in gaudy colors squeezed past, their arms full of boxes; one of them elbowed Miner in the side and cackled excitedly before being urged forward by his colleagues.

They had to pull Miner up the ladder by his armpits, and as soon as he was above deck, they threw him down. He rolled to his knees, groaning, and looked around.

Much of the noise had abated; the fight was over. The ship's crew were seated in a huddle on the deck, wrists tied behind them with pieces of rope. A few men—one in purple, one in sky blue, and one, surprisingly, in white—stood guard over the crew, swords swinging loosely in their hands. More of the pirates (because they were pirates, Miner supposed) hurried back and forth, carrying boxes and bundles to the railing and tossing them to men who waited on a ship tethered alongside the *Eclipse*. The pirates were jovial, shouting and laughing and singing snippets of songs.

Miner turned and twisted on his knees, frantic for any sign of Ennek. His heart leapt into his throat when he saw three bodies alongside the railing, each sprawled in a puddle of blood, unmoving. He couldn't see their faces. One of them had Ennek's build—broad and not very tall—but the unmoving man's head was obscured by the torso of another of the victims. He was coatless and his rough brown shirt was identical to those Ennek and many of the sailors wore. It was impossible to tell the man's identity.

"Ennek!" Miner shouted, earning a heavy blow to the head from Red Shirt. Miner was knocked off balance and fell over; when he righted himself, he saw Captain Eodore among the captive sailors, sadly shaking his head and then gesturing with his chin at the railing opposite the pirate's ship.

No! Miner refused to accept that. "Ennek!" he called again, his voice breaking.

Red Shirt hit him again, harder, and this time Miner stayed down when he toppled. The rough planks were wet and the splinters dug into his cheek. "He's gone, son," he heard the captain say.

After that, things became fuzzy and sounds were muted, as if Miner were watching the ships from very far away. He could barely feel it when he kicked out at any pirate who came within range, when his foot connected with shins and knees but not hard enough to do any harm, when Red Shirt dealt him a third blow to the head and then used a length of rope to bind Miner's ankles and tie them to his wrists.

Some immeasurable time later, a particularly large pirate with a bald head and complicated beard grabbed Miner and heaved him onto his shoulder. He began to stride toward the railing.

"No!" Captain Eodore called. "We surrendered and you agreed not to harm any more of my men. Take the blasted cargo but leave him be."

"He not you man," replied one of the pirates, this one slightly older than the others and wearing a black shirt with large silver buttons. "He slave."

"No, he's a free man now. Let him go!"

The pirate pointed at his own neck. "Slave. Cargo." Then he said something to the man who was carrying Miner, and the man continued walking until he reached the railing.

As the pirates handed him precariously over to their comrades on the other ship, Miner wasn't even afraid of the gray water he saw beneath him. In fact, he wiggled as best as his bindings allowed, hoping he'd squirm free and fall into the ocean and drown. At least then he'd be joining Ennek in the sea's cold embrace.

But he didn't get free, didn't fall, and soon he was being dropped unceremoniously to the deck of the pirate ship among the piles of their other loot. Someone grabbed his knees and dragged him away from the railing. His sweater bunched up against his chest, and Miner buried his face in it. It smelled of Ennek, who had given him the sweater as a gift. It was warm and soft and finely made, and it must have cost a fortune. More than that, it was deeply symbolic: the afternoon it was given to him, as Ennek blushed and smiled after Miner pulled it on, that was the afternoon Miner had begun to believe that the man truly cared for him.

Ennek had loved him, in fact. Miner knew that now. Ennek had risked everything, had given up his entire life for Miner's sake. And look where that had gotten him—dead at the bottom of the sea. As dead as Camens, the only other man Miner had ever fallen for, the man who was also a Chief's younger son, and who had been executed at his own father's orders.

Miner vowed that as soon as he could manage it, he'd be dead as well.

KIM FIELDING is very pleased every time someone calls her eclectic. Her books have won Rainbow Awards and span a variety of genres. She has migrated back and forth across the western two-thirds of the United States and currently lives in California, where she long ago ran out of bookshelf space. She's a university professor who dreams of being able to travel and write full time. She also dreams of having two perfectly behaved children, a husband who isn't obsessed with football, and a house that cleans itself. Some dreams are more easily obtained than others.

Blogs: kfieldingwrites.com and www.goodreads.com/author/show/4105707.Kim_Fielding/blog

Facebook: www.facebook.com/KFieldingWrites

E-mail: kim@kfieldingwrites.com

Twitter: @KFieldingWrites

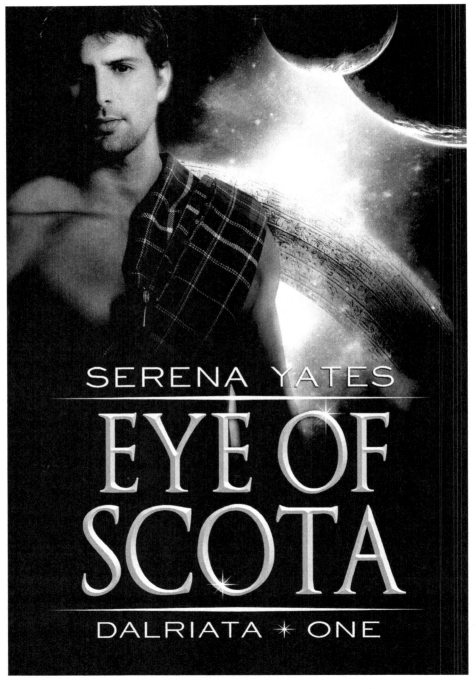

By Serena Yates
Dalriata: Book One

In 845 a group of Gaels fleeing the Vikings stumbled through the mystic Eye of Scota and found safety on a planet they named Dalriata. Seven centuries later, the arrival of the Crìosdaidh religion changed everything. Fugitives stopped appearing, and the newly established Council of Priests used the energy of Slànach Stones to enforce their religious laws. But by 2500 the Stones' power is dwindling. The High Priest is desperate—none of the warriors sent to find more Stones have returned.

Cináed MacAlpin, a young healer priest, is chosen to undertake another attempt. He hopes that new Stones will reduce the pressure to heal only those deemed worthy by the priests. But his task is not easy. Cináed must travel to the land of Bunádh and find the Eye that is the source of the Stones. Once there he meets Tadeo Banderas, a spaceship captain exploring the newest Earth-like planet discovered by the Solar Exploration Fleet. Cináed and Tadeo soon find out that the spark of energy between them may hold the key to Dalriata's future.

Azgarth's
Chosen
BOOK ONE

HIS MASTER'S
SUMMONS

CASSIE SWEET

By Cassie Sweet
Azgarth's Chosen: Book One

At the chasm between life and death lurks the art of reanimation.

When world-famous violinist Andres Valentine is pushed from a window to his death by Herr Maestro Wilhelm Kering, he is snatched back from the abyss by a doctor well-versed in reanimation. Contrary to popular belief, Andres's life up to this point has not been filled with opulent soirees and adoring fans, but is controlled by a hellish force, a being of the dark fae—Azgarth.

Henri Vauss is a medical student who works for a man capable of raising the dead. Even though the practice is controversial, Henri sees the revolutionary side of the science and enjoys the challenges he finds in Dr. Stanslovich's lab. Ever since taking on the case of Valentine, though, odd occurrences have infected the manor, making Henri question everything he believes about science and the world.

When Valentine confides to Henri that he wants to be rid of Azgarth's bonds, Henri vows to find a way to free him, never expecting to get caught in the snare of the fae master.

By B.A. Brock
The Godhead Epoch: Book One

No one can outrun destiny or the gods.

In Epiro, a kingdom in Greece, Perseus is prophesied to be a great demigod hero and king, with a legacy that will shape the world of Gaia. When he was born, his grandfather exiled him, and his mother brought them to Seriphos, where she created an academy for demigod youth. Perseus trains there and waits for the day when he will be able to take the throne of Argos.

Despite potential future glory, Perseus's fellow students think he is weak. By the time he reaches manhood, he has given up the hope of having any real friends, until Antolios, a son of Apollo, takes an unexpected interest in him. Perseus and Antolios fall in love, but Antolios knows it cannot last and leaves Seriphos.

Perseus, grief-stricken and lonely, rebels against the Fates, thinking he can avoid the prophecy and live his own life. But when the gods find him, he is thrust into an epic adventure. With his divine powers, he fights gorgons and sea serpents, and battles against his darker nature. Perseus strives to be his own man… but the gods have other plans.

Ash AND Echoes

Book One of the
BLESSED EPOCH

AUGUST LI

By August Li
Blessed Epoch: Book One

For the past few years Yarroway L'Estrella has lived in exile, gathering arcane power. But that power came at a price, and he carries the scars to prove it. Now he must do his duty: his uncle, the king, needs him to escort Prince Garith to his wedding, a union that will create an alliance between the two strongest countries in the known world. But Yarrow isn't the prince's only guard.

A whole company of knights is assigned to the mission, and Yarrow's not sure he trusts their leader.

Knight Duncan Purefroy isn't sure he trusts Yarrow either, but after a bizarre occurrence during their travels, they have no choice but to work together—especially since the incident also reveals a disturbing secret, one that might threaten the entire kingdom.

The precarious alliance is strained further when a third member joins the cause for reasons of his own—reasons that may not be in the best interests of the prince or the kingdom. With enemies at every turn, no one left to trust, and the dark power within Yarrow pulling dangerously away from his control, the fragile bond the three of them have built may be all that stands between them and destruction.

RAGE: BOOK 1

SAM C. LEONHARD

By Sam C. Leonhard
Rage: Book One

Rage is a seasoned assassin, and he lives by his own rules. One of them forbids him to kill children, and at sixteen, his new target is definitely too young to die. Instead of breaking her neck, he kidnaps Lucinda of Babylon—and soon finds out the girl has the knack to annoy the hell out of him.

As if taking care of a stubborn girl isn't enough of a burden, Lucinda's best friend Keiran joins their escape. And falls in love with Rage. And totally ignores the fact that the man in black, who cannot and will not use magic even to save his own life, does not love him back.

Staying one step ahead of a madman who is desperate to end their lives, Rage and his unwilling companions travel to the Forbidden Monastery, a place where horrible magical experiments once took place. There are ghosts screaming for their blood and dangerous, wild magic is always ready to strike. At the end of the day, two people are dead, and Rage realizes with bitter clarity that his heart can break just as easily as it did when he was young.